o n e
is a promise

TANGLED LIES

PAM GODWIN

dedication

For my readers
When you find the book
that changes the tempo of your heart,
dance to that rhythm.
Never let it go.
Thank you for reading my stories.
Thank you for recommending them to your friends.
Thank you for believing in me.

one
present

My hands shake so badly the lip gloss slips from my fingers and clatters in the bathroom sink. Dammit, the doorbell's going to ring any second, and I'm wracked with jitters. And other things. The horrible tilting sensation in my chest quakes with apprehension, grief, guilt. All the usual shit.

Breathe, Danni. It's just one night. No expectations. No promises.

I brace my hands on the edge of the sink and stare at my frazzled, rawboned reflection. Jesus, I haven't been this nervous since I danced at the mayor's Christmas party.

Raising my arms, I sniff each armpit — *sticky and odorless* — and adjust the strapless top of my maxi dress. Am I showing too much skin? I glance down. *Too much nipple.*

I need a bra. But the straps will show. I'll have to change the dress. Do I have time?

The doorbell buzzes, and the sound hits me directly in the stomach.

Shit, I can't do this. I'm not ready.

I'll never be ready.

I snatch the lip gloss. Dot, smear, rub. Then I roll Nag Champa oil on my wrists and neck. That'll have to do.

Gathering the floor-length skirt of the dress, I exit the bathroom and pause in the square hall that adjoins the rooms of my tiny one-story bungalow. I close my bedroom door on the left and let my hand linger on the glass doorknob. If I have sex tonight, it won't be in the bed I shared with Cole.

In the guest room on the right, racks of leotards, tutus, and sequined bra tops line the walls. No reason to shut that door.

Two steps take me past the galley kitchen, and I veer left into the dining room. There's no furniture in here in lieu of the black Harley-Davidson softail that sits on a rug in the center. Shiny and polished as the day it was rolled in, it's the only thing in this house I keep meticulously clean.

Out of compulsion, I stroke the soft leather seat and breathe through the deep agony it evokes. *I miss you so damn much.*

The silver band on my finger glints in the fading light from the window. I yank my arm back and move the engagement ring from my left hand to my right. It's one of the many ways I torture myself, constantly switching the band from one hand to the other, testing my resolve. I should stop wearing it altogether, but the thought strangles me with godawful finality.

Baby steps.

Forcing my bare feet across the honey-wood flooring, I enter the sitting room and peer into the peep hole in the front door.

Outside, my date shoves his hands in the front pockets of his jeans and squints upward. Is he scrutinizing my droopy gutters? If I remember correctly, this guy installs vinyl siding for a living.

Mark Taylor.

He looks just like the photo my sister sent me. Late twenties. Clean-shaved complexion. Thin lips. Slender build. The setting sun reflects off his jaw-length hair, highlighting blond strands against the waves of brown. He's handsome enough, but he isn't Cole.

Stop it.

With a galvanizing breath, I plaster on a smile and open the door. "Hi."

He stiffens, moving only his eyes as he gives me a full-body once-over. "Danni Angelo?"

"That's me." I step back and wipe my clammy palms on the dress. "Come in. I'm almost ready."

His canvas sneakers remain rooted to the brick porch. "Wow. You're..." He drags a hand over his mouth. "So much prettier in person."

What picture did Bree show him? My sister's been so obsessed with my nonexistent love life I let her set me up with one of her husband's friends. I don't know

3

anything about this guy. I really don't care. I just want to get this over with so she'll stop nagging.

"I mean, your photo had me agreeing to the date immediately." He grins and peruses my body again, lingering on my chest. "But Danni Angelo in the flesh is a knockout."

"Thank you." I shift uncomfortably.

Why is he staring at my boobs? I barely have enough meat to hold the dress up. Certainly nothing to gawk at. Must be the nipples. A peek down confirms it.

He seems to shake himself out of his stupor and steps into the front room. I twist the ring on my right hand while he takes in the brick fireplace, red velvet couch, orange armchair, and purple rug. He skips over the side table that holds the only picture frame I couldn't bring myself to put away for tonight's date.

I stare at the photo longingly. It's my favorite selfie of Cole and me, taken at Busch Stadium three years ago when he surprised me with tickets to see the St. Louis Cardinals.

"Damn, that's badass." Mark approaches the dining room.

"Hmm?" Shoving away memories of baseball and Cole, I trail after him.

He circles the motorcycle and raises a brow. "You know how to ride this?"

I know how to ride on the back of it, clutching tightly to the man who left it behind.

"No." I arrange my mouth in a smile. "Just holding it for someone." Straightening my spine, I inch toward the hall. "I'm going to go slip on some shoes and—"

"I was thinking…" He steps toward me with his hands in his pockets. "Maybe we could hang out here?

Order in some food and..." The corner of his lips crook up. "Get to know each other without trying to talk over the noise in a bar or restaurant?"

"Oh. Um..."

I actually prefer staying here to going anywhere with a man I don't know. If this date goes to hell, it would be easier to kick him out of my house than try to catch a ride home.

Other than the blatant way he checked me out, he seems polite and unassuming. But what if I'm missing an undertone in his suggestion? Does staying here mean he expects sex? God, I need that. Like really, really need the hard, consuming sensation of a man inside my body.

Emotionally, however, I'm not prepared for that. The idea of intimacy with anyone but Cole feels like betrayal.

"It was just a suggestion, Danni." His green eyes search my face. "If you'd rather —"

"I haven't been on a date in three years." I touch my flushed forehead, cursing myself for admitting that out loud.

"I didn't know." He gives me a gentle smile. "I should definitely take you out then."

"No, that's not what I mean." I run my fingers through my hair, holding the blonde mess away from my face. "I'm just nervous and a little rusty at this. Or maybe a lot rusty. How does this work? Is sex expected on a first date?"

He chokes and covers his shocked grin beneath the cup of a hand. Then he clears his voice and sobers his expression. "You're a straight shooter, huh?"

"So I've been told. You want a beer?"

"Sure." He follows me into the kitchen. "To answer your question, I'm not expecting sex tonight. But I'm not gonna lie. I'm crazy attracted to you."

With my head in the fridge, I glance over my shoulder and catch his eyes on my ass a half second before he looks away. It doesn't bother me. I work hard to keep my body fit, and it feels nice to be appreciated.

I hand him a Bud Light and open one for myself. "There's a cozy place to sit out back. Beer and conversation without the noise. I can order pizza. No promise of sex. Sound good?"

"Perfect."

Grabbing my phone, I lead him through the narrow walkway between the parallel kitchen counters and head toward the door at the other end.

"Love the style in here." He taps his fingers on the green stove top and turns in a circle to take in the matching retro green cabinets, green tiles, and yellow-flowered wallpaper.

Five years ago, I bought the house from an old lady who hadn't updated since the seventies. Room by room, I slowly remodeled but ran out of money to tackle the kitchen and bathroom. The vintage green in both rooms has grown on me.

"I like it, too." I hold the door for him and step into the addition on the back of the house.

Once upon a time, this was my favorite room. The floor-to-ceiling mirrors, wall-mounted ballet bars, and varnished wood flooring were installed during the happiest year of my life, every screw and bracket set by the strongest, most loving hands I've ever known.

Mark chugs a gulp of beer and looks around. "So this is where the magic happens?"

A lot of magic happened in here, but that was before my entire world was ripped away. "I run a dance company out of this room."

Cole made love to me tenderly, viciously, panting and grinding against every inch of this space. Now, the creaks in the floor, scratches in the wood, the shattered hole in one of the mirrors, every echo and dust mote is a painful memory scraping at the wound inside me. On the worst days, it's impossible to walk in here without doubling over with grief. Tonight, I just feel…lost.

"No way." Mark's attention zeroes in on the pole at the edge of the room. "You have to dance for me."

"I'd rather not." I haven't touched that pole in three years.

"Please?" His smirk twists with dirty ideas as his tongue slips out to wet his bottom lip.

"You know I'm not a stripper, right?"

"Your profile says you're a dance instructor, but it doesn't say what kind of dancing." He meanders toward the pole and gives it a shake, testing its sturdiness. "*This* is a stripper pole."

"Hate to ruin your fantasy, but I teach ballroom, jazz, ballet, and cardio dancing."

I also belly dance twice a week at Bissara, a local Moroccan restaurant. But I won't tell Mark that and give him a reason to start eating *pastilla* on weekend nights. Especially since I don't know how this date will end.

"My classes require clothing." I turn toward the nearest mirror and scrutinize my posture. Even when I'm not dancing, I'm conscious of proper poise and body alignment. A compulsion every dancer has. "The pole is for muscle toning."

7

Not a lie, but not the full truth. I have a stripper pole in my house because Cole was a pervert in the best way possible.

An unwelcome ache trembles inside me.

"This way." I open the back door and step onto the blacktop driveway that runs along the side of my house.

Mark joins me outside and nods at the yellow convertible MG Midget parked a few feet away. "What year is that?"

"1974." I gather my hair against the soft breeze, relishing the warmth in the late-spring air. "It's almost nice enough to take the top down."

Driving with the wind on my face never grows old. I love it almost as much as riding on the back of a motorcycle.

He strolls along the winding brick pathway to the cushioned wrought-iron furniture. A massive hundred-year-old oak tree stands at the center of the small yard, mantling the sitting area with thick branches of foliage.

"How long have you owned it?" His gaze roams over the car as he reclines on the loveseat. "It's in great condition."

"I bought it my last year at Washington University." I lower beside him, cradling the beer in my hands and battling the anxiety in my belly.

"You went to WashU?"

"Yeah. Four-year dance degree. I was twenty-two when I bought the Midget. So I've had it…six years. I've replaced almost everything on it just to keep it running. The Midwest winters eat away the undercarriage, but I can't bring myself to sell it."

I can't afford a new car. Not that I care. The Midget gets me where I need to go, so it's all good.

"Have you always lived in St. Louis?" he asks.

"Yep. My sister lives with her husband and daughter ten minutes away. My parents moved to Florida a few years back. You?"

"Born and raised here. Lots of family scattered around town."

We fall into friendly conversation, order pizza, and finish off several more beers. I lose track of how much I drink, but I know I exceed my limit when my nerves and inhibitions give way to heavy limbs and flushed skin. He's easy to talk to, has an attractive smile, and the beer tastes better than it has in a long time.

Over the course of the next hour, he inches closer and closer. So close his thigh presses warm and hard against mine.

"Is that patchouli?" His nose brushes the juncture between my neck and shoulder.

"Nag Champa." My head tips back, and goosebumps pebble beneath his breath on my skin.

"You smell so good. Intoxicating." Long tapered fingers skim over my collarbone. "So sweet and sexy." He touches the hollow of my throat. "Incredibly beautiful." His other arm slides along the back of the loveseat, hooking around my shoulders. "I want to kiss you."

In the cloak of night, lulled by the hum of singing insects and the numbing effects of alcohol, I want that, too.

Turning my head, I pause with my mouth a hairbreadth from his, but I don't have the courage to close the gap. It's so dark his face is a nondescript shadow. He could be anyone.

He could be Cole, if only for a fleeting kiss.

I part my mouth, breaths quickening, and he dives in. A touch of lips. A hand in my hair. Fingers curling around my neck. I hold still, eyes closed, and imagine tattooed muscles and a dangerous smile.

Mark pulls in a shaky breath and traces his tongue along the inside of my bottom lip. A tiptoeing touch, hesitant and inquiring. Nothing like Cole.

"You can kiss me harder," I whisper. "Deeper."

He presses closer, bending over me and slanting his head to lick inside my mouth. Rolling my tongue with his, I try to surrender beneath the invasion, but the mechanics feel wrong, like I'm leading instead of following, straining instead of letting go. He doesn't taste right. His lips are too malleable and thin. His jaw is too pointy, and his shoulders feel bony beneath my hands.

I keep at it, pretending his mouth isn't pooling with saliva, hoping to fall into a mindless groove. That hope is dashed the moment he shoves a hand between my legs, hindered only by the long skirt of my dress.

I've never been a prude, but I'm reminded why the dozen lovers I had before Cole never lasted. Seduction is everything, and Cole knew how to ravish me with a single look.

Then he abandoned me.

I need to get over him. I know this, and to do so, I need to forget about sentimentalities and just have sex. It doesn't have to be great. It doesn't even have to be good. I just need to fucking do it already.

So I let Mark prod and dig at my crotch through the folds of the dress, mentally urging my body to play along.

Ten minutes of groping and sloppy kissing, and

my pussy's still as dry and frigid as my emotional state. Is it me? Am I so messed up that I'll find a thousand faults in every man I try to be with?

I break the kiss and press my lips to Mark's shoulder, discreetly blotting off his spit. "I'm going to grab another beer. Want one?"

"Okay." He must think I can't see him adjusting his dick in the dark, because he does so with an unsexy-like tug.

I slip my phone off the coffee table and make my escape inside. When I reach the kitchen, I dial Bree.

My sister answers on the first ring. "You're supposed to be on a date."

"It isn't working."

"Which part?"

"All of it. He's nice, but I don't feel anything."

Her sigh billows through the phone. "You've known him all of ten minutes."

"Two hours. There's no chemistry. No sparks. Nothing. Nada."

"Give him a chance." Something crashes in the background, and she muffles the speaker through her shout. "Angel, I told you not to touch that!" Rustling noises scratch through the phone. "Danni, look, try to have an open mind, okay? These things take time."

"It only took a fraction of a second with—"

"If you say his name, so help me God."

"I'm trying, Bree." I prop my elbows on the kitchen counter and move my engagement ring back to my left hand where it belongs. "This guy… He's not right for me."

"Are you attracted to him?"

"He's cute."

"So he's cute and nice. Let him use those traits to clean the dust out of your vagina."

I scrunch my nose. "I don't understand how you teach first-graders with that mouth."

"I'm looking out for you, Danni. Just think about all the orgasms you can have without worrying about batteries. Remember what that's like?"

"Yeah." I remember with sweet, agonizing longing.

"Then go jump on his dick." She disconnects.

Kill me already.

At this rate, I'll die alone, waiting for a man who's never coming back.

I blow out an exasperated breath. It's just sex. Or not sex. Either way, hanging out with Mark is the opposite of *alone.* I need this.

After a couple more minutes of waffling, I return to the backyard with my heart sprinting in my chest.

"You forgot the beers." His lanky silhouette prowls toward me.

Shit. My mind is so flustered I can't even think of an excuse.

He veers around me to stare down the driveway at the street. "You expecting someone?"

"No." I join him on the side of the house and squint at the luxury sedan parked on the curb.

The back door of the mysterious car opens, and a woman steps out. Her heels turn toward us and clickety-clack along the driveway, sounding her advance.

Is she lost? It's too dark to make out her features, but she'll pass under the motion-sensor mounted on the roof in the three, two…

The floodlight illuminates her tall slender frame.

Dark brown hair sweeps into a low bun. Sleeveless black dress, flawless golden skin, heavy makeup. A blank expression on a face I've never seen before.

"Miss Angelo?" She pauses within arm's reach.

"Yes?"

In her late-twenties or early-thirties, she lifts her nose with an air of snootiness. As pretty as she is, she's probably used to people staring at her.

"I'm Marlo Vogt, a representative of The Regal Arch Casino and Hotel." She shakes my hand with limp fingers. "Mr. Savoy would like to meet with you."

"I don't know who—"

"He owns the casino."

The owner? Of the largest casino in the Midwest? My jaw drops. "Why does he want to meet with me?"

"He wants to discuss"—her sharp gaze flicks over my body—"your services."

My hackles bristle. "If he wants dance lessons, he can set up an appoint—"

"He's waiting."

"He's what?" My eyes widen. "He wants to meet now?"

"I'm here to escort you to the casino."

Everything inside me rebels against her high-handedness. "He can make an appointment like everyone else." I cross my arms over my chest. "I have plans tonight."

Marlo casts a disinterested glance at Mark, who watches the interaction with an arched brow.

"Mr. Savoy is a busy man," she says in a bored tone. "The offer is now."

I can't afford to turn down a job. I'm barely

keeping my dance company afloat, and private dance instruction is an easy way to bring in money. But I'm not going to instruct someone who expects me to drop everything at the snap of his fingers.

"Send my regrets to Mr. Savoy." I grasp Mark's hand. "If he's interested in my services, I'm listed under Danni's Dance Company on the Internet." I turn away and leave her glaring after me.

Mark follows me back to the loveseat behind the house. "That was weird, right?"

"Very weird." I sit beside him, wondering how much money I just turned down. "The bulk of my business is private ballroom lessons. Rich old men. Couples looking to spice up their marriage. I could really use the income, but that was... I've never had someone show up at my house like that." My stomach knots. "My address isn't publicly listed."

"He owns The Regal Arch properties. If a man that wealthy wants to hire you, he can easily find out where you live." He rests a hand on my knee. "You've never met him?"

"Not that I know of. Have you?"

"I've heard of —"

Footsteps echo along the driveway, the scuff of soft-soled shoes growing nearer. I didn't hear Marlo drive away and stupidly wonder if she changed out of her heels.

I stand just as the trespasser rounds the back corner of my house, and my breath stalls.

A tall imposing man in a suit steps onto the brick path, backlit by the nearby floodlight. Shoulders back and hands clasped behind him, he's a scowling pillar of intimidation.

one is a promise

Is this Mr. Savoy? Was he in the car the entire time? Why is my heart beating so frantically?

I'm instantly drawn to him, to the way he pauses at the edge of the light without speaking. The way he lowers his chin and lifts only his gaze to look me straight in the eyes. The way his severe expression doesn't twitch, doesn't expose a hint of emotion or intent.

My feet move cautiously, as if commanded by his steady focus. As if he's gathering every molecule in the air, summoning all energy from every living thing around him, demanding the world's attention merely through the presence of his dominance.

His blond hair is styled to perfection, longish on top, trim around the sides. His fair complexion, chiseled jawline, full lips, and stern brow work together to form a compelling scowl.

How I can be so captivated by a scowl is beyond me, but it stirs something inside me. Something raw and achy and so very lonely.

I step within inches of him and tilt my head up, up, up. Holy shit, he's at least a foot taller than my five-foot-four frame. Over six feet of gorgeous Norse god in tailored twill.

It's as if the crisp suit was fitted to emphasize the hard lines of his legs, the cut of toned thighs, the sizable bulge of his groin, and the width of his chest. All of it wakes me from a foggy, ghostlike sleep.

Blinking once, twice, I crane my neck to peer up at his face.

Crystal blue eyes.

My stomach erupts in a flurry of tremors. My God, I know those eyes. I curl my toes against the brick pavers as excitement and trepidation spikes through my nerve endings. There's something in that gaze, something in the forever pools of blue that knows me, too. But how? Where have I met him?

A voice clears behind me, and my spine goes rigid. *Shit. Mark.*

I toss an apologetic smile over my shoulder and return to the sculpted physique under the white shirt. With the silver tie hanging loose and the top few buttons open, there's a gorgeous expanse of strong neck and hairless pecs exposed. Not that I'm staring.

"How do I know you?" I lift my eyes to the icy blue of his.

"Everyone knows me." He offers a large hand. "Trace Savoy."

The casino owner. "I've never been to your casino." I place my palm in his and gulp at the electricity zipping up my arm. "I don't know how..."

My voice fragments as a memory surfaces. Crowded dining room at Bissara. Dark suit. Blue eyes. He's watched me belly dance at the restaurant.

"You like Moroccan food?" I slide my hand away and flex my fingers at my side.

"I do." His scowl deepens, and it makes him look even sexier, if that's possible. "I purchased Bissara."

"When? Why wasn't I notified?"

"I own it as of this morning. I want to discuss your employment at the casino."

I shake my head, confused. "I don't work at the casino."

"You will. We'll finish this conversation in my office." He glances at my bare feet. "Put some shoes on." Flicking his wrist, his gaze falls to his watch. Then he folds his hands behind him. "Don't keep me waiting."

two

present

Don't keep him waiting?

A surge of righteous anger rattles my insides, but I can't afford to explode and risk losing the belly dance contract.

With a calming breath, I jut my chin. "I'll meet with you, Mr. Savoy—"

"It's Trace."

"—at a scheduled time and place." I feel so damn short beneath his freakishly tall frame I'm tempted to lift on my toes to better compete with his stark glare.

"Maybe I didn't make myself clear." His head tilts, expression stony. Like a marble statue. "You work for me now, and I require your presence in my office."

I anchor my fists on my hips. Trace might've bought the restaurant I dance at, but I work for myself. He can take his inflated sense of superiority and shove it up his ass.

"Hi, I'm Mark Taylor." My date holds out a hand to my unwanted visitor.

Trace glances at Mark, a millisecond assessment and dismissal, before returning to me. "Say goodnight to your friend, Danni."

I release a shocked laugh. "Don't tell me what to do." *You insanely handsome, overbearing Neanderthal.* Sweet mercy, why does his bossiness turn me on so much?

The intensity of his eye contact sucks me into a spinning vortex. This isn't like the fleeting looks I exchange with men I pass on the street. It goes beyond any of those few-seconds-too-long gazes shared between strangers. This is dialog without words. Absorption without expression. Foreplay without so much as a twitch of a finger. I feel him in places that haven't been touched by a man in years.

"I own a vinyl siding company." Mark pulls a business card from his wallet and offers it to Trace. "We do commercial jobs, so if you're looking to renovate any of your properties, I'd love to work with you."

I gape at him. Did he seriously just turn this into a business opportunity? If Cole were here, he would've muscled Trace off my property with steam billowing from his ears. Not that I expect a hot-tempered reaction from Mark, but a *Hey, man, she's spending the evening with me* would've gone a long way in earning a second date.

Trace pockets the business card, and Mark grins like he just won the lottery. They can both go to hell.

"Mark, I hate to cut the evening short." The lie tastes like sweet relief. "But I need to deal with this."

"No worries. I have an early morning anyway. I'll call you, okay?"

He leans in to kiss me, and I turn my head, letting his lips graze my temple. As I watch him amble toward his truck, the potency of Trace's gaze hijacks my traitorous libido. He stares at me as if he just staked his claim, and God help me, that notion awakens such a deep-seeded need inside me it takes all my strength to not surrender to it.

Heat tingles across my cheeks, pulses in my breasts, and swells between my legs. My lungs work harder, and a phantom caress sweeps over my skin. I imagine his lips coasting down my neck and nipping at the curve of my shoulder. His breaths would be steady, patient, hovering over the pulse point in my throat and electrifying me with desire. I wouldn't be able to stop myself from fisting his perfect blond hair and bringing his mouth to my chest, where my nipples are now tightening and throbbing beneath the thin fabric.

My heart pounds against my ribcage, kicking up the dust of abandoned emotion. I want to pursue this…this crazy possibility. But if my job is going to be entangled with him, I can't. I don't even know him, for Christ's sake.

When Mark pulls away from the curb, I head toward the back door and pick up my pace at the sound of footsteps trailing behind me.

"You're not going to see that schmuck again." His silken voice kisses down my spine.

That's exactly what Cole would've said, and the

familiar possessiveness wobbles my knees. I hurry inside the house and spin on the threshold, forcing my gaze to the intruder's flinty stare.

"My dance company is listed online, along with my phone number. Goodnight, Mr. Savoy." I shut the back door on his beautiful brooding expression and lock it. "Fucking fuck, that was…just…*fuck.*"

I lean my back against the wall, thankful there aren't windows in the dance room. Because his eyes… Holy hell, he has that look. The one that makes my blood run so hot everything inside me melts and trembles. It's the same look Cole gave me the day we met. The *You're mine, and there's not a goddamn thing you can do about it* stare that owned me instantly and completely.

Soft shivers of yearning flow through me as I head toward the bedroom. I consider calling Bree, but I'll wait until morning. Conversations about Trace will be better with a clear head. As it stands, I'm drowning in a jumble of nonsense and conflicting emotions.

It's been so long since I've been this affected by a man I question how much of it is my desperate imagination. After the lackluster make-out session with Mark, anyone could've strolled down my driveway and captured my attention.

But Trace isn't just anyone. He's the epitome of eloquent power and affluence, intimidation and mystery. A modern lord at ease with commanding and conquering, and for a knee-weakening moment, his sights were trained on me.

Jesus, what am I doing? He probably looks at every woman with the same burning focus, and right now, he's driving away with Marlo Vogt, his gorgeous colleague. He could be taking her back to her place this very second with his hand between her legs and his name gasping on her painted lips.

Shutting down those images, I change into a purple camisole and cotton pajama pants with black-and-white polka dots. Then I pad into the kitchen, twisting my messy blond hair into a knot on my head. I need something to mellow my brain and put me to sleep. A full bottle of Riesling should do it.

Filling my largest wine glass to the rim, I gulp down half and carry it back to the bedroom. As I pass through the hall, something moves in my periphery beyond the dining room.

I spin toward it, and my line of sight narrows on the sitting room and the arrogant suit reclined on the couch. A yelp freezes in my throat.

"What are you doing in my house?" I charge toward Trace, sloshing the wine in my mad dash.

He glances down at the picture frame in his hand. "If you're engaged to this one, what are you doing with the foreveraloner with a boner?"

Foreveraloner? "Mark wouldn't be alone right now if you hadn't shown up. And what gives you the impression I'm engaged…?" Following his gaze to the engagement ring on my left hand, I curl my fingers.

"Are you cheating on him?" He narrows his eyes at me.

"No." My stomach knots with irrational guilt. "How did you get in here?"

"The heavy-duty deadbolt on the front door is useless when it's unlocked. A tiny woman living alone should never—"

"I'm not helpless."

"*Never* leave your door unlocked." He sits forward, eyes flickering with blue flames. "How can you be so careless?"

My nostrils flare. "An unlocked door isn't an invitation to walk in."

This conversation is unnervingly familiar. I need to stop comparing guys to Cole, but seriously, Cole reamed my ass every time I forgot to lock up.

Trace holds up the photo. "What would your fiancé think about the dipshit you were with tonight?"

He would've smashed Mark's face for a thousand reasons but first and foremost for leaving me unprotected with an invasive suit-wearing Viking.

I snatch the picture frame from his hand and return it to the side table. "Is trespassing a habit for you?"

"Never. I'm also not in the habit of waiting." Icy blue eyes flick over my pajamas and sharpen when they reach my bare feet. "I told you to put shoes on."

"Mm." I rest a hand on my cocked hip and sip the wine, watching him over the rim of the glass. "I'm not going anywhere."

He taps the screen on his phone and lifts it to his ear. "Take Marlo back to the casino and return for me."

Outside, an engine roars to life, and images of Trace going home with Marlo vaporize. I hide my stupid smile behind the wine glass.

He pockets the phone with controlled grace in his movements, at odds with the muscle straining the shoulders of his suit jacket. He's all strength and hard lines buttoned up in a pretentious package. What I wouldn't give to unwrap him and find out exactly what he's hiding beneath those tailored clothes.

His legs are spread, taking up space like he owns

it, with his knees brushing against the coffee table.

At this point, a normal woman would've reached for her phone and dialed 911. I consider doing that, for maybe half a second, and decide to deal with him my own way.

I've been called reckless, shameless, audacious, and even naive, but I think those name-callers live in fear and paranoia. I prefer to view things with open-minded optimism.

Trace Savoy, with his fancy suit and personal driver, isn't here to turn my life into a horror movie. He's not going to stab me, rob me, or tie me up in an abandoned cabin. Anything else, I can deal with. Especially with the liquid courage coursing through my blood.

Which is why I don't hesitate to step over one of those muscular thighs and sit on the edge of the table, putting my legs between his. I don't expect him to lean away, and he doesn't disappoint.

Bent forward at the waist with his hands folded together between us, he immerses me in the endless oceans of his eyes before lowering his gaze to my lips. "Are you going to offer me a drink?"

"Nope." I lean closer, a kiss away. "Why are you here?"

His scowl darkens. "I already told you."

"Your mouth says one thing, but your eyes say another."

Raw, unguarded turbulence stirs the air around us, and I glory in it, breathing it in with deep inhales. I never thought I'd experience this feeling again—the feverish thrill in my belly, the throbbing lust between my legs, the reckless hope blooming in my chest.

His lips part. The angles of his face soften, and something passes through his gaze. Something he doesn't want to give me, because it falls away with one slow blink, replaced with an uncompromising expression and resting frown.

"I'm closing Bissara and reopening it at the casino." He removes a folded document from the interior pocket of his suit jacket.

"What?" I straighten and set the glass on the table beside my hip. "What about the employees?"

"Most will be offered jobs at the new location. Including you." He hands me the paperwork. "These are the terms of your employment."

For the next few minutes, I read through the multi-page contract. I only dance at Bissara twice a week, but according to this, he's tripling my hourly wage? I'm goddamn giddy until I reach the section about my required schedule. "Five nights a week? No way. I teach dance classes on—"

"You're barely scraping by on the revenue from those classes." He sweeps his haughty gaze over my yard-sale furniture and scuffed-up wood floors. "I'm offering you an opportunity to earn a more comfortable living."

"I've been scraping by for years. That's what people do." Irritation heats my cheeks, and I suddenly wish I wasn't sitting so damn close to him. "I think your level of comfort looks a whole lot different than mine, Mr. Savoy."

"Trace."

"Do all your employees refer to you by first name?"

"None." Only his lips move, his eyes steady as ever, drilling into mine.

"Do you treat your employees with personal visits to their homes?"

"No." He bites the word.

I fold the contract, set it aside, and lean in, drifting so close the mint on his breath tingles my lips. "I'll ask you again. Why are you here?"

A muscle flexes in his jaw. The only response he gives.

"Okay, I'll take a stab at the answer." I slide my fingers beneath his silver necktie, caressing the fine silk. "You watched me dance at Bissara. You liked what you saw. Maybe you assume a woman who gyrates her hips like that is an easy lay. Or maybe it doesn't matter, because the powerful Trace Savoy always gets what he wants." I give the tie a yank that doesn't move him. "You came here for me, and it has nothing to do with that contract."

He grips the silk above my fingers and tugs it. Tug, tug, tug, until the end slips from my hand. "I find your forwardness off-putting."

My neck goes taut. "I could say the same thing about your fuck-me eyes."

"Fuck-me eyes." His deep unflappable voice swirls around me in a smoky mist. "Curious conversation for someone wearing an engagement ring."

I press my thumb against the silver band and picture the woman I used to be. Free-spirited, happy, and forward as hell. She's been curled up in the fetal position for too damn long.

"I'm not engaged anymore." I avert my gaze.

"Then he's as idiotic as the one you were with tonight."

The need to defend Cole sizzles in my stomach like a hot ember. "Maybe I'm a total raging bitch and drove him away."

"Now I know you're lying." He brushes an errant strand of hair behind my ear, making my breath catch. "You, my tiny dancer, are an erotic dream dipped in the sweetest honey. A man only needs to look at you to become fiercely protective of your smile." His finger traces the ridge of my bottom lip. "Of every limber curve." He feathers a path over the heaving swell of my chest. "Every delicious tremble."

He lifts from the couch to bow over me, forcing me backwards with his massive frame. My spine presses against the coffee table, and I squeeze my legs together between the straddling *V* of his. No part of him touches me, but he doesn't have to. His bedroom eyes are enough to crank my pulse and plunge my senses into delirious disorientation.

"I've watched you dance." He bends closer, arms braced on either side of my head with the silk tie dangling like a teasing caress across my exposed midriff. "I've memorized every shimmy and thrust of your hips, the sensual movements of your arms, the flirtatious tosses of your head, and the limitless flexibility of your spine. You're a flesh and muscle articulation of sex. Each vibrating hip drop, quiver in your thighs, and bounce of your tiny tits plants filthy thoughts in a man's head. His mouth waters, so he orders more to drink. His slacks become too tight, so he remains at the table, hiding the swollen evidence of his intentions. And he's hungry, so very hungry he stays and he watches and he eats."

28

My insides thrum with the velvety cadence of his timbre, every word stirring, seducing, working me into mindless anticipation. The scent of his skin floods my lungs, smothering me in a wicked haze of spicy aftershave and masculinity.

I can't remember the last time I was this turned on. I'm so fucking wet my pajama pants stick to my thighs. The ache between my legs is unbearable, and my voice is a goner beneath the rapid gasps of my breaths. I want this man. Tonight. Right now.

Have I lost my damn mind? Try as I may, I can't rationalize my reaction to him. Only a few hours ago, I wasn't prepared to take this daunting leap with anyone. Now I'm arching my back and panting like a hussy? "What are we doing, Trace?"

I hold my breath as he teases his nose down my neck, along my collarbone, and across the top of the camisole where cotton meets quivering skin.

He studies me with so much concentration it feels like he can see through my clothes, my flesh, to examine my deepest wildest desires. "We're finalizing the interview."

Interview? My stomach hardens, and I push at his chest. "What does that mean?"

He doesn't budge against my hand, his voice void of emotion. "You're an acquisition. One that will earn me a lot of money." His head cants at a slight angle. "Don't look so surprised. Were you not listening to anything I said?"

He orders more to drink...he remains at the table...he watches and eats.

Realization dumps cold water on my arousal. Trace

wasn't referring to himself. He was talking about the patrons in the restaurant.

He sits back on the couch, nonchalantly adjusting the suit jacket around his narrow hips as if his cock isn't straining the shiny fabric of his slacks.

"If you're here strictly on business..." I lurch off the coffee table and stand on the opposite side. "Explain that." I point at his erection.

"Making money gets my dick hard."

Where did this heartless douche in a tin can come from? I feel like a damn fool. How did I melt beneath his manipulations so easily? Am I really that naive? And why does he think I'll make him money? I'm a nobody. My belly dance routine earns good tips, but it's just ambiance, much like a mariachi band in a Mexican restaurant.

"I'm confused." I pace through the sitting room. "Patrons might enjoy my dance routine, but they come for the food."

He eyes me impassively. "Have you ever gone to Bissara on the nights you're not dancing?"

No. I glare at him.

"It's a ghost town." He stretches an arm along the back of the couch. "The overcrowded dining room you're used to seeing? That only happens on the nights you dance. You know why?"

Given the incisive look in his eyes and the cruelty in his scowl, I can guess.

"Sex sells." His gaze migrates from my face to my thighs and back again. "And you're dripping with it."

Humiliation sets my cheeks on fire, and I'm acutely aware of the cold wet crotch of my pajama pants. All his talk about my smiles and curves was just his sick way of making a point. My body serves a purpose, *his purpose,* and it has nothing to do with romantic interest. I really am a fool.

"Why not just open your own restaurant and offer me a job?" I chew on the corner of my thumb nail. "You didn't have to buy Bissara."

He stares without a crease or tic in his rock-hard expression, and the answer becomes clear.

"You want to own the only Moroccan restaurant in town." Bitterness clips my voice. "To eliminate competition? Or to force me to work for you?"

"Both. But I'm not forcing you. I'm just making the decision easy for you."

"Oh, it's easy all right. Easy to tell you to go fuck yourself." I stand taller and stab a finger toward the door. "I want you to leave."

"You're overreacting." He releases a patronizing breath. "This is just business. I'm offering a salary that's more than fair, so lose the attitude and take the job."

Heaviness seeps into my limbs and tightens my stomach. I'm attracted to him, and he sees me as nothing but a financial deal. I'm mortified for trembling and gasping beneath his touch, but I need to get over it and either kick him out or consider his job offer.

I snatch the contract off the table and read it again without looking at him. "Why is the owner of the casino making this offer and not some middle manager?"

"I'm hands-on," he says in a deep, rumbling voice.

A voracious shiver grips my body, and I'm certain it's the response he intended to elicit. His assertive stares, inappropriate touches, and suggestive words are all meant to persuade. I'd have to be comatose to not be affected by it. But it's not just his actions. It's *him*. He's compelling, gorgeous, powerful. The kind of man a woman wants at her side, united and tangled, fighting for her, not against her. I cringe at the thought of making an enemy of this man, but if I keep my emotions out of this, he can't hurt me.

As I reach the end of the contract, my head is all over the place. It's a lot of money to turn down, and I suspect Trace Savoy won't accept my rejection without a fight. Doesn't mean I'll back down, but I need to consider every angle.

Shoving a hand through my hair, I lift my gaze. Our eyes connect, and we freeze. Everything stills. We don't blink, don't move, don't breathe. There's something there, something fragile and gritty and complicated creeping between the lines of personal and business. I know he senses it, too. Part of me wants to demand he acknowledge it, but the other part, the smarter part, knows that nothing good can come from involving myself with this man.

His phone buzzes in his pocket, breaking the trance. He glances at the screen and returns his attention to me. "Why do you dance?"

"It's my passion."

"Elaborate."

Despite his curt tone, I don't mind answering. Dancing is the piece of myself I will never suppress or hide.

"I love creating art through movement. Not only does it allow me to express my feelings, it makes others feel." I lower onto the coffee table, bending a leg across the surface to face him. "It's not about the job or the money or the accolades. I dance because I have to.

Because it's who I am — the artist, the athlete. It's my outlet to let go, to just *be*."

"And you achieve this through teaching?"

"Yeah, but honestly, I'd rather focus on honing my own talent. In an ideal world, I'd perform on stage with dancers I can learn from. But Beyoncé has yet to knock on my door and offer me a position on her dance team." I snort to myself. *As if.* "We don't always get the job we want. So I teach dance lessons and entertain restaurant patrons. It makes me smile and keeps a roof over my head."

"There's a small stage at the center of the restaurant's new location, and that stage will be visible from the most active gaming areas in the casino." He leans in, eyes hard, a business man poised to seal a deal. "The casino averages over six million in admissions every year. That's six million patrons strolling through my doors and resting their eyes on the art you create through movement."

"Art or male desire?" I squint at him. "Your spiel about selling sex sounds exactly like you intend to objectify me to promote your goods and services. I'm a person, not a commodity."

"You're whatever I want you to be." The controlling controller controls his gait to the front door. "We'll finalize the contract tomorrow night. Seven o'clock sharp."

It takes great effort to not recoil from the cutting snap of his voice. "What the fuck is your problem?"

"My office is on the 30th floor of the casino hotel." He sweeps open the door, bringing with it the sound of the idling car on the curb. "Don't make me wait."

"I'm scheduled to dance at Biss — "

"Bissara is closed until the remodeling is finished at the casino."

"Wait. Back up." I approach him with suspicion edging my voice. "Didn't you just purchase it this morning? You'll lose money if you don't keep it open."

"I'll lose money if I don't get the employees relocated and up to speed immediately." He palms the doorframe, towering over me. "The new Bissara will be a fine dining restaurant. Full-service, high-quality, catering to wealthy clients with refined palates. The staff must undergo thorough training to meet the specifications."

Well la-di-da. I don't care about his rich and important agendas. I'll go to his office tomorrow, only because I want to hand him a counteroffer that'll make his eyes bulge and his ego explode with indignation.

"Lock the door." He steps outside and shuts it behind him with a victorious glimmer behind his scowl.

I glare at the deadbolt until my vision blurs. Why does he care if I lock it? What the hell is his angle? There's something going on beyond him wanting my employment. He chased away my date. Trespassed in my house. Offered me a job that pays triple the normal rate. It feels like he's gone out of his way to put me directly under his thumb.

Am I reading too much into this?

The door cracks open, and his crystal blue eyes fill the gap. "Lock. It."

Oh my God. I shove it closed, turn the deadbolt, and flip him off through the door.

A moment later, the muffled sound of his car fades into the distance. That's when it dawns on me I didn't ache for Cole once while Trace was here. It's both disturbing and remarkable. There isn't a chance in hell I'll ever forget what I lost, but for the last hour, Trace's assjackery extinguished the grief I carry for the man who owns my heart.

But as the silence creeps in, so does the emotional pain I've been wallowing in for years. Self-pitying, soul-gutting, wishing-for-death pain. Sometimes it feels like all I have left is an endless well of tears and bitter loneliness. Sometimes it's easier to give into the anguish than to hold it at bay. I'm tired. So fucking tired of missing Cole with every agonizing breath.

Am I fading? Becoming less of who I was? Cole's absence cast me in darkness, but this solitude and discordance is of my own making.

I trudge through the dining room and rather than giving into the urge to straddle and hug his bike with all my might, I keep walking. Passing through the hall, I strip off the pajama bottoms. In the spare bedroom that serves as my closet, I slip on a pair of low-rise booty shorts. Then I enter the dance studio through the door between the rooms.

My emotions unravel with each step across the wood flooring. Burning chest, tightening throat, pressure behind the eyes — it's all there, threatening to turn me into a useless blob.

I rush through my stretches before powering on the sound system and selecting an empowering song.

The instrumental intro of *Dangerous Woman* by Ariana Grande trickles through the speakers. I stand in the center of the room, rolling my shoulders and measuring my breaths. The instant the smoldering vocals begin, I move. Arms, legs, abs, neck, every muscle is engaged, sweeping in wide fluid motions and channeling my emotions.

I don't need to focus or think about the steps. I simply let go, give myself over to the moment. The music floats through me, possesses my body, and carries me to better days.

three

four years ago

"Here he comes." Virginia wraps a liver-spotted hand around my arm and points her filmy eyes at the vacant street. "Hear that?"

All I hear is the too-damn-early squawk of birds telling me to go back to bed.

"He's bringing the marijuana into our neighborhood." The saggy skin on her neck quivers. "I just know it."

A smile struggles behind my pinched lips. When my hundred-and-ninety-year-old neighbor isn't complaining about the Bosnians moving in with their pink flamingos and loud music, she's fretting over alleged drug activity. I love Virginia dearly, but her over-imagination is horribly discriminatory.

For the past few weeks, she's had her floral smock all twisted up over the tattooed devil on a motorcycle who rides down our block. She can't see two feet in front of her, but her hearing is sharper than a bat. And she says he's coming.

A gentle fog blankets the sleepy road. The giant oak trees and quaint brick bungalows in this neighborhood date back to the 1920's, as do most of the residents. Since I'm the only one under the age of seventy, they all come to me when there's a problem. Last week, I spent an entire afternoon chasing a poor squirrel out of Jackie's basement. And Wilson, the Vietnam vet who lives across the street, needs help programming his TV on a weekly basis.

I still don't hear the offending motorcycle, which Virginia claims *rattles her fine china before the Lord has risen for the day*. She also swears the *pot-smoking heathen* tries to run her over when she steps off the curb. Of course, she chooses to alert me of his misbehavior at six every morning.

Seeing how I'm not an early riser, I'm prepared to do anything to put an end to her banging on my door.

So here I am. Armed with coffee—I can't function without it. Standing in my front yard—it's cold enough to freeze my tits off. Dressed to kill—I know how to rock a slouchy crop top and cheeky boyshorts.

The plan is simple. I'll wave down the biker with a little flash of skin. He'll pull over because he's a man. We'll have a friendly stop-pissing-off-my-neighbors conversation, and I'll be back in my warm bed in no time.

"I'll take care of it, Virginia." With a grip on her

bony elbow, I guide her across the driveway.

Her house slippers shuffle along the pavement, chafing my patience. By the time I coax her into her home next door, I'm shivering so violently my bones hurt. I consider slipping back into my house to pull on some leg warmers, but an engine rumbles in the distance, maybe two…three blocks away.

Curling my hands around the warm coffee mug, I tiptoe through the chilly grass and step into the middle of the empty street. The gray sky casts the fog in a wintry glow, making it feel colder than it should in late September.

The purr of the engine grows louder, and after a few shivery breaths, the motorcycle thunders like a black stallion out of the mist at the end of the street.

I'm hoping for a bald, grizzly-bearded biker dude. Never met one I didn't like.

He motors toward me, straddling a beast of a bike and maintaining the prudent speed limit. Heavy boots, faded denim, and a black leather jacket come into view, but that's where the stereotype ends. Beneath the half-shell helmet is a young, clean-shaved face and huge brown eyes.

At twenty feet away, I know I'm in trouble, because this man is fucking gorgeous.

It's his smile. A heart-thudding, sexy-as-fuck, world-changing smile that shines from the inside out. It lifts his cheeks, illuminates his entire expression, and damn if I don't feel it pulling on my own lips.

He slows his approach and stops on the curb beside me. With his eyes on mine, he turns off the engine and kicks a leg out, balancing the bike between muscular thighs wrapped in frayed jeans.

I float toward him, and his gaze follows, tracing my face as if absorbing every detail. We're both smiling, locked in a wonderfully bizarre introduction.

Our eyes dance over each other, greeting, exploring, and connecting in a moment of silent fascination, where time and words are inconsequential. I hear the crescendo of possibilities, feel the vibrations answering inside me, and everything just…clicks.

His grin, complete with dimples, grows impossibly wider as I drink him in. Golden complexion, pillowy lips, straight white teeth, square jaw—every symmetrical feature renders a sculpture of masculine beauty. Carved to perfection, rebellious around the edges, and flirtatious without opening his mouth, oh baby, he's all that and a lit fuse on dynamite.

"I expected the black jacket, shit-kickers, and faded jeans." I step close enough to feel the heat of his body. "But those dimples…"

"If you pinch my cheeks and tell me I'm adorable, you'll never see them again." Amusement gleams in his eyes, but something else sifts through his gravelly voice, something dark and sinful. "Christ, your smile is beautiful."

"Thank you for giving it to me."

He gives me more than a smile. The look that follows marks the before and after in my life. The air ceases to exist, and the only thing between us is the anticipation of what is coming. In that flicker of time, with something as inconceivable as a look, he claims me, owns me, and ruins me for all others. It's a look so defining it puts quotation marks around *mine, his, us,* and *forever.*

one *is a promise*

My pulse pounds. My skin tingles, and a cocktail of desire circulates and multiplies in my blood. This is it, the suspended moment I will forever remember. The one that determines my ultimate happiness or demise. The pinnacle point that reveals who I am and what I want.

He releases the chin strap of his half-helmet and lets it dangle against his neck. "You're shivering."

Am I? I snap out of my daze and lift the mug to my lips. "Are you married?"

"I will be." Resting a leather-sleeved forearm on the gas tank, he leans in. "Does five o'clock tonight work for you?"

I sip the coffee and hum. "Is that a proposal?"

"It's a foregone conclusion." He rubs his jaw with a gloved hand. "I always wondered what you would look like."

"You wondered what *I* would look like?"

"My forever."

His response triggers giggly chemicals in my brain, but I do my best to behave like a twenty-four-year-old woman.

"I can't tell if you're being sincere or fucking with me." I wish the coffee would kick in so I could keep up. "I'm leaning toward mental patient. Did you escape the hospital on your bike?"

"Mental patient? You're the one standing in the street, freezing your ass off, and smiling like you were waiting for me."

"I *was* waiting for you."

"Perfect," he murmurs, his gaze transfixed on my mouth.

I bounce on my toes, trying to work some blood

into my iced-over muscles. "We need to talk."

His eyes fly to mine. "Is that right?"

"Yep." I roll back my shoulders. "It's about to go down."

"I can't wait." He grins.

"Hold this." I hand him the mug and reach for the lapels of his motorcycle jacket.

He lifts the coffee to his lips, watching me with curiosity as I slide down the heavy zipper and expose his black t-shirt beneath.

Tendrils of ink snake along the side of his neck and disappear beneath the cotton that stretches across his wide chest. My fingers itch to feel the carved ridges of those pecs, so I surrender to it, flattening a palm against the cement wall of his torso and gliding over the rippling terrain of his abs.

Broad through the shoulders, narrow at the waist, he's all testosterone-fueled muscle wrapped in leather and denim and heat. I'm definitely going to curl up against that. For warmth, of course. Not because I'm under the hormonal influence of *holy-shit-he's-sexy*.

"You make a damn good cup of coffee." He takes another sip, smiling around the rim as his eyes follow the movement of my hand.

"Thank you." I hook a leg over the bike, slide onto the wide spread of his thighs, and straddle his lap, chest-to-chest. Oh my, he's big…everywhere.

He doesn't balk at my boldness, and instead balances the mug in one hand so he can wrap the heavy jacket around my back. "Better?"

"Way better." I sigh at the heat radiating from his shirt and grip his biceps, folding my legs around his waist and making myself at home.

We could fuck in this position, with our chests pressed together, groins aligned, and his steel-hard thighs flexing beneath me. He only needs to pull himself out and thrust his hips. My hunger for him pulses, hot and reckless, between my legs. Such an outlandish reaction to someone I just met, yet it feels so impossibly *right*.

He tucks me tight against him inside the jacket and runs his nose through my hair. "Is this how it's going down?"

"Depends on how you do with that talk we need to have."

"All right." He chuckles, and the sound vibrates through me. "Get on with it then."

I tilt my head back and peer at him through my lashes. "I hear you're trafficking drugs through my neighborhood."

With his face angled down and inches from mine, his gaze drifts up, ticking over the surrounding homes. "Is that the rumor in the knitting circles?"

No doubt my neighbors are leaning over their walkers and squinting out their windows. But none of them have the eyesight to see the intimate cocoon of man and leather I'm indulging in.

"Never underestimate a concerned citizen with a knitting needle." I wink.

He tips the mug back, his throat working as he drinks. The deep swallow, bouncing Adam's apple, and taut tanned flesh over corded muscle—it's all so captivating. Why am I spellbound by a man's neck? I want to sniff it. Lick it. Mark it with hickeys.

Passing the coffee back to me, he stretches the

zippered flaps tighter around my shoulders. There's not enough room for both of us in this jacket, but his gloved hands span over the bare skin of my lower back, minimizing heat loss.

"Tell your concerned citizens," he says, "they're welcome to search my person anytime they want."

I'll be the only one searching his…everything. "They won't go near you. Something to do with your habit of running over old people."

"Why did the old lady cross the road?"

I laugh, startled at the absurdity of the question. "To get to the other side?"

"One would think. But the old lady in question crossed the street to beat me with a rolled-up newspaper as I rode by. Lucky for her, I have ninja reflexes and avoided a collision."

Eeesh. That sounds like Virginia. She's a shit-stirrer, which is why I don't take her complaints seriously. But if I ever want to sleep in again, he needs to find a new route to wherever he goes at six in the morning.

"Where do you live?" I reach for the lip of the half-helmet, dying to see his hair.

"Renting a house a few blocks away on Lemona." He nods behind him and lifts his gaze to my hovering hand. "Go ahead. Take it off."

I remove the helmet and widen my eyes at the skin-fade hairstyle. Clipped close on the sides, it could almost be a military cut, but the thick brown strands on top are long enough to suggest his hair would be wavy if he let it grow.

"Going for the Marine look?" Juggling the helmet and the mug between us, I run a hand over the softly sheared hair above his ear.

His eyelids grow heavy, and he leans into my touch. "Something like that."

Does that mean he's military?

I position the helmet back on his head, straightening the straps against his chiseled jawline. "Where do you go every morning?"

"Work." He points his chin in the direction of the city behind me. "Downtown."

There aren't any large military bases in St. Louis, but I ask anyway. "Armed forces?"

"Non-intelligence agency. Boring government worker."

I have a hard time imagining that. "Desk job?"

"Sometimes."

"And you cut through this neighborhood because it's quicker?"

"Yup." His eyes stay on me, penetrating in their perusal.

"If you jump over to Mackenzie, it might add like…thirty seconds to your drive. It's a main drag, so you won't be stirring up quiet little neighborhoods, and more importantly, I'll be able to sleep in. Would you be willing to do that?"

"Only if you say yes." His dimples deepen.

"Say yes to what?"

"Whatever I want." Gruff and thick, his voice electrifies the currents pinging between us.

"That sounds dangerous." *And gloriously naughty.* "How about we start with a date?"

"We can call it anything you like." He pulls me closer in the circle on his arms, crushing the coffee mug between us.

"There's eleven things you should know before dating me," I say.

"Eleven?"

"No more. No less." I'm making this shit up as I go.

He laughs with delight twinkling in his eyes. "Okay, lay them on me."

I gather a deep breath, as if preparing to give a long-winded speech. I'm playing with him. Stalling him, if I'm honest. He doesn't seem to be in a hurry, and despite the chill creeping over my exposed legs, I don't want him to leave.

"I can't walk past a mirror," I say, "without checking myself out."

"As beautiful as you are—"

"It's not vanity." Though the compliment has me beaming. "It's a matter of professional growth. Dancers live, breathe, and thrive by watching their reflections."

"Ah." He glances at my thighs where they hook around his waist. "That explains why you're so fucking fit."

"Straight-up cardio, all day, every day." I finish off the last swallow of lukewarm coffee. "Your turn."

"I didn't realize I was participating."

"Tell me eleven things I need to know. Feel free to start with the most scandalous ones first."

His smile is infectious. "I have a huge appetite. For food and other things."

"I exercise for a living, which means I'm always hungry. For food and other things."

He groans. "I'm ready to start that date now."

"You haven't heard the rest." I cock my head. "The

next thing you should know is the only movie genre that exists is *Dirty Dancing*."

"That's not a genre."

I arch a brow.

"Okay, I get it," he says. "There'll be no discussions about what we watch on movie night."

"Unless *Dancing with the Stars* or *So You Think You Can Dance* is on. Those take precedence."

He shakes his head, smiling. "I can live with that, if you can live with my mode of transportation."

I crane my neck to peer at the sexy lines of the Harley we're straddling. "What if it's snowing?"

"We stay in bed."

Well, damn. I press my grin against his chest. I've been smiling so hard and so long my cheeks hurt. Who knew an unexpected moment with a stranger could be so agreeable. I want to pour this feeling into a fireproof box and keep it under my pillow.

"Give me another one," he says.

"I have a tendency to break out in dance." I wriggle on his lap. "Anywhere. Anytime. If there's an opportunity for spontaneous dancing — in the supermarket, at a bar, on the toilet, you better be prepared."

"This, I have to see." His gloved thumb strokes the skin along my spine, making me shiver. "You should know I'm not a good dancer."

"That's *my* job. As long as you have rhythm and you're not afraid to let loose, we'll get along just fine." I tilt up my chin and sink into his warm brown gaze. "I own a crapload of beauty products and clothes. My spare room overflows with dance costumes I can't part with, stockings of every color and style, beaded bras, double-sided tape, false lashes, dance shoes… You get the idea. Dressing up is my job, so don't expect me to give up a drawer for your sleepovers, because it ain't happening."

His lips bounce between mirth and contemplation. "I don't wear underwear."

Oh, sweet Jesus. If I dipped my finger down the back of his jeans, would I slide right into his crack? I might be on the extreme side of outgoing, but I should probably wait for our date before playing with his butt cleavage.

"I don't share," he whispers.

"I don't cheat," I whisper back. "But there's no place for jealous cavemen in my line of work. I dance with guys. Wear skimpy clothing around guys. Shake my ass in rooms filled with guys. Can you deal?"

He groans and slides his cheek against mine. "I'll deal."

We continue our back-and-forth conversation, and I lose count of how many things we share about ourselves. He admits to being a mercurial hothead, a workaholic, and an opponent of alcoholic beverages that require a corkscrew, while I express my love for stretching, body massages, and all things Beyoncé.

"As far as corkscrews are concerned," I say, "I love a late-night glass of vino, but I'm all for the screw-cap, economy-jug variety."

"You're adorable."

"So are your dimples."

He sighs, and the sexy hollows in his cheeks fade away. "I have to go to work."

I don't like it, but I knew it was coming. Untangling my legs from his waist, I prepare to brave the cold.

"Ask me to stay." He touches a knuckle beneath my chin.

So tempting, but I need to process. Alone. I've never climbed onto a stranger's lap and flirted like a crazy person. It calls for analysis of feelings and sanity. Maybe some meditation for good measure.

I lean up and hover my mouth a kiss away from his. "Anticipation," I whisper, "heightens the pleasure."

His entire body goes hard against me, but he doesn't close the gap between our lips. "I hear the same applies to trouble."

Trouble heightens pleasure? With him, I believe it. "Are you trouble?"

"Absolutely."

"Then come back tonight."

I pull away, and his mouth chases mine.

"Tonight." With a hand on his chest, I stop his advance.

The frigid air creeps in as I slip off the bike and walk backward across my front yard.

"Tonight," he says, holding my gaze.

It's almost painful to continue my retreat, but I'm hopeful about seeing him again. Somewhere between a smile and a name, I let myself imagine a future filled with deep brown eyes and seductive dimples.

As I reach for the front door, he calls after me, "Mrs. Hartman."

Hartman? That must be *his* last name.

"Yes, Mr. Hartman?" I glance over my shoulder.

"I need a first name to accompany the thoughts that will distract me all day."

"Danni." I open the front door and lean against the doorframe. "Yours?"

"Cole." He buckles the helmet strap beneath his jaw.

"See you tonight, Cole Hartman."

The motorcycle sputters with a vibrating growl, and he watches me, smiling, until I step inside and shut the door.

I rest my forehead against the wood, replaying every second of my introduction to Cole Hartman.

And I grin.

The moment has come to an end, and I know it's just the beginning.

four

present

I wake from a deep sleep with the sensation of someone watching me. I must've overworked myself dancing last night, because it takes a helluva lot of effort to lift my face from the pillow. Or maybe it was all the wine I drank. Body cramps. Pounding head. Cotton mouth. Yeah, I need coffee.

Dragging my eyes open, I groan at the sunlight exploding through my bedroom window. There's no one in view, but the heavy breathing behind me suggests whoever is in my room isn't trying to be stealthy about it.

I roll over and come face to face with huge brown eyes.

Standing beside my bed, my niece tucks her chin to her chest and glares at me from beneath thick lashes. After my run-in last night with Trace Savoy and the subsequent bottle of wine, I'm not equipped to deal with a four-year-old demon named Angel.

Worse is the off-tune drone of my sister's humming in the kitchen. The interrogation awaits.

Maybe I should steal back the house key she stole from me. Or change the locks.

I narrow my eyes at Angel. Long black curls, rosy cheeks, and a dark complexion inherited from her Hispanic father, she's the prettiest little girl I've ever seen. That is, when she's not speaking.

"It's creepy to watch people sleep," I mumble.

She lifts a tiny shoulder, and I swear a mischievous smirk lurks behind those doll-like lips.

"Why don't you run along and get Aunt Danni a cup of coffee?" I tuck the pillow beneath my throbbing head.

"Jesus hates you." Angel blinks, expressionless.

"Did he tell you this himself?"

"This is God's house."

"Actually, it's my house, and I work hard for the money that pays for it."

"It's God's money."

"Do you even know what that means?"

She turns toward the door and bends at the waist. "Toot *this*." A farting noise sprays from her mouth, and she races from the room.

Birth control. That's what this is. If my bighearted, grade-school-teaching sister can give birth to the spawn of the devil, God knows what I would produce. Call me selfish, but I'm not even tempted to find out. I have a ten-year IUD to make sure of it.

Of course, I need to have sex to get pregnant in the first place.

Still wearing the booty shorts from last night, I throw my legs over the side of the bed and follow the aroma of sizzling grease into the kitchen.

"You look like ass." Bree smiles and shoves a mug of coffee at me.

"Thank you." I sip the creamy beverage and sigh. "For the coffee, not the comment."

"Eggs are almost done." She turns back to the stove.

She's not here to cook me breakfast. She wants the scoop on the date, and I'm surprised she hasn't asked yet.

Dressed in her usual gear—baggy gym shorts, tank top, hair in a high ponytail, complete with an elastic headband—she takes her role as a soccer coach's wife seriously. Eighteen months younger than me, she shares my height, build, facial features…everything. Only she's darker. Darker complexion—*fake bake*. Darker hair— *L'Oreal No.5*. If she embraced her naturally pale skin and blonde hair, we'd pass as twins.

"You didn't get the *D* last night." Gray eyes—same as mine—squint at me over her shoulder.

I had two chances to get laid. Final score 0-2. Man, I suck. But she only knows about the one.

"You don't know what happened." I finish off the coffee with a couple of aspirin.

"You woke alone and grumpy." She prepares two plates of eggs, bacon, and toast. "I know what *didn't* happen."

"I'm always grumpy before coffee."

"Not if you got the *D*," she sings and casts a glance at Angel, who glowers from a shadowed corner in the hallway.

"I wasn't impressed with the guy you picked." I might've jumped on the other *D*, if he weren't such a... Well, a dick.

"Eat." She slides a full plate in front of me. "And tell me what happened."

"Mm." I grab a fork and shovel in a fluffy scrambled bite of eggs. "Another guy happened."

She chokes around a mouthful of bacon. "Anuffer guy?"

I hop onto the counter and gesture at the watchful silhouette in the hall. "You gonna feed the little person?"

"Angel already ate." Bree wipes a paper napkin across her mouth. "What other guy?"

I launch into the story, starting with Mark's arrival, his groping, and Marlo Vogt's appearance. As I reach the part about the casino owner trespassing in my house, a noise from the hallway distracts me.

Angel sits with her back against the wall and hugs her knees to her chest. With her head tilted down, she stares up at me, whispering something under her breath.

I try to ignore her. "Trace Savoy bought Bissara and offered me a job with a pay raise."

As I explain the terms of the contract, Angel's indiscernible muttering grows louder.

"Jesus." I set my plate aside. "She's really distracting."

"She's practicing her alphabet." Bree smiles at her daughter. "Aren't you, sweetie?"

"Mm-hmm," Angel says without moving her judgmental gaze from me.

The whispers begin again. I strain my hearing and don't detect a single recognizable syllable.

"It sounds like Latin." Not really, but I love to give Bree shit about Angel's disturbing personality. "Are you sure she's not knee-deep in demonic possession?"

"Stop with the demon references, Danni. I'm not okay with it." Bree puts her plate in the sink a little too roughly. "You're giving her a complex."

Can a sociopath get a complex?

"Anyway..." I finish walking through the events of the prior night and end on a sigh. "Trace left with that stupid scowl on his face.

Bree blows out a breath, her expression pinching. "Sounds like Cole."

"Cole never scowled."

"Except when his temper flared, which was all the time. And he was always on you about locking the door."

"What's your point?" I slide off the counter and pour another cup of coffee.

"Can you separate business from pleasure? I don't want you to...I don't know, to get involved with this guy *just* because he reminds you of Cole."

She was never a huge Cole fan. He was too mysterious and rough around the edges for her tastes.

"I'm not doing anything, Bree." I stir cream into the coffee as a twinge stabs in my chest. "Trace is nothing like Cole, and I'm not accepting his job offer."

"But you need the money." Her voice is soft and motherly, scraping on my nerves.

"I'll find other jobs."

"Paying jobs?"

"Yep." I sip the coffee, relishing the bold flavor.

"Are you going to Gateway today?" She pins me with her school-teacher glare.

"Of course." I go to the homeless shelter every Saturday. What's the big deal? I turn toward the demon-whisperer in the hall. "You want to go dance at the shelter with me?"

"No." Angel hunches into a ball, peering at me over her bent knees.

"You can wear one of my tutus."

Her eyes widen with interest. *Got her.*

"No way." Bree steps in front of me, hands on her hips and blocking my view of Angel. "You're not taking her downtown."

"It's good bonding time."

"Whenever you *bond* with her, she comes home with bad habits."

"Is that true?" I ask Angel.

"*Redrum,*" she whispers in a fiendish voice, curling a tiny finger in front of her face like she's holding an imaginary finger puppet. Exactly how I taught her.

Laughter snorts past my nose. "Come on, Bree." I yank her ponytail. "It's funny."

"Whatever. It's time to go, Angel. Give Aunt Danni a hug."

"Nuh-uh." She jumps to her feet and spins away, arms folded across her chest.

"Angel," Bree says sternly. "Give your aunt a hug. *With arms.*"

"No thanks." I mimic Angel's pose. "I don't want forced affection."

Bree makes an irritated noise in her throat. "Fine."

I walk her out, rubbing the chill from my arms and bouncing in place as she helps Angel buckle up in the backseat. With her bent over and leaning into the car, I can't resist jabbing my toe into the back of her knee and forcing her leg to bend.

With a huff, she straightens and steps around to the driver seat. "Grow up, Danni."

"That sounds horribly boring and lame."

She rests a hand on the open door and looks at me over the top of the car. "What are you going to do about the meeting at the casino tonight?"

"I'll go if I feel like it." I shrug. "I have a counteroffer that'll make his ass clench."

Her disapproving glare rolls off my shoulders. "You have no idea what you're doing."

"Not knowing what I'm doing is kind of my superpower." I grin.

"Yeah, that's what I'm afraid of."

five
present

"Look at all those smiles." Father Rick Ortez leans against the wall beside me, his own grin twitching his gray mustache. "I'm always amazed at how many of them you can get on the dance floor."

It's not easy. No one at a homeless shelter has a reason to dance or smile. But I'm persistent, because when they finally give in and participate, they focus on learning the steps and laugh at their fumbling feet. In those small moments of levity, they forget about the tragedies that thrust them onto the streets.

Rick runs the shelter, and he doesn't wear his white collar here, so it's easy to forget he's a priest.

Which is the point. He wants all people to feel welcome, no matter their religion, race, or background.

On any given night, there are about fifteen-hundred homeless people in St. Louis. Since Gateway's occupancy permit only allows seventy-five beds, the shelter is always maxed out.

I recognize some of the faces tonight. Those I've never seen before are the hardest to coax into dancing. They don't know me, don't trust my intentions, and I don't blame them. But I have a strategy that works.

Line dancing. Anyone with two working legs can do it. I always start off alone, traveling through the steps and explaining each movement. After I draw a crowd, I cajole the most enthusiastic ones into joining me. Eventually a few more jump in. Then more and more.

I've been at it for hours, but they're finally warming up and letting go.

"Don't you have to dance at the restaurant tonight?" Rick runs a hand over his bald head, watching twenty people of various ages and dress teeter through the Cupid Shuffle.

I don't know what time it is, but my seven o'clock meeting with Trace Savoy is probably nearing. Or passed. I rather enjoy the thought of him waiting.

"My schedule changed." I guzzle the remainder of my water bottle. "Don't worry, Rick. I'll still be here a couple of times a week." I wish I could donate more time, more money.

"You have a good heart, Danni."

Good and broken. But no one here knows my background. I came to Gateway after I lost Cole, and I always move the engagement ring to my right hand before walking in. No questions. No past.

Two years ago, I started in the kitchen, hoping the volunteer work would direct my focus to other people's misery instead of my own. The line dancing lessons evolved from there. I figured if my goal is to put smiles on troubled faces, I'll find my own happiness in the process. It mostly works out that way. Sometimes I leave here feeling sadder than ever, but those times are rare.

I slide back into the dance line, rolling my hips and grinning at the elderly woman beside me. She's stiff and hunched over, her weathered complexion knitted with a lifetime of hardship. But her toothless smile makes my heart soar.

"Look at you." I touch the paper-thin skin on her elbow, guiding her through a turn. "You caught on quick."

"Oh, I..." She sidesteps, staggering and laughing at herself. "I don't know about that."

With my music player set on repeat, the Cupid Shuffle loops two more times before my phone vibrates in my back pocket. I stay in the line, twirling through the steps as I glance at the screen.

Unknown: You're late

According to my phone, it's only *7:01 PM*. A grin lifts my cheeks. If Trace had to pull my number from my website, I bet it really puckered his scowl to do so.

I step out of the dancing line and add his number to my contacts list. Not that I intend to talk to him after tonight. But I might be in the mood to make prank calls.

Flexing my hand, I type a response.

Me: Well-timed lateness is an art.

Trace: Punctuality is a professional courtesy.

Me: You're scowling, aren't you?

Trace: Where are you?

Me: Between here and there.

Trace: Your here better be in the casino.

He types fast, his texts pinging within seconds of mine.

Me: What do I get if it is?

Trace: A job.

Me: Oh right. The one that objectifies me. Tempting.

Trace: Tell me what you want.

Me: A smile would be a good start.

A heartbeat later, the ringtone on my phone plays *Try* by Pink, and his name flashes on the screen.

Oh man, he's persistent, and damn if that doesn't make me feel all bubbly inside.

I accept the call. "911. What's your emergency?"

After a moment of silence, his deep voice growls through the line. "What's that noise?"

I hold the phone toward the portable speakers for a few seconds and put it back at my ear. "Recognize it?"

"No."

"How do you not know the Cupid Shuffle?"

"The Cupid—? Never mind." His voice sharpens. "You're late."

"You already said that. Don't be tedious."

"This is fucking—" Something thumps through the connection, and he blows out a breath. "You're testing my patience."

"You're being presumptuous."

"What's that supposed to mean?"

"You assume I agreed to this meeting."

"Get. Your ass. In my office." His low even tone might lend power to his command, but it only makes me want to push all his buttons.

"Hmm." I sashay back into the dance line, synchronizing my steps with the song. "How about you try that again with *professional courtesy?*"

He sniffs and clears his throat on a heavy exhale. "Can I expect you this evening?"

"Much better. You can expect me later." I disconnect the call and dance through three more iterations of the shuffle before saying goodbye to my new friends.

Thirty minutes later, I leave my phone and keys in a hidden pocket beneath the driver's seat of the Midget. Then I make my way through the parking garage of The Regal Arch Casino and Hotel and step into the lobby.

Bright bursts of electronic sound and color assault my senses, and the stale scent of smoke tickles my lungs. An industrial theme dominates the decor, accented by numerous steel archways that curve and stretch overhead. Painted black and pinpricked with light, the domed ceilings twinkle like starry skies over thousands of glowing slot machines.

Tinkling, clinking, beeping noises clash in a battle of conflicting melodies. It's the discordant song of desperate people stuffing Trace Savoy's pockets with money.

As I stroll around the flashing machines, no one socializes or glances my way. Row after row, the gamblers lean back, bend forward, and puff on cigarettes. Brows grooved in concentration. Hands poised to punch a button or pull a lever. It's mesmerizing. And kind of sad.

A path of swirly-patterned carpet leads to a bank of silver elevators on the far side of the gaming area. Instead of heading to the 30th floor, I wander toward the restaurant on the opposite end.

Slipping inside the vacant dining room, I sidle around piles of construction materials and plastic sheeting. The overhead lights are off, the workers gone for the day. If this is Bissara's new location, Trace didn't waste time starting the renovations. When a small round stage at the center comes into view, I know I'm in the right place.

I stride toward the platform, circling the eight-foot diameter. It rises to chest level without steps to climb on. So I kick off my flip-flops and hoist myself up to stand on the dark acrylic surface.

Glass walls separate the restaurant and gaming area, dampening the blaring beeps and tinkles of slot machines. But I can see them—the kaleidoscope of neon lights illuminating the serious faces of addicts doing what they need to do.

That's six million patrons strolling through my doors

and resting their eyes on the art you create through movement.

The stage is certainly visible from the most active gaming areas, but gamblers aren't looking around at the scenery. They sit in a trance, focused on their drug, determined to win. None of them would notice a belly dancer in the restaurant.

"Are you lost?" An unfamiliar masculine voice drifts from the shadowed corner near the entrance.

I turn and spot a dark figure reclined at one of the tables. "Nope. Are you?"

"I work here." The man stands and walks toward me, dressed in a white collared shirt, black pants, and black vest. "I'm a blackjack dealer."

He nods at the casino tables beyond the glass, where men and women wear uniforms like his, their hands busy with cards and chips.

As he approaches, I lower to the edge of the stage and dangle my legs over the side.

Dark hair, slim build, and trimmed beard, he's neither ugly nor handsome. But I don't trust that smile. It's too assertive and greasy.

"I'm James." He holds out a hand.

"Danni." I clasp his clammy fingers and pull back, keeping the exit behind him in my periphery. "Shouldn't you be working?"

"I'm on break." He licks his lips as his eager gaze sweeps over my skinny jeans and pauses on my shoulder, which is bared by the wide neck of my slouchy shirt.

Dancers aren't shy about showing skin, and I'm no exception. James can leer all he wants if he keeps his hands to himself.

He bends closer, resting a hand on the stage beside my hip. "This might come across as a little aggressive…"

"It's only aggressive if you have something aggressive in mind."

"Go out with me tonight."

"Why would I do that?"

"Well, you're a beautiful woman." He leans a hip against the platform. "It just so happens I have a thing for beautiful women." His smile twists suggestively. "I get off work in an hour. What do you say we get to know each other?"

A smart girl would tell him to get lost, but I'm a glutton for mischievous conversation. "What would *getting to know each other* involve?"

His eyebrows jump up, and he quickly smooths his expression. "Dinner?"

"I already ate."

"Drinks?"

"Then what?"

He rubs the back of his neck. "Uh…"

"Tell me exactly how you imagine getting to know me, James." I trap my bottom lip between my teeth and release it. "Or are you afraid to say?"

A shadow moves at the edge of my vision. It's out of focus, but I make out a tall silhouette in the doorway behind James. I don't shift my gaze. I don't have to. The sensation of being lividly and intensely glared at tells me exactly who lingers at the entrance of the dining room.

"I have lots of ideas." James scratches his beard and scrutinizes my body with slimy intent, oblivious of the casino owner standing behind him. "I don't know if I should say —"

"You better spit it out before my employer gets

here. He hasn't had sex in years, and it's turned him into an intolerable, angry ogre."

"You work here?"

"Nope. What happens after drinks, James?"

"Okay, so I'm thinking..." He fiddles with his necktie. "I'll take you home. And kiss you. And touch you. And make sweet love to you."

I don't even try to hide my cringe. "Boring."

"What? Which part?"

"Make sweet love? Dude, you can do better than that."

"I don't know wha—"

"Do you like anal play?" Knowing Trace is listening makes it damn hard to keep a straight face, but somehow, I manage it.

James sucks in a breath and flattens a hand over his heart. "Yes! I mean, what man doesn't?"

"*Your* rectum, James. Not mine. Have you ever been pegged by a thirteen-inch dildo?"

"No." A flush rises up his neck, and he retreats backward a step. "Fuck, no."

"That's too bad. We could've had something beautiful together."

"Enough." Trace appears beside James, his murderous glare trained on the other man.

Recognition widens James' eyes as *Oh-Jesus-I'm-fucked* contorts his expression.

"You're fired." Trace bares his teeth, towering over James. "Gather your things and—"

"Stop it." I poke a toe against Trace's rock-hard thigh then lean toward James, whispering loudly around the cup of my hand. "He can't get it up. Makes him

67

unbearably bad-tempered."

"Danni." Trace growls.

"Don't worry about him," I say to James, leaning back. "You're not fired."

"Mr. Savoy? Sir?" He drops his chin, practically bowing. "I need this job. I didn't mean any harm."

Trace clasps his hands behind him, his glower firmly directed at James. "You harassed a casino employee —"

"A casino *guest*." I cross my legs at the knee and bounce my foot. "*I* harassed *him*. The poor guy didn't stand a chance."

"That's not what I overheard."

"Sounds like a *you* problem. Get your hearing checked."

"I have zero tolerance for this kind of behavior in my casino." His voice is steady and controlled as it snaps through the room.

"So authoritative and manly." I feign a shiver and blink doe eyes at him. "Being the weak vulnerable female that I am, I would've never been able to handle this conversation on my own."

A muscle ticks in his jaw. Maybe he'll grab at his hair and mess it all up. As is, every blond strand flawlessly molds into a textured slick-back style. But he doesn't scrape a hand through it, doesn't clench his fists, or do anything to suggest an unraveling composure. I can't decide if his indomitable self-control is sexy or aggravating.

"James." I prop an elbow on my thigh and rest my hand beneath my chin. "Will you hit on casino guests in the future?"

"No." James looks from me to Trace. "I promise,

sir."

Trace points his scowl at me, and I give him a playful wink.

"Consider this your only warning." He stabs a finger toward the door. "Get back to your station."

"Yes, sir. Thank you." James races out of the restaurant like hell's breathing up his ass.

Reclining back with my arms braced on the stage behind me, I meet Trace's stony stare. "Waiting for someone?"

His nostrils widen and relax as he glances at his watch. "She's fifty-three minutes late."

"She sounds important. Especially if she dragged his lordliness out of his royal tower to consort with the commoners."

"She's a royal pain in my ass. I'm rethinking the job I offered her."

"Rock on. She wasn't going to accept it anyway."

His eyes narrow. "Then why are you here?"

I squint right back. "How did you know I was here?"

He huffs a sharp sound and flicks a finger at the ceiling.

Elaborate glass fixtures of every color create a mosaic design overhead. A closer look reveals tiny black globes amid the art work. *Cameras. Of course.*

"You were spying on me? I could have you arrested for stalking." I arch a brow. "And trespassing in my house. Any other crimes I should be aware of?"

"Cut the shit, Danni."

"Oh, Trace. I wouldn't shit you. We're just getting to know each other."

"Yeah?" He strokes his bottom lip, tempting me to kiss it. "I heard how you get to know men."

"Anal play?"

His frown jerks, as if an invisible finger yanks it up at the corner.

"You smiled!" I feign a gasp, pointing at his mouth. "Did it hurt?"

He grunts.

Maybe I can coax another one. "Do you fancy a thirteen-inch dildo, Mr. Savoy?"

He glances at the empty doorway and composes his expression into that of an imperious casino boss. "I see you found the stage. Is it adequate for your routine?"

Ugh. So stiff. I'd love to see him loosen up. I bet it's glorious.

"Depends." I swing my legs around and stand at the center of the platform. "Still rethinking that job offer?"

His gaze latches onto my mouth before it makes a slow descent along my neck, tracing the shape of my breasts, my hips, and the apex of my thighs. My entire body reacts, igniting deep within my core and spreading outward to inflame my skin. My nipples tighten. My pulse kicks up, and a throbbing ache flares between my legs.

Jesus, this man is potent. All he has to do is stand there in his tailored suit and transmit displeasure like it's foreplay. His sculpted lips part naturally, forming an enticing fracture in that scowl, which is framed by a jawline carved in right angles. So commanding. Masculine. Way too hot for a stuffed shirt.

He hasn't moved his focus from the vicinity of my crotch, so I snap my fingers in his line of sight.

Those stark blue eyes jump to my face, and there's something glowing in the depths. Something needy and compulsive and...*resentful.*

"You don't like me very much, do you?" I anchor my fists on my hips.

"That's negligible." He paces around the stage, hands folded behind him. "Let's go to my office so you can sign the contract and —"

"I don't think so, Scoot McGoot." I stretch my arms out, encompassing the 360-degree panorama of crowded casino tables and one-armed bandits. "I hate to break it to you, because this really is a great stage, but no one out there cares about a dancer in a restaurant. Doesn't matter how much you pay me."

His pacing veers toward the bar, where he bends behind the steel counter, vanishing from view.

Before I can ask what he's doing, a column of soft light envelopes me from head to toe. The source shines from beneath my feet, and as I step forward, the light follows me, effectively encasing me in a glowing tube.

"So cool." I bounce from side to side, captivated by the accuracy of the motion sensor.

He messes with something on the back wall, and a sultry, fast-tempo pop song streams from hidden speakers. I recognize it immediately. The deep vocals of the Haitian rapper. The stately resonance of brass instruments. The vibrating *clap-clap-clap* of percussion. The high-energy composition of *Hips Don't Lie* by Shakira. It's a song I practice to often, and my body twitches to ride the rhythm.

"Dance." Trace stalks toward the stage and stares up at me. "Please."

Saturated in the beam of light beneath my toes, I tremble with excitement. His *please* isn't the only reason I pull off my shirt, but it's a powerful incentive. I doubt he uses that word often, and standing before him in a sports bra and low-waist jeans, I'm happy to oblige.

The music thumps through me, setting the pace of my breaths. My arms move first, lifting sensuously, flowing like a lazy wave from one hand to the other and taking my shoulders with them. I hold my hips still, concentrating all movement above my chest. Making him wait for it.

The way he stares up at me... Sweet hell, it says everything he doesn't. Grave and serious, his blue eyes devour my body with naked interest, as if I'm beautiful, as if he desperately wants to touch me, grab me, fuck me.

Buttoned up and crisply starched, his suit molds to the muscled form of his body, as if challenging me to stare. To want. To conjure images of my hands stripping every immaculate layer.

The volume grows louder, and I engage my abdominal wall, undulating the muscles in a rippling shiver. His thick shoulders lift with an intake of air, a breath he holds for several counts before releasing, relaxing, and inhaling again.

I affect him—my body, my art, my command of both. It gives me a sense of power over him. Not that I intend to see him again, but for one night, in an empty restaurant, it's invigorating.

When the song reaches a staccato rhythm, I punctuate the beats with vertical hip drops, outward hip hits, shoulder accents, and ribcage lifts. The fluid motion of my body aligns with the instruments, pulling me into a state of hypnosis that carries me across the platform, floating on a column of light and curving my lips from corner to corner.

I smile because I appreciate the sensual gestures, the mellifluous lines and bends of my frame. I smile because as Trace watches me, his eyes glow at max voltage, electrocuting the short distance between us.

Leaning toward him, I shimmy what little I have on my chest and meet his gaze. Bending deeper, I hang my head and roll my shoulders in a dance of their own, caught in the music, held by the moment.

Upside down, my hair sweeps the floor, arms hanging beside my face as my deltoids, lats, and traps contract and bounce in a textured choreography of muscle.

Slowly, I rise, raising my arms above my head and rolling my hips in infinity loops. As I lower my hands alongside my face, I writhe my fingers in sinuous, seductive waves, tilting my head, gyrating my pelvis, and making his jaw dip lower, lower…

He snaps his mouth shut, his chest rising and the rims of his eyes tightening with tension.

I know what he sees. I've memorized my reflection in the mirror as I sway and rock through the serpentine maneuvers. The shimmies, shivers, and flexibility of my hips. The female form moving in a way that simulates flexibility, promiscuity, and sexual energy. I'm an actress on a stage, eliciting emotion and feeding off the reactions. Or in this case, one reaction.

I put an extra kick in my hip tilts and laugh as his jaw twitches toward a smile. "You like that?"

His face instantly cements back into stone, his eyes thunderous.

The song winds to a close, and I slow my movements, lowering my arms and gazing to the side and at the floor until silence blankets the room. Then I bend in a customary bow and blow him a kiss as I straighten.

He reaches for the knot of his tie and drops his hand. "Turn around."

"Why?"

His lips clamp together, darkening his expression, as if I committed blasphemy by questioning him.

Our silent standoff doesn't last long. I'm too curious to not turn around, and when I do, my breath hitches. "Whoa."

Twenty, thirty…maybe fifty people gather on the other side of the glass wall. Most are men, but women congregate, too. And employees. Others linger near the tables farther back, eyes pointed in my direction, watching.

I wave at the crowd and smile. "Why are they — ?"

"You're good, Danni." His timbre comes from somewhere near the bar behind me.

The light beneath my feet blinks off, veiling me in shadows and signaling the audience to disperse.

"You really think I'm good, huh?" I hop off the stage and slip my feet into the flip-flops.

"Not just good. You're captivating." Trace strides toward me and grabs my shirt from the floor.

I reach for his hand, but he yanks it back and proceeds to guide the shirt over my head. The gesture stutters my breath, and when my face emerges through the neck hole, I stare at him with wide eyes.

Focused on his task, he lifts my arm, then the other, sliding each of my hands slowly, gently, through the sleeves. Letting him do this feels so strangely intimate I'm at a loss for how to respond. It's such a small thing, but it's been a long time since I've been tended to like this. Too long, apparently, given the swarm of bees diving and whirring in my stomach.

He straightens the shirt around my hips and drifts closer, his finger trailing oh-so-softly along my jaw. "Watching you dance is an exquisite experience. The freedom in your movements, the pleasure on your face… it evokes feelings that are deeper, hotter" — he bends so close his lips brush my ear — "better than sex."

Shuddering warmth curls through me. "You must not be having very good sex."

He touches his brow against my temple, his hand sweeping back to trace my spine as his minty breath bathes me in heat. "I imagine sex with you would annihilate every experience a man has ever had."

Holy hell, I feel every raspy word like hungry kisses along my neck. "What are you doing, Trace?"

He steps back and smooths a hand over his tie, his scowl harder, angrier than before. "I want to finish this meeting in my office. The contract — "

"And just like that, you completely ruin a good moment." From the back pocket of my jeans, I hand him a folded scrap of paper. "I have a counteroffer."

He takes it and strides toward the exit, leaving me standing there with my mouth open.

What the shit just happened?

"Wait." I trail after him. "Aren't you going to read it?"

"Yes."

I chase him all the way to the elevators. And by

chase, I mean sprint, because damn his long legs.

His unapproachable demeanor allows him to move through the casino without being stopped or interrupted with idle conversation. The crowd actually parts to move out of his way.

He attracts attention from everyone he passes, especially from the women. His towering height and expensive suit are noteworthy, but it's his arresting looks—the sexy blond hair, sculpted features, broad shoulders—that weaken knees and drop jaws. Alluring and mysterious, he's an orgasm for the eyes.

Bypassing the public lifts, he strides down an empty corridor, where another elevator waits. He punches in a passcode, and the doors slide open.

"Your own personal lift?" I step inside the mirrored box.

"Yes." He follows me in with my counteroffer folded in his hand.

How much longer is this going to drag out? I'm ready for him to read my demands, lose his shit, and send me on my way.

The panel of buttons only provides access to the 30th floor, 31st floor, and a few underground levels. He presses *30*.

"What's on the top floor?" I lean against the wall opposite him.

"My residence."

He lives in the hotel? In the penthouse, evidently. How disappointingly prosaic.

As the elevator shoots upward, he unfolds the paper. His eyes flick over my handwriting, his features stoic and indecipherable. When I'm certain he's read through all of it, my nerves kick in. He doesn't look up, doesn't react at all.

My preposterous counteroffer demands a salary that rivals that of a tenured surgeon. It also includes other requirements, such as a wardrobe budget, private dressing room, retirement contribution, health care, paid vacation, and free alcohol at the casino bars. The health insurance would be nice since I haven't had medical coverage since college, but I don't give a fuck about the rest of it.

With slow exacting movements, he folds the paper and tucks it into the interior pocket of his suit. Then he rests his hands on the guard rail behind him, crosses one shiny shoe over the other, and meets my eyes.

His expression is firm, leaning toward unkind, but there's a hint of deviousness deep in the brackets around his scowl. I can't decide if he's going to kiss me or say something hateful.

It's curious how he always tilts that strong chin downward, a mannerism that forces him to look up. Since he's so tall, maybe bowing his head is a matter of practicality. Or maybe it's deliberate because he knows that upward glare appears darker and more intimidating beneath the brooding mantle of his brow.

I wish he wasn't so damn attractive or that I wasn't so enthralled with his severe personality. Because as I wait for him to push the button that will send me back to the lobby and out of his life, part of me regrets sabotaging this opportunity. I need the job, but more than that, I need someone with his impenetrable resolve in my life. A partner who will challenge me. A man who will stand up to me. A lover who will inspire me out of my celibate funk.

It's not that I'm good at reading people. I'm not. But there's a subtle air about Trace Savoy, one he tries to stifle. On the surface, he's too cavalier. Too arrogant and apathetic. It's a facade. Beneath that callous shell lurks an interested, impassioned, sexual man. I've glimpsed it in the creases of his expression, in his heated words, and in the caress of his touch on my face. I want more of it. I need to know if there's something between us, something that could grow and stretch and take flight.

I search his beautiful face, looking for clues to what he's thinking and find nothing. "You're toying with me."

"Your counteroffer suggests…" He pushes off the wall and in two strides, he puts his face in mine with his hands on the guard rail behind me. "*You* are toying with *me.*"

He's deliberately crowding me. My head doesn't even reach the knot on his tie, so I have to angle my neck way back to meet his gaze. It's a position meant to make me feel smaller, more vulnerable. Little does he know, he can't hurt me. I've been hurt — a hurt so mortally, inconsolably excruciating there's nothing left in me to break.

The elevator dings, and the doors open. He doesn't move.

And that glare. That hostile, infuriating, sexy goddamn glare makes my thighs clench and my skin heat.

"Maybe I *am* toying with you." I want to feel the curve of his scowl, so I give into the indulgence and stroke a finger across his full bottom lip. "What are you going to do about it, Mr. Savoy?"

He flashes me a scathing smile that isn't a smile at all as it sends chills from my tailbone to my neck. "I'm

one *is a promise*

going to accept your demands."

six
present

"Accept my demands?" I chase Trace out of the elevator and through the unlit lobby on the 30th floor. "Are you serious?"

His gait is driven and focused as he passes a small sitting area, swerves around a steel reception desk, and vanishes into a dark corridor.

I slam to a halt in the empty lobby, reeling from shock and confusion. Should I leave? Instinct urges me to return to the elevator, because no one in their right mind offers a belly dancer that kind of money, let alone all the benefits I outlined. Did he even read the counteroffer?

Turning toward the window beside a leather

couch, I lower onto the cushion and face the glass. In the distance, the St. Louis Arch rises over the banks of the Mississippi River, its curved silver shape like a handle on the twinkling metropolis. Buildings of various heights spread out around it, and among those structures is Gateway Shelter. With its seventy-five beds already occupied, they'll be turning away homeless people for the rest of the night.

I can't stop thinking about that as I stare out the window and analyze my feelings. I donate every extra penny to the shelter, which isn't much. But if I accept this job, if Trace is serious about meeting my ridiculous salary requirements, my God, I could help the shelter expand, add more beds, healthier food, softer blankets. Oh, the possibilities!

I'm getting ahead of myself. Trace is up to something, and it can't be good.

Would a belly dancer increase the revenue in his casino? Maybe. I saw the crowd gathering downstairs, and that was without my costumes or the fine-dining services he intends to provide.

Am I the best belly dancer in St. Louis? For sure. But he could find a better dancer outside of the city and pay her just enough to relocate.

That leaves me with one conclusion.

He wants *me,* and his interest is personal.

"Danni!" he bellows from somewhere down the hall. "I'm waiting!"

I pinch the bridge of my nose. If I take this job, I'll have to train him. The Marlo Vogt's of the world might jump at his grunting, barking, glowering bullshit, but I work for myself and cower to no one.

The question is, do I have a personal interest in

him?

I turn my attention to the view outside the window, admire the glimmering reflection of the cityscape on the river, and come to terms with the situation. I'm drawn to him in a way I haven't been drawn to anyone since Cole.

Trace could be both a job and a solution for my loneliness. Maybe we'll fuck. Maybe we won't. What's the worst that could happen? If it gets complicated, I'll quit the belly dancing gig and focus on teaching and other side jobs.

But before I seriously consider this, I need a better feel for his intentions.

A short walk takes me down the hall and into the only open doorway at the end. Inside a huge lavish office, he sits behind a glass desk with steel supports shaped like mini arches. His attention doesn't leave the laptop in front of him, his fingers tapping over the keys.

"I'm on to you." I stroll toward him and circle the desk to stand beside him.

He doesn't acknowledge me as he sends what appears to be a revised contract to the printer across the room. Seated in a stiff leather chair, he's almost eye-level with me, his sexy blond hair close enough for the woodsy aroma of his shampoo to reach my nose.

After a few more clicks on the keyboard, he shuts down the laptop and swivels the chair to position his knees on the outsides of mine. "You're on to me?"

"Sure am." I cock a hip and hook my thumbs in the back pockets of my jeans. "This thing you're cooking up between us? With the house visit and the stage in your new restaurant and the obscene salary? It's more than a business deal."

He props an elbow on the armrest, rubs his jaw, and stares at me with disinterest. "How does that make you feel emotionally?"

"Emotionally?" I jerk my head back, grappling for what to say. "Do you say random shit just to keep things interesting?"

"Depends. Are you interested?"

He has contempt and sarcasm down to an art, but I think, maybe, this might be his attempt at humor?

"You're a lot of fun, Trace," I deadpan. "You're also strange." *Strange in an elusive, intriguing, I-bet-he's-kinky-as-hell way.* "Did you actually read my counteroffer?"

"I did." He rolls the chair back, rises to cross the room, and returns with the document from the printer. "I met all your demands except the schedule. I'm not paying you three-hundred grand a year to work two nights a week."

I choke at the mention of the salary, even though I'm the one who wrote it into the offer. It was just a number I pulled out of my ass. What if I'd asked for more? What's his breaking point on this deal?

He places the contract on the desk beside me, and there, stated in bold print is his requirement of five nights per week. Wednesday through Sunday. Three to midnight, with a one-hour break.

"I have a busy schedule." I cross my arms. "I'll give you two nights."

"Five nights, and you'll agree to a one-year contract with the option to renew." He stands over me by sheer height and taps the signature line on the contract. "Sign here."

No way in hell will I agree to a year. "Three nights, and you'll get a two-weeks notice whenever I grow bored of your sparkling personality."

He clasps his hands behind his back and stares at the document. "Five nights a week, and you can have your two-weeks notice."

Fuck, how can I turn that down? I pace away from him, walking a circuit through the office as I think.

Who is this man, this modern-day overlord, who sits behind a desk, beckoning people to his presence and casting down hirings and firings? His simple yet luxurious corner office with its gray tones and architecturally-themed lamps and furniture validates his rich and powerful status. But there are no pictures or awards. No memorabilia or framed degrees. Not a trace of the man behind the suit.

"How old are you?" I glance over my shoulder and find him facing the wall of glass that frames the Gateway Arch in the distance.

"Thirty." He doesn't look at me, though he can probably see my reflection in the window. "You?"

"Twenty-eight." I pivot, making my way back to him. "How did you become the owner of…" I wave a hand at the office. "All this?"

"All this?"

"The largest hotel and casino in the Midwest."

"Wealthy parents."

I'm not sure what surprises me more — his candidness or the icy chill in his tone.

"Trust fund?" I rest a shoulder against the glass beside him.

"Inheritance. They died a couple of years ago."

Oh. My chest clenches. "I'm sorry." I soften my voice. "How did they — ?"

"You've wasted enough of my time tonight." He tosses a pen on the desk behind him. "Sign the contract, Danni."

I suck in a breath. "Don't do that. If I cross the line with you, just tell me. You don't have to be a dick about it."

He bends down, putting his face in mine and forcing my back against the cold window. "You're having a hard time understanding the roles here, so I'll make it clear for you." He brushes his nose through my hair. "You don't know me, and you're not going to know me. From this point forward, you'll do what I say with a great deal more respect than you've shown me so far."

"I don't know about that last part, but I do know you." I slide my fingers beneath the lapel of his suit jacket.

"Is that right?" He doesn't push my hand away and instead rests his weight on an arm braced against the window above my head, his mouth inches from mine.

"Yep." I tilt my chin up to meet his arctic eyes. "You don't date or do relationships. You fuck. Then you send them home with a pat on the ass."

He scowls in a way only he can make look indecent.

"You exude intimidation and upper-class superiority," I say, "because you want everyone to think you're aloof and untouchable. And maybe you are." I push against the rigid wall of his chest. "But being aloof and untouchable is kind of like being an asshole, and that's not a special trait. The world is overrun with assholes. You don't have to be smart or wealthy or good-looking to join that club."

His gaze narrows, cutting like blue lasers. "I know you, too, Danni Angelo."

"Oh yeah?" I feather my fingers down the buttons of his shirt. "Do tell."

His eyes follow the movement, one blond brow arrogantly arched. "The only thing you hate more than an asshole is a guy who isn't an asshole."

I flatten my spine against the window. "That's not—"

"Sensitive guys bore you, and their flattery gets them nowhere. Assholes make your pulse race and your panties wet, especially when they tell you when, where, and how hard."

Heat coalesces between my legs, and my molars crash together. Damn him.

"You're the kind of dish that looks enticing, smells delicious, and tastes even better." He gives me a chilly once-over bristling with judgment. "But after a few bites, it festers in the gut like a bad decision."

An abrasive breath lodges in my throat, and my face tightens. "What's the matter, Mr. Savoy? Too scared to sample something deep and stimulating for a change?"

He smirks, and I don't like the satisfied glimmer in his eyes. I slip out of the confined space between him and the window, seeking distance.

"You're messy." He glares at my hand where I twist the silver band on my right finger.

I drop my arms to my sides as outrage spikes through my blood. "I'm not—"

"I could fuck you right now, right here, and give you more pleasure than the son of a bitch who gave you that ring." His arm snaps up, and his hand wraps around my throat.

How dare he insult Cole and manhandle me like this? I should rage at him, but as my heartbeat jumps against the fist shackling my neck, my entire body throbs erratically, excitedly, wantonly.

"Tease," I choke out.

He uses his grip to force me backwards until the edge of his desk hits my legs. "Doesn't matter how hard I make you come, you'll go home and cry yourself to sleep over the man you're still in love with." He releases me and straightens. "You're an emotional mess, and I don't want any part of it."

Anger flares, burning up my cheeks.

"I'm human." I lurch toward him and shove at his chest. "A feeling, passionate, warm-blooded human, you callous prick."

He allows me to push at him, his expression volcanic and breaths coming hot and fast, steeping the air between us.

If he doesn't want *any part of it,* why did he demand I come here and take this job? His mixed signals are maddening.

"I don't understand what you want." I spin away and move to the desk where the contract waits. "I'll do the job under the negotiated terms, but I'm not signing anything."

I don't hear him approach as the scorching proximity of his body envelops my back. He brushes my hair to the side, and his fingers glide with diabolical pressure over my nape, around my throat, stretching toward my breastbone and slipping beneath the neck of the shirt as his thumb strokes the base of my skull. Then his breath is there, a furnace of seduction tickling my ear and racing shivers across my skin.

"I want to watch your body move." His mouth grazes my bare shoulder. "Five nights a week. In my casino."

Watching you dance… It evokes feelings that are deeper, hotter, better than sex.

Is this a kink of his? Watching a woman undulate her hips without touching her? Except he *is* touching, his hand slipping from my neck, down my shoulder blade, and snaking around my ribs to clutch my waist. It feels so good to be in strong, masculine arms I arch back against him and sway my hips.

Instead of pulling away, he rocks with me — a slow, instinctual grind that vacillates to the rhythm of our breaths. It's unexpected, drugging, and insane. But I sink into the groove, glorying in the feel of his powerful frame cradling my backside.

He runs the heel of his free hand across my collarbones, banding my chest with his forearm and hugging me against him. "I fucking love your body."

"But not my *messy* personality?" My head falls back on his shoulder.

"Exactly."

My stomach hardens. "What a cruel thing to say."

"You don't look offended." He touches his lips to my neck and rolls his hips against me.

The steely length of his erection prods and rubs, leaving little to the imagination. Hard and thick, the man is hung.

But I'm stuck on his words. He's interested in my body, in watching me move, but nothing else? He's embracing me, roaming his hands over my curves while avoiding my breasts and everywhere below my waist. If another man touched me like this with his arousal pressing against me, I'd know his intent. But Trace has made it clear he doesn't want me, at least not in a tumble-between-the-sheets way.

So why is he holding me? His desire is evident in the heave of his breaths and the swell of his cock. I want to demand an explanation. But I'm afraid he'll push me away, and dammit, I'm not ready for cold isolation to slip back in. It's been too long since I've been held by a powerful, sexy man.

Not only that, he knows how to move. We're not actually dancing, but there's freedom and natural rhythm in the sway of his hips, both of which are deadly temptations for my music-loving soul.

"Do you dance?" I ask.

"When the need arises."

"Ballroom dancing at fancy parties?"

"Correct." He nips at my neck.

"Dance with me. I want to see your moves."

"No." His teeth press against my skin.

I rest my hands on his hips behind me, following the narrow lines of his suit and relishing the contours and indentations of taut muscle beneath the fabric. "You only want to watch?"

"That's right." He drags his nose along my throat.

"After you watch me dance, then what?"

"Then nothing." The hand beneath my breast shifts upward, dangerously close to cupping me.

"I feel your erection, Trace. What would you do if I grabbed it?"

"Try it and find out."

His voice is raspy and thick, but I hear the threat sharpening the syllables. If I grope him, this little dance ends. I might be bold enough to wrap my hand around his cock, but the rejection would sting.

He seems content to just stand here, rocking and molding his hands to the bends and dips of my body. It's both confusing and comforting. If he were simply fondling me like Mark had done last night, I would know how to respond. But this is different. His lips caress my neck adoringly, erotically, luring me into a trance that messes with my head.

If I had any self-control, I'd end this meeting and go home. But I crave his small doses of affection, hunger to kiss him, and ache to strip out of my itchy clothes and melt beneath his touch, his mouth, his thrusts. Sex with him would be turbulent, pyretic, and wholly satisfying.

My pulse hammers at the thought of fighting with him, wrestling and fucking in a tangle of sweat-slick limbs. Maybe he's right. I do enjoy a challenging asshole, and I'm compelled to explore the enigma of this infuriating man.

But he thinks I'm messy. The more I roll that around in my mind, the more I want to prove him wrong. In fact, I'm starting to think he's intentionally trying to get under my skin.

Twisting in his arms, I lift on tiptoes and search his glacial gaze. "You're up to something."

"I'm not." His tone is stringent, unmoved.

"You are. You're gambling with my emotions. Taking bets on my libido."

"Are you making casino jokes now?" He huffs a laugh—a single humorless pulse of sound.

His impassive expression further enrages me, and I shove at his chest. He steps back, but I stay with him, pushing until he bumps into the window behind him.

"You can't love my body," I say, holding my palm against the lapel of his jacket, "and not want to fuck me."

Dear God, what's gotten into me? I really do need to get laid. It's like he's triggered a chemical in my brain that's robbed me of all shame.

His breathing speeds up again, and he raises his arms against the window on either side of his head, as if opening himself up to me. Or holding himself back.

"I want full disclosure." I press my palms against his, crowding him in the cage of my arms. "Just tell me what this is so we can move on."

If someone walked in, they would think I'm pinning him to the glass, but that's not the case. Though his back and hands are pressed to the window, he's stronger, bigger, and more aggressive. He's allowing this, and the flicker in his eyes tells me he likes it.

"You want to know if I intend to fuck you?" His fingers curl around mine.

Then he dips his head. Before I can blink, he kisses me. A brutal whiplash of a kiss that sucks the air from my lungs and skyrockets my pulse. I anticipate the lash of his tongue, but it never comes. His teeth catch my bottom lip, a sharp twinge of pain, and he leans back.

"No," he says coldly. "I will not have sex with you."

But that kiss. It lingers on my mouth like a trail of fire.

"What?" I dig my fingernails into his palms. "Why the fuck did you kiss me?"

"Because I can." He swings us around, reversing

our positions. Rather than closing in, he breaks away and lowers in the chair at his desk. "Good night, Danni."

My gaze falls to the thick column of his neck, the starched white collar, and the squared shoulders beneath the stiff fabric of his suit jacket. Focused on his laptop, he wakes the screen and launches a spreadsheet, his demeanor all business, his dismissal unquestionable.

Maybe I'm delusional, but it feels like I made a tiny bit of progress, if I count that angry kiss. My curiosity is more piqued than ever, my fascination not even close to being satisfied.

It's not like I want a relationship with him, but I can't stop myself from recalling the torrid sensation of that huge hand wrapped around my throat or imagining it spanning over my bare ass, slapping and reddening my skin as he plows into me with hard-hitting thrusts. No doubt he's massive, rock-hard, and strong everywhere, an image that produces ripples of pulsations through the long-neglected muscles between my legs.

Christ, I need to get out of here.

"Call me when the restaurant is open." I stride toward the door.

"You'll be here tomorrow morning." He doesn't glance up from the laptop.

"Why would I—?"

"You'll meet with HR and fill out your paperwork. Eight o'clock." He reaches under the glass ledge of the desk, and a sharp buzz sounds overhead. "Don't be late."

The door releases from the wall and swings toward me. I shuffle backward into the hall to avoid colliding with the swinging wall of steel. It clicks shut, and the sound of electronic tumblers announces that he locked me out of his office.

A shocked laugh escapes my lips. I bet that dick move makes him feel all powerful and authoritative. I want to be annoyed by it, but instead, I find his social ineptitude oddly addictive.

As I exit the 30th floor and amble through the parking garage, my blood sings and my heart thumps wildly, enthusiastically, for the first time since Cole.

seven
three years ago

Stay by Rihanna plays on my phone where it sits on the plywood subfloor in my brand-spanking-new dance studio. The aroma of sawdust and sweat and excitement infuses the air as I rock my hips and study my reflection in the newly hung mirrors.

Cole kneels several feet behind me, installing the final ballet bar in the room he recently added on the rear of my house. Dust coats his Converse and faded jeans, his torso scrumptiously bare and rippling with overworked muscle.

I still can't believe he built me a dance room. Who does that? When he showed me the designs and told me he was paying for everything, I sobbed hideous snot-laden tears of joy. Then I tried to talk him out of it, which I've learned is a wasted effort when his mind is made up.

It's been nine months since we met in the street on that fateful morning. We fucked like animals that first night, and he moved in a month later. To say it's been a whirlwind is an understatement. Every second of every day is a combustible haze of touching, kissing, intoxicating delirium that obscures our awareness of the world around us.

Inseparable to the point of infatuation, we're sickeningly, obsessively, can't-get-enough-of-each-other in love. I can't imagine this fever ever fading. It's too strong, too real, too deeply and intricately woven into the fiber of my being.

His dense lashes lift, and his brown eyes connect with mine. The need to kiss him hits me directly in the chest, and my pulse kicks into a wild crescendo. Is it possible for two people to kiss *too* much?

When our mouths aren't locked together in aggressive passion, we're grinning stupidly at each other. Like now.

That smile of his puts me in my feelings, and his dimples dare me to come closer, for a taste, a touch, for a full-body saturation in all things Cole.

"You're distracting me, baby." His gaze darkens, drifting lazily over my body.

"And?" I lift the hair off my damp nape and hold it on top of my head.

Now that I have his attention, I work my stomach muscles, contract my spine, and let my hips flow sensually to the provocative vocals.

I feel silly dancing around in his heavy work boots,

but he demanded I wear them to protect my feet. Always so demanding and protective, but he does it in a manner that makes me feel cared for and loved. A girl could get use to this. She could become attached.

What am I thinking? I'm way past attached.

Sitting back on his heels, he swipes the back of a hand over his glistening brow. "If you're going to tease me with that sexy ass, do it on the pole."

He surprised me with the stripper pole a couple of hours ago, having installed it while I was running errands. I haven't danced on it yet, deciding to save that erotic show until after we've both showered.

"What do you have left to do tonight?" I sashay toward him, singing along with Rihanna, twisting my hips, and sensually moving my arms above my head.

"Danni, you're killing me here." He groans, and his fingers clench around the drill in his hand. "I was going to start on the wood floors tonight."

I'm tempted to pout, but I won't. He's doing this for me, and I'm so damn grateful. I'll be thanking him with my body all night long, because holy hell, he wears dirt and sweat like a sexy tatted-up rock star.

"Stop looking at me like that." His jaw flexes, his expression a storm of unrestrained desire. "Christ, you're making me hard."

"I wish I could stop, but when I see you, all I want to do is rip your clothes off and wrap my pussy around your cock."

He curls his fingers against his thigh and looks around the unfinished room, an internal battle straining his gorgeous face. Oh, he wants to fuck me, but he knows as well as I do that anticipation makes it so much hotter.

"If you behave," he says, his tone hard and uncompromising, "I'll give you my cock. When *I* am ready."

A shiver pulses through me. One thing's for certain. He'll fuck me rough and dirty, overpowering me in a way I never imagined wanting or enjoying. Now that I've experienced Cole's brand of sex, I won't ever go back to grunting and groping in the dark with a passive man. I hope to never touch another man again.

He returns his attention to the ballet bar, but I know he's aware of my every move. Each time I shake my hips, flick my wrists, or swipe my tongue along my lips, a smile takes hold of his mouth.

His jeans sit so low on his hips the *V*-shaped cut of his torso stands out in stark relief. I want to trace the sculpted ridges with my lips and lick that thin trail of hair into the shadowed dip behind his fly.

Now my heart is fluttering. My mouth dries, and my nipples tighten against the itchy lace of my bra.

I continue to dance around the room, and his breathing speeds up. The muscles in his shoulders go taut, drawing my gaze to the black serpent tattooed around his bicep and along the side of his neck. He's covered in ink—both arms, pecs, back, and a full wrap around one thigh. All black snakes. He had a pet snake in high school, which he claims gave him a dangerous reputation. A reputation that got him laid. A lot. I think he's full of shit. His sex appeal alone drops panties everywhere he goes.

My playlist switches to the next Rihanna song, *We Found Love*. The quicker tempo lifts my cheeks and revs my body into a faster pace. I twirl through the room, bagging construction scraps and storing unused tools.

I'm so lost in the music I barely feel the summer heat.

The A/C ventilation isn't finished in the new room — a task in an endless list of tasks to complete before I can start teaching in my very own studio. Just thinking about that opportunity fills me with so much love for the man who gifted it to me.

I spin and bounce to the music, dripping with perspiration. I've been vigorously shaking my ass through the last five songs. So I pull off my shirt and fling it like I'm doing a striptease.

The sound of the drill screeches to a dying halt.

"Shit." Cole rubs a finger over the errant hole he stabbed in the wall and narrows his eyes at me. "That was your fault."

"Mine?" Standing before him in a white lace bra, ratty short-shorts, and oversized work boots, I give him an innocent look. "Why?"

"You know why." His gaze drops to my chest, and he runs a hand over his face. A look of contemplation crosses his features, and he points at the far corner. "Bring me the tool box."

I drag the heavy metal container to him and kneel beside it. "What do you need?"

"You." His eyes flash.

"You have me. What else?"

"There's a small box at the bottom." He fiddles with the attachment on the drill.

A small box? I dig around, and my hand bumps something soft and square. Something out of place amid the metal edges of his tools. As I lift the tiny package, my heart catapults to my throat.

A black unmistakable box that can only contain

one thing.

"Cole?" My voice croaks.

"Open it." He inches toward me on his knees, and as his shadow falls across my face, I feel washed in blinding light. It's his smile. My very own ray of happiness. The first and last thing I ever want to remember.

My fingers tremble as I open the lid, and a ring glimmers beneath the overhead lights. A plain silver band without diamonds or stones. My chest constricts, and my throat catches fire, burning with unshed emotion.

"I didn't get a diamond because of something you said once. *For every finger to receive a ring, another finger must pull a trigger.*" He cups my face, his eyes searching mine with unnecessary worry. "You said you abhorred the human price of precious gems."

"I did," I whisper. "I do."

"I researched and found that even non-conflict diamonds come from corrupt industries that do horrible crimes against humanity."

I nod, hands shaking, eyes welling with grateful tears. "You're right, Cole. Thank you." I reach for his hand. "Thank you so much for taking the time to understand that. This ring is… It's perfect."

He releases a held breath and rises on his knees, pulling me against him, chest to chest, heart meeting heart. His hands slide around me and splay over my backside. Then he lowers his forehead to mine and issues the command I yearn to hear. "Marry me, Danni."

Tearful laughter bubbles up as I repeat his words from the day we met. "It's a foregone conclusion."

"It is." He grins wickedly. "But I need you to say the appropriate response."

"Yes." I smile with tears in my eyes. "I'll be your Mrs. Hartman."

He snatches the box from my hands, grips the back of my neck, and pulls my mouth to his.

"I fucking love you," he breaths into the kiss with so much adoration it makes my heart hurt.

I say it back, but the plunder of his tongue garbles my voice, steals my air, and scrambles my brain.

I've kissed a lot men in my twenty-four years, and every kiss applied the same mechanics. Parting lips, swiping tongues, and the dreaded sharing of spit. Since meeting Cole, I realize a real kiss is more than the motion of mouths. It's an inspiration. A creation of something unfathomable and timeless. And the art of kissing begins and ends with Cole Hartman.

He kisses like his mission in life is to devour every breath I take and give it back with an infusion of love. His lips are firm, his hands active, his entire body bunching and rocking against me. Intensity lives in his blood, dominating his emotions and attitude. He doesn't do anything half-ass, especially when it comes to me.

"I need you," he says gruffly as his mouth veers along my jaw to latch onto my neck.

"I'm filthy."

"No question about that. You're my dirty little fuck doll." He grips the backs of my knees and flips me onto my back.

I don't slam against the floor, because his arm is there, catching my fall. I don't know when he removed the ring from the box, but it's in his hand as he crawls over me and slides it onto my finger.

"Perfect fit," we say together.

His possessive smile is worth more than a mine filled with precious stones. My chest overflows with more love than it can hold.

"I'm going to break you tonight." He bites my nipple through the bra.

"Is that before or after I drain your balls?"

"Yes." He moves to my other breast, sliding down the cup to lave at my taut bud.

"Good." I moan, arching against the wicked sensation of his talented mouth. "I don't want to feel my face or hands after you're finished with me."

"I'm going to use you." He unbuttons my shorts and pulls them off, taking my panties with them. "And abuse you."

"Do it."

"I'm going to split you in half." He kneels between my legs and spreads my thighs wide, taking full advantage of my flexibility.

"Any time now would be great." I writhe beneath him, wanting, aching, throbbing with wet arousal.

"When I pull your hair, you'll scream for it, begging me to fuck you harder, deeper."

"Because I love your dick. Now stop teasing me and serve it up, you dirty bastard."

He laughs thickly, hungrily, and falls on top of me, attacking my mouth with breathless urgency. Whatever restraint he was holding onto snaps. The arm at my back keeps my bare skin from sliding against the splintery subfloor, but he's shaking now, struggling to suspend me as he grinds the fly of his jeans against my pussy.

"Just put me down." I reach between us and try to open his jeans.

With a deep growl, he surges to his feet, hauling

me with him. The room spins, and my back crashes against a mirrored wall. He lifts me, wraps my legs around his waist, and shoves a hand between us, fumbling with his zipper.

The ragged sound of his breaths permeates the air, and the balm of hard labor and masculine musk fills my lungs. All of it makes me crazy with need. I palm his hard buttocks through the jeans and grind against his hand, rubbing my wetness all over him.

"Goddamn, you're soaked." His muscular backside flexes in my grip, and he abandons his fly to shove his fingers inside me.

Holy fuck, I feel him everywhere, stroking inside me, his tongue in my mouth, his skin slick and hot slipping against mine. I want to kiss and lick every inch of him, but he's covered in a golden layer of sawdust.

"Shower," I breathe against his lips.

He grunts in agreement and works off his shoes and jeans. Commando, of course. My sexy rebel doesn't own a single pair of underwear.

Naked, he holds me against the swollen length of his cock and exits the dance studio through the kitchen, heading toward the bathroom. I cling to his shoulders, sucking on his full lips and clenching my thighs around his waist.

We don't make it far before he finds a sturdy surface — the front of the refrigerator — and slams his cock into me. The vicious thrust rips a hoarse groan from his throat, and his hands shake and flex on my thighs.

"Fuck! Ohfuckohfuck!" I spasm around the thick invasion and stab my fingers in his hair, holding on. "Fuck me like you own me."

"I do own you." He kicks his hips, driving into me ruthlessly, while wrenching my head back and forcing my eyes to meet the feral gleam in his. "I want your come. Your screams. Your pleasure. Give it to me."

I do. I scream his name as a swell of lust rises and builds into an unbearable pressure that detonates in rippling sparks of sensation. The hammer of his hips propels me through the toe-curling orgasm, pounding me against the fridge and sending beer bottles tumbling and clanking inside.

His chest heaves, and his pupils dilate as he holds me in unwavering eye contact.

"You look so fucking hot coming on my cock." He smiles savagely and continues to thrust while aftershocks of pleasure twitch and jerk through my limbs. "God, I love your cunt."

"My cunt loves you," I say through labored breaths. "You should put a ring on it."

He tenses, and his response rolls out like a growl. "A piercing?"

"Sure."

His dick gives a hard jerk inside me. "Tomorrow. We're busy tonight."

He peels my sticky body off the fridge and carries me through the hall and into the bathroom. It's a tiny space, and it seems even smaller since he moved in. With his broad bulky frame, he's like a bear bumping into the walls and stumbling against the tub and toilet.

As I stretch out an arm to dial in the water temperature in the shower, he holds me on his cock, thrusting me up and down and sucking on my neck.

"I want to fall asleep inside you tonight." He draws my earlobe into his mouth and circles a finger around my clit, working me into Cole-induced orgasm addiction.

Any woman who claims she doesn't like sex hasn't been on the receiving end of Cole's cock. Unfortunately, I'd be hard-pressed to find many of those women, because he's plowed his way through the greater St. Louis area.

My molars slam together, and I inwardly curse my ill-timed thoughts.

His fingers pause on my clit, and he leans back. "What's wrong?"

"Nothing." I kiss his parted lips.

"Bullshit." He steps into the tub and positions my back beneath the warm spray.

I sigh and relax against his chest, sliding my cheek against his scruffy jaw. "I was thinking about your slutty days."

"I don't think about that. Ever." He shifts, pressing me against the tiles so he can cradle my face in his hands. "My life began the day we met. There is no *before*. Only *you*."

I trace a finger along his dark brow, around the outer corner of one deep brown eye, and follow the chiseled angle of his face. "You're beautiful."

He squints. "I'm not a fan of—"

"Handsome."

"Better." He crooks a sexy grin and drags his nose alongside mine.

"And manly." I grip his rock-solid ass, delighting in the feel of soft skin over steel.

"Now you're talking."

I love the way he tilts his head to follow me with his eyes. Whenever I'm in his arms, he keeps his face close to mine, always watching, studying, touching his brow, lips, nose, or cheek to mine, as if he can't get close enough, breathing me in, smelling me, and tasting my skin. His attentiveness is unparalleled. I've never met anyone like him.

"Fuck me, Cole." I suckle on his mouth and rub my tongue against his. "Fill me up."

He pulls out of me and spins me around to face the wall. His arm swings toward the built-in ledge beside us, sending shampoo and soap to the floor as he grabs what he's looking for. *Lube.*

My stomach flip-flops, and I push my ass out like a wanton thing. He oils up his cock and drops the bottle. Then his hand slides over my abs, between my legs, and three fingers sink inside. I rise on tiptoes and flatten my palms against the tiles, my legs trembling against the pleasure sweeping through my body.

His other hand presses against my ribs, just beneath my breast, holding me tight to him. I clutch that hand, lacing our fingers together and squeezing hard.

"I'm ready, Cole."

He took my anal virginity two weeks after we met and fucks my ass every chance he gets. It's his weakness. One glimpse of that puckered hole and he can't control himself. He's already panting at my ear, grinding and rubbing himself against me while his fingers plunge in and out of my pussy. He's a goner.

"I won't be able to hold back," he growls.

As if he knows another way. Not only is he hard as a rock, he's well-endowed. Long and wide with a big fat head. I'm going to feel every inch of that gorgeous cock.

He seats the broad tip against my tight ring of muscle and bites the sensitive skin beneath my ear. "Push back, baby."

I edge back, relaxing into it. His fingers curl inside me, gripping my pussy and maneuvering me where he wants me as he sinks into my ass.

"Jesus, fuck." It's a tight fit. I'm not going to last. My body's already primed, inching toward to the fall into bliss.

By the heaving, groaning noises at my ear, he's right there with me. He loves anal, but he never lasts long when he takes me this way. It feels too good, so fucking tight and erotic he always finishes within minutes.

"Danni." He pumps into me frantically, erratically, his entire body shaking with the need to release. "I'm going to…"

He moans, dropping his head on my shoulder and slamming to a stop inside me.

"Are you coming?" I ask.

"Trying not to, but fuck, you feel incredible." He resumes thrusting, fingering me with urgency while his thumb does devilish things to my clit. "You need to come."

"I can't." Not yet.

"You will." His hand untangles from mine and moves to my breast to tweak my nipple. "One more."

I melt against him, clear my mind, and ride the pleasure of his thrusts, the play of his muscles against me, and the heat of his breath on my neck.

"Kiss me." I angle my neck toward him.

His mouth latches onto mine, forcing my head back to deepen the kiss. Then I feel it. The tiny pulses of rapture skittering between my legs and blooming outward, flooding my nerve endings, strengthening, consuming, taking over all thought.

I tear my mouth away. "Ahhhh, God, Cole. I'm coming, I'm coming, I'm coming."

A gust of air escapes his lungs, and he chokes, jerks his hips, and shouts, "Danni! Oh, goddamn. Unnnngh!"

His cock throbs and swells inside me, and I wish I could see his face, the pout of his lips, the complete and utter look of satisfaction that I know is morphing his expression. He's insanely beautiful when he comes.

But I feel him — the tension slipping from his body, the lingering shock waves creeping over his skin, and the caress of his hand easing from between my legs to affectionately rub my body.

This is when his sweet side makes an appearance, when he's loose and satiated and wrapped around me without the driving need to fuck. It's a fleeting moment — the man has a ridiculously fast recovery rate — but I'll take it. I'll take him anyway I can get him.

He washes me, and I wash him. Then we towel off and collapse naked in bed. I lay sprawled on top of him, legs entwined, with my chin propped on my fist on his chest.

We stare at each other, content to do so without words or motion for long minutes. His hands rest on my lower back, and every once in a while, his fingers creep along my butt crack, as if seeking that opening he loves to play with.

When my eyelids start to grow heavy, his timbre breaks the silence.

"How's your ass?"

"It misses your cock."

"Insatiable."

"Says the three-times-a-day guy."

"You're the only woman who can make me hornier after sex."

"Am I supposed to take that as a compliment? I'm starting to think I'm not satisfying you."

He yanks me up his chest and hardens his eyes. "I'll never get enough of you."

My bones turn to goo, and I lower my face to his Cole-scented neck. "I was going to dance on the pole for you tonight, but you wore me out."

"You can do that tomorrow after I put a ring on your pussy."

How do I feel about that? I chew the inside of my cheek, trace a finger in the hollow of his throat, and decide it sounds like fun. "I'll do a labia piercing. I don't want any needles in my bean."

"Perfect. That piercing doesn't require abstinence from sex." He stretches beneath me, stroking a hand across my bottom. "They wouldn't be able to pierce your clit anyway. Yours is too tiny."

"It is?" I lift my head to see his eyes.

"Incredibly tiny." He leans up and kisses my lips.

I had no idea. It's not like I go around comparing clit sizes with my friends. And I don't want to think about how he knows the female anatomy well enough to make such a claim, but the thought is already there, gnawing at my confidence. He knows his way around a pussy because he's unbelievably attractive with a sex drive that rivals Genghis Khan, who is reputed to have sired hundreds of children.

"Did you know Genghis Khan had two- to three-thousand women in his harem?" I twist the silver band on my finger.

His brows pull in as he watches me fidget. "I haven't been with *that* many women, Danni."

He doesn't sound so sure, and my nerves flare. He's never worn a condom with me. Not even the first time. He swore he was clean, and I have an IUD. It's pricked at me for a while, but not enough to bring it up. Until now, with his ring on my finger.

I slide off the band and rub the shiny surface. "Is there a chance little Coles are running around in the world? I mean, it wouldn't change anything between us. I just want to be prepared and—"

"No." He grips my hand. "Danni, look at me."

I lift my eyes and sink into the devastating depths of his.

"I've always been careful," he says with earnest. "I've always used protection."

"But you didn't with me."

He pries the ring from my hand and holds it in front of my face, catching the light from the nearby lamp.

Is something etched on the inside? An inscription?

I clasp his wrist and angle it closer, twisting it in his grip.

One Promise ~ One Forever

My chin quivers, and my voice abandons me.

"You're my forever, Danni." He returns the ring to my finger and caresses my cheek. "I didn't need protection with you."

I nod and inch closer, touching my lips to his. "Thank you."

He holds me for several minutes before taking a breath that hitches his chest. "We need to talk about the wedding."

"We have plenty of time—"

"We don't." He nudges me up, and the wrinkles around his eyes alarm me.

"What is it?"

"I have to leave town for a while."

"What?" I slide off him and sit up. "When? For how long?"

He shifts, putting his back to the headboard and pulling the sheet across his waist. "It's work. I have to take these trips sometimes. Out of the country."

If it was a weekend or even a week-long trip, his expression wouldn't be so grave.

My stomach sinks. "For how long, Cole?"

"A year."

My heart stops. "No. Tell them you can't do it."

"Can't do that, baby." He bends forward, dropping his head and avoiding eye contact.

A dead giveaway. When he can't look at me, it means the worst news is coming.

"Why?" It's all I can ask. My entire body is in shock.

"I work for a government agency that deploys—"

"You're a fucking auditor!"

"Let me finish."

I sit back and cross my arms to hide my shaking. This shouldn't upset me so much. We've only been together nine months, but dammit, I haven't been separated from him for a single night since we met. I've never been this person, this dependent, needy creature who can't live without a man. But now I am, and I hate myself for it.

"I'm sorry." I roll back my shoulders and meet his eyes. "Go ahead."

"I audit records for freedom of information, and I've been assigned to the al-Bashrah oil terminal in the southern waters off Iraq. I'm stepping in as a project manager to make sure the government isn't getting screwed by the contractors."

"You're going to Iraq. For a year." I let that sit for a second and measure my breathing. "When do you leave?"

"Next month."

"Next month," I echo hollowly.

"When do you want to get married?"

"I don't know." I can't even think about that, but I know I have to. *He's leaving.* "I kind of hate you right now," I say without conviction.

"Hate me all you want." He grips my chin and waits until I meet his eyes. "We're getting married. We can do it now or a year from now, but it's happening."

I'm going to spend a year alone. I can do it as his fiancé or as his brand-new bride. Tears flood my eyes and spill down my cheeks, collecting in a salty pool at the corner of my mouth.

"Damn you, Cole." I lift a hand to shove his touch away, but my fingers curl around his forearm instead, holding on with aching desperation. "A fucking year."

He hauls me onto his lap, arranges my legs around his hips, and hugs me tight to his chest. "I can't stomach the thought of being away from you."

"I'll go with—"

"No. It's not even an option."

My eyes widen. "Will you be in danger?"

He laughs—an empty sound I've never heard him make—and strokes a hand through my hair. "No."

"Then why can't I go?" Mother of God, am I

whining?

"You have a dance company to run. Besides, civilians aren't allowed near the offshore oil platforms. You can't be there."

The gravity of the situation sets in, and the lump in my throat burns red-hot.

No Cole smiles for a year. No riding on the back of his bike. No strip teases on the pole. No holding hands at Cardinals games. No sharing beers in the backyard.

"No sex for a year." I trail my fingers across his bottom lip.

"I'll be jerking off to memories of you dancing naked."

I smile sadly. "You'll come back to me?"

"Yes." He lifts my hand and touches his lips to my ring, his eyes bright and unyielding. "I promise."

One promise.

One forever.

"I'll wait for you." I fold my arms around his neck and touch my mouth to his ear. "I'd wait for you forever."

eight

present

I didn't see Trace at the casino when I met with HR the morning after our confrontation. In fact, I haven't seen him or heard from him for the past three weeks. I've spent that time shuffling my schedule, moving evening dance lessons to days, and merging classes together.

So I can belly dance five nights a week.

At The Regal Arch Casino.

For three-hundred-thousand dollars a year.

Holy.

Fuckamoly.

"Waz up with you, *hoss?*" Nikolai O'Shay releases my hand midway through a left-and-right Samba whisk, his Caribbean accent thickening with exertion. "You need to grease dat waistline."

In other words, I'm not moving my hips like they're oiled. I hoped he wouldn't notice. But of course, he did. We've been dance partners since college and entertain at ballroom functions a couple of times a year, like the mayor's Christmas party. We landed a gig at Anheuser-Busch's upcoming Fourth of July celebration, and we only have six weeks to nail this routine.

One More Night by Maroon 5 thumps through the speakers in my dance studio. The choreography is tricky, but the beats per measure work for the Samba. If I find my groove, we'll be golden.

"I have a lot on my mind." I bend at the waist and rest my hands on my knees, trying to catch my breath.

"Tell your boy all about it." Nikolai shuts off the music, takes a running leap, and slides across the dance floor, ending flat on his back with his legs between my feet and his silver eyes staring up at me.

Perspiration glistens in his tight curly hair, which he keeps cropped close to his skull and bleached blond. Half-Irish, half-Afro-Caribbean, he was born and raised in Trinidad. His accent sounds like he likes to sing when he talks, and his pale eyes and dark skin give him a head-turning exotic look.

"I'd rather focus on the routine." I place a foot on his chest and lift his chin with the toe of my high-heeled dance shoe. "Let's take it from the top with the traveling lock."

He curls a hand around my calf, and his gaze journeys up my bare legs to my spandex shorts and sports bra. "You need to release some of that tension, girl." He winks. "I can help with that."

one is a promise

Nikolai is one of the best dancers in the Midwest. He also models, and recently finished an ad campaign for United Colors of Benetton. But his natural-born skill is flirtation. Coming on to women is as involuntary for him as breathing.

We had sex on and off through college, and over the past few months, I've considered taking him up on his advances again. But I know I'd regret it. One, he's the closest thing I have to a best friend. Two, monogamy is a language he doesn't speak. And three, he's really not that great in bed.

"How about I dump all my problems on you," I say, stepping toward the sound system, "after we run through the routine again."

"All right." He jumps to his feet, brushes off his loose pants, and rolls his neck. "Let's do it."

As the song begins, we take our positions and slide through the small light footwork. Swaying right and left, always turning, bending, and straightening, we create a unified twirling motion, two bodies swinging forward and back like a pendulum.

I concentrate on adding little lifts at the end of each beat, the subtle kicks that bounce in my pelvis and sex-up the movements. My feet ache in the heels, my soles covered in callouses. But I muscle through it, pushing against the floor to roll up on my toes and absorb that lift in my core. Soon, I'm oiling my hips and slipping into the zone.

"There's my girl." Nikolai beams, rolling me in a full turn out and back.

A knock sounds on the exterior door of the dance studio.

He pulls me into a closed position, bending me backward as I shout with my head hanging upside-down, "Come in! It's open!"

It's a Friday afternoon. The visitor could be any one of my students. Or my sister stopping by after school. Though she never knocks.

I sidestep through a circular volta, spinning to wrap my legs around Nikolai's waist with my back to the door. He gyrates against me, hands spanned across my backside and bare chest flexing beneath my fingers. Then he stops abruptly and drops my feet to the floor, staring at whoever walked in.

Chest heaving, I turn and come face to face with Trace Savoy.

Hands on his hips and expression stormy, he aims his crankiness at the other man.

Oh, now this is interesting. Cole hated Nikolai, but that was a jealousy problem. Who knows what crawled up Trace's ass?

"What are you doing here?" I adjust the spandex shorts where they gather uncomfortably around my upper thighs.

"Checking in." Trace shifts his testy gaze to me.

Nikolai turns off the music and joins my side. "Who's the stiff upper-lip?"

"The reason my evenings are no longer available. Nik, meet Trace. Trace, this is Nikolai."

They don't shake hands or exchange customary greetings. Nikolai crosses his arms over his nude chest. Trace maintains his wide stance, hands behind his back, spine straight.

He's wearing a black suit today, the shirt stiff and blue like his eyes. No tie. The top few buttons are open, offering a tempting view of his strong neck.

"I'm gonna go." Nikolai slips around me, pulls on his shirt, and changes into his street shoes.

"No, wait. We need to—"

"I've been here before." He moves toward the door, gesturing between Trace and me. "Once was enough."

Trace raises a brow in question. I'm sure he'd love to hear all about the night Nikolai met the bloody end of Cole's fist, but it's none of his business.

"There's nothing going on here." I give Nikolai my angry look, which works on exactly no one.

"Right." He laughs and shakes his head. "Call me, *padna*. We'll have that talk you promised."

I fist my hands at my sides as he gives Trace a chin lift and steps outside, vanishing beyond the door.

"What happened to the mirror?" Trace nods at the splintering hole that's been there for two years.

"Self-pity happened." I leave the broken mirror as a reminder of what I used to look like, so that I never let myself reach that level of numb, grieving drunkenness again.

"I can have it repaired."

"No, thanks." I grab a towel and wipe the sweat from my face and neck. "For the record, that's the second time you've chased a man from my house."

"I did no such thing." He steps through the room, scanning every detail of Cole's hard work with his infuriating eagle eyes. "It seems you have trouble hanging onto men."

My blood simmers, and my pulse shoots through the roof. "Nikolai is one of my many lovers. He always comes back."

He pauses, turns his head toward me, and narrows his gaze. "You're not fucking him."

Though he's right, the conviction in his tone makes me want to cold cock his clenched ass. I spin away and stride through the door that leads to the kitchen.

"You know how I know that?" He trails after me, zinging electricity up my spine.

"I don't care." I grab a bottled water from the fridge and chug it on my way to the shower.

"If you were spreading your legs for him," he says, leaning against the door jamb of the bathroom, "he wouldn't have left so quickly."

"You don't know —"

"You've turned him down so many times he's conditioned to accept your rejection."

How does he know that? And why is he still here? Even more troubling, why haven't I kicked him out?

The black suit hugs his tall muscled frame. As hot as it is outside, I bet his skin is damp and warm beneath the expensive fabric. And hard. Like sun-soaked marble. His chiseled jaw, defined cheekbones, and straight nose form a regal backdrop for the blizzard churning in those cerulean eyes.

With the collar of his shirt open and a few blond strands falling haphazardly from his raked-back hairstyle, this is the most casual I've seen him. He's arresting in a deliberately edgy yet effortless way that makes it so easy to stare at him.

"You need to stop doing that." He rests a hand in the front pocket of his slacks.

"Doing what?"

"Giving me the look. I'm not going to fuck you."

Then he opens his mouth, and I'm reminded why I don't like him.

"You're confusing the *look* with annoyance." I reach into the shower and turn on the water. "Why are you still here?"

He regards me in a way that makes me feel defensive and brittle. But he can't hurt me. He can stand there all he wants in silent judgment. I'm taking a shower.

I hook my thumbs beneath the waistband of the shorts and ask with my eyes, *Are you going to watch me undress?*

He turns and ambles into the hall.

I listen for the sound of the back door as I strip and step into the tub, but I can't hear shit over the spurting water. It would be better if he left.

Except I'm dying to know the real reason he showed up. *Checking in,* he said. What in the ass does that mean?

Is he wandering through my house right now? Other than Cole's bike and the spare room crammed with dance costumes, I don't have anything of value. Not that I'm worried about a man of his wealth stealing anything.

But he can steal information, can glean my weaknesses from the shrine in my bedroom.

Which is exactly where I find him after I shower and wrap myself in a towel.

Perched on the unmade bed with the sheets tangled beneath him, he holds a photo of Cole and me in his hands.

I yank it from his grip and return it to the dresser where countless others clutter the surface.

"What are you doing in here?" I storm toward the closet, collecting bras and panties from the dirty clothes scattered across the floor.

"Waiting on you. It's become a dirty habit."

I glance over my shoulder and find him lifting a black thong from the floor. I dash toward him and snatch it from his hand right before he presses it to his nose.

"Add panty-sniffing to your list of dirty habits." I tighten the towel around my chest and return to the closet. "Really, Trace. Why are you here?"

The closet is deep enough to stand out of his line of sight as I slip into a white lacy tank top and a pair of denim cut-offs.

"The new Bissara is almost finished. It opens next week, and I want you to see it."

"You could've called." I slide my feet into gold flip-flops and exit the closet, running fingers through my wet blonde hair.

He watches my approach, his eyes shockingly unguarded and wild, like a snow storm in hell. Then slowly, they dip, tracing my hips, my legs, and lifting to linger on my breasts.

My nipples tighten against the thin fabric, and my chest feels heavy and itchy. "Trace."

He blinks, shifts his focus to the shrine of Cole pictures on my dresser, and clears his throat. "Are you waiting for your fiancé to return?"

Air whooshes from my lungs, and I clutch the engagement ring that hasn't moved from my right hand since the night I met Trace.

"I waited for him for a long time." My chest squeezes with ugly emotion. "He's not coming back."

Ask me why, Trace. Make me tell you why I've been so

lonely.

He stands and breezes out of the room. "Let's go."

I flinch, wobbling at his sudden change in mood.

"Go where?" I follow him through the kitchen. "I have plans today."

"Change them." He grabs my phone from the counter and hands it to me. "Where's your purse?"

"I don't carry a purse, and I'm not changing my plans." I pull a ponytail holder out of the junk drawer and twist my hair into a knot on my head. "Maybe I'll swing by the casino later. Maybe I won't."

I squeeze by him in the narrow walkway between the counters, pass through the dance studio, and step outside.

"Where are you going?" Blond eyebrows form a *V* above impatient blue eyes.

"Errands." I circle the yellow MG Midget and remove the key from the pocket beneath the seat.

His eyes widen, and he flattens a hand to his forehead. "You keep your car key *in* your car?"

I shrug and unlatch the convertible top, folding it back as the sun beats down on my shoulders.

"Did you even lock up the house?" he asks, exasperated.

"No, Dad. I won't be gone long." I climb into the driver's seat.

"Where's your house key?"

Under the flower pot beside the door. "I have it."

As I roll down the windows, he strides inside the house. He's gone a few seconds, presumably locking the front door, before returning to lock the back door.

My smile comes with a heavy rush of nostalgia. His

paranoia is so much like Cole's. It should be unnerving, but instead I find comfort in it.

"You live minutes from downtown." He grips the driver's side door, bending over it to glare down at me. "You're going to get robbed."

"In case you didn't notice, I don't have anything to steal." I slide the key into the ignition. "I don't even own a TV."

Unless I count the one Cole left behind, which is locked in the basement.

"You have an expensive motorcycle in your dining room," he says. "And what's stopping a thief from waiting inside to take *you* when you return?"

He sounds just *like Cole.*

I slip on a pair of cat eye sunglasses and drop my head back on the seat. "I need to get to the bank before it closes."

He straightens, studying me for a moment with frustration written across his elegant features. Then he removes an envelope from his suit jacket and offers it to me.

"What's this?" I clasp it, but he doesn't let go.

"An advance on your pay." He still hasn't released it.

"Afraid I'm going to back out?"

"You didn't sign the contract." He relinquishes his grip.

"I told you I'd be there, and I will." I open the envelope and peek at the check.

Oh sweet baby Jesus, that's a lot of zeroes. An entire month's pay. My heart slams against my ribs, and my hands tremble.

"I'll drive you." He opens the door.

In the rear-view mirror, I spot a sleek black sedan sitting on the curb. "You mean your driver will take me?"

"Yes."

"No, thanks." I pull on the door handle, attempting to shut it.

He pulls back, stopping me. "What's the problem?"

"It's a beautiful day. I want the wind on my face."

Most guys would give in. *You want to be a pain in the ass? Fine. It's not worth arguing over.* But not Trace. He's stubborn, confrontational. A man who gets his way.

"Get out." He opens the door wider. "I'm driving."

My head jerks up. "You're driving...*this*?"

He stares at the tiny spartan interior like he can't believe he suggested the idea.

I burst into laughter. "What about your perfect hair?"

He blows out a breath and swipes a hand over those sexy textured locks.

"Will you even fit in here?" I'm still laughing, recalling the first time Cole crammed his massive body behind the wheel.

Trace is leaner than Cole, but leg room will be tight. Really tight.

"We're about to find out." He plucks me from the seat like I weigh nothing and drops me on the other side of the gear shift.

As I tumble against the passenger door, he reaches beneath the driver's seat and slides it back with a rusty screech. Then he shrugs out of his suit jacket and looks at the non-existent space behind the seats, as if trying to figure out where to store his designer threads.

"Try the trunk." I peer at him over the top of my

sunglasses, grinning.

One long-legged stride takes him to the rear of the Midget. The trunk groans open.

"You got to be kidding me." He slams it shut and returns empty-handed.

I slide the envelope into the center console and meet his eyes. "Sometimes I fill the trunk with ice and use it as a cooler for beer."

"That explains the rust." He lowers his six-foot-five frame behind the wheel. After a little wriggling and a lot of huffing, he works his knees around the wheel and shuts the door. "This thing is a death trap."

"If you're going to complain—"

"Where are we going?" He reaches for the key in the ignition.

I give him the directions to the bank. "You know how to drive a stick?"

He casts me an aggravated look, but beneath the heavy scowl lurks a glimmer of mirth. *His disguised smile.*

"Be careful, Trace. I might get the impression that you're having fun."

"Right." He latches his seatbelt, waits for me to do mine, then we're off.

As he backs onto the street and pulls away, the sedan follows behind us.

"Is he going to tail us the whole time?" I kick off the flip-flops and prop my feet on the dash.

"Yes. My driver knows CPR, so he'll be able to resuscitate us when we get run-over by a Mini Cooper."

I snort and glance at his face. The almost-smile at the corner of his mouth turns my snort into laughter, and holy shit, he chuckles. It's a gravelly sound, with a full grin and everything.

What a breathtaking sight. His hair ruffles in the wind, his complexion glowing beneath the sunlight. I might not like him, but my God, I wouldn't mind scratching all my itches with him. This thing we're doing, this pushing, pulling, flirty dance is the best foreplay I can remember having in a long time.

When we arrive at the bank, he stays in the car to make a phone call. I originally wanted to come here to withdraw some money to live on for the next week, but as I deposit the massive check, I add another purpose to my visit.

After the bank teller cuts me a certified check made out to Gateway Shelter, I head back to the car with the taste of happy tears in the back of my throat.

"A few more stops." I spot the black sedan a few parking spaces away. "Schnucks Pharmacy on Gravois is next."

He merges the Midget into traffic, shifting through the gears like a pro. "What do you need there?"

The nosy bastard doesn't need to know I buy prescriptions for my neighbors.

"I'm out of condoms." I flash him a smile.

It's hard to tell what emotion those aristocratic features are conveying, but I'm certain it's not enthusiasm.

"We're stopping by the casino on the way back," he growls.

At the pharmacy, he goes inside with me, glowering like an ill-mannered barbarian when I add a package of Trojan Magnum XL condoms to Virginia's arthritis prescription.

"Quit scowling." I pull some cash from my pocket.

"They're not for you."

The young man behind the register watches us through his hipster glasses.

Trace grabs the bag from the man's hand and storms out of the store in all his temperamental glory.

I pay the cashier and take my time wandering through the aisles. When I step outside, he's not in the car or anywhere in sight. My throat tightens. Did he leave?

As I scan the parking lot for his driver, an arm hooks around my waist from behind. I glimpse the blue sleeve of Trace's shirt before he crashes my back against the building, wraps a hand around my throat, and covers my mouth in a searing kiss.

nine
present

Perfect lips slide over mine. Perfect biceps flex beneath my hands. Perfect insanity spirals through me and spins the world off its axis.

Trace sinks his tongue into my mouth, punishing me with beautiful, brutal, intoxicating strokes. His hand slips around my neck, joined by the other at the back of my head, holding me to him as he deepens the kiss.

All thought is gone, decimated completely beneath the fury of his assault. I taste his low-simmering anger, but there's also possession, acceptance, and desire reverberating through every curling caress.

The hum of sexual energy pulses between us as he

lifts me, presses my back against the brick wall of the pharmacy, and licks deeper, faster, inside my mouth.

He feels wild and reckless beneath my skin, in the fingers biting my backside, in the teeth clashing against mine. I surrender to the rising frenzy of hunger, lips brushing, chests heaving, our moans low and muffled with need.

Somewhere nearby, a car door slams. Traffic rumbles in the distance. The rattle of grocery carts come and go. And Trace shows no sign of pulling back.

He feeds from my lips like he's starving, his mouth hard and unforgiving, his hands kneading the muscles of my butt. He pins me so tightly against him I feel the steel flanks of his waist between my thighs, the length of his erection swelling against my pussy, and the rush of his breaths consuming my own.

The need to cling to this moment curls my fingers into his shoulders, demanding he keep going. *Don't stop.*

His lips press harder against mine, and I kiss him back with a fevered madness that convulses through me like an earthquake, vibrating my limbs and burning me up.

Desperate sounds of greed rise from my throat, and he groans in response, his powerful body wrapped up in mine and shaking against me. I arch away from the wall as pleasure radiates through my core, pulsing between my legs and drenching my panties.

The intensity of the kiss is shocking, the feel of his hot satin tongue overwhelmingly erotic. It sweeps against mine viciously, masterfully, and I gasp, my breasts crushed against his chest and my lips tingling and swollen.

Too soon, his mouth breaks away, sliding to my

ear, panting, growling, whispering, "Fuck."

He lowers my feet to the ground but stays close, crowding me as he yanks on the cuffs of his sleeves and glares down at his erection. "Where to next?"

"Second base?"

"That's not what I mean." He braces a hand on the wall above my head and inconspicuously adjusts his bulge with the other hand.

"Need help with that?"

He steps back and scowls at me with full, wet, pouty lips. Then he turns on his heel and strides toward my car.

"No, no, no." I run after him. "We're going to talk about this."

He continues along his determined path and removes the car key from his pocket.

"Dammit, Trace." I jog faster. "That kiss" — *that explosive smoldering kiss that rocked the ground beneath our feet* — "changes everything."

"It changes nothing." He lowers into the Midget.

The car groans and rocks beneath his weight. I might've laughed if I weren't so fucking irritated.

I'm still trembling with the aftershocks of bliss, which only ignite the flames of purpose. I refuse to let him pretend that didn't happen.

"Do you kiss all the women you don't want to fuck like that?" I climb into the car and angle over the console to face him.

"I kiss a lot of women." His eyes cut to me, hard and imperious. "Whoever, however, whenever I want." He fires up the engine. "Put your seatbelt on."

My heart feels like it's shrinking, but it doesn't

hurt. It's just disappointment, an emotion I know how to deal with.

"You say you don't want messy." I lean in, shoving my face in his. "But you're flirting with it, and honey, I will flirt right back. So put that in your pocket and fondle it when you're alone at night."

"You were right about one thing." His scowl twists into something ugly and implacable. "I don't date. I fuck. Which means I'm never alone at night."

My breath lodges in my throat, and I ease back, straightening in the seat and latching the seatbelt. A burning sensation ripples through my jaw. Jealousy, probably. But the feeling is quickly squashed by the stab of an old unhealed wound. A wound inflicted by another man.

I rotate the silver band on my finger, dragging the inscription of lies against my skin. It's easy to blame Cole for my deepest hurts, because I never felt real pain until he vanished from my life. That's the ache crushing my airway right now. Grief. Hopeless, irrevocable grief for the man I lost.

"Next stop is downtown." I give Trace the address for Gateway Shelter and slide on the sunglasses, hiding the moisture pricking my eyes.

"That's not a safe area at any time of day." He tilts his head, regarding me out of the corner of his eye. "What do you need to do there?"

"If you don't want to drive me, your car is right over there." I flick a finger toward the black sedan parked a few feet away.

He stares through the windshield, his thumb sliding back and forth on the steering wheel. Then he shoves the Midget into gear and peels out of the parking lot.

Five minutes into the drive, the silence between us grinds against my bones, but I have nothing left to say to him. So I plug my phone into the upgraded stereo system, select a song, and crank up the volume.

Down by Marian Hill taps through the speakers, and I move with the rhythm, humming, swaying in the seat, and lifting my hands as the wind whips at my hair. He flicks glances my way, but I avoid his eyes and the unkindness I'm certain I'd find there.

By the time he pulls up to Gateway Shelter, I feel more empowered. Balanced.

With the certified check in hand, I breeze through the side door and find Father Rick taking inventory of the food supplies in the kitchen.

"Danni!" He sets down the clipboard and smooths his mustache. "I wasn't sure if you'd be in today."

"I'm not staying to dance tonight." Not with Trace and his withering conjecture hovering at my back. "Just wanted to drop this off."

Rick accepts the folded check, his gaze locked on Trace. "Are you going to introduce your friend?"

"Trace Savoy." Trace steps forward and offers a hand.

"Nice to meet you, Trace. I'm Rick." They shake, and Rick directs his grin at me. "Danni's our very own bona fide angel. Her ability to make people smile is a gift from God."

"I don't know about that." I point my gaze at the eternal scowl on Trace's face. "Seems I have the opposite effect on some people."

Rick glances back and forth between us with

grooves rumpling his bald head.

"I need to go," I say. "But I'll be back later this week."

Trace holds the door for me, and I almost make it outside before Rick makes a choking sound behind me.

"What is this?" he whispers.

A glance over my shoulder confirms he's staring at the check.

"It's a donation." I pat Trace's rigid arm. "From Trace Savoy."

Rather than playing along, Trace strides over to Rick and glares down at the check. A glare that blisters with disapproval as it lifts to me.

"Give us a minute," I say to Trace. "I'll meet you at the car."

His jaw works, as if fighting back a retort. He straightens the collar of his button-up with a sharp, angry yank and charges out the door.

"Don't worry about him." I shift back to Rick. "We bicker like siblings."

"That man doesn't look at you like a sibling." Rick narrows his eyes. "Are you okay, Danni?"

"I'm great." I grip his forearm and give it a reassuring squeeze. "Trace bought the restaurant I dance at. We just have some disagreements to work through."

"And this?" He holds up the check.

"It's honest pay." I back up, retreating toward the door. "You're going to do amazing things with this place."

His cheeks redden. "Thank you, Danni. There's a special place waiting for you in heaven."

"Don't write me off yet, Father Rick." With a laugh, I slip through the door and brace myself for Hell in the form of fiery blue eyes.

"Ten grand?" Trace whirls on me the instant I step outside.

So much for waiting at the car. I shake my head and walk past him.

"That's over half your paycheck." He grips my elbow.

"*My* paycheck." I yank my arm away. "To spend however I want."

"You need to—"

"Save it." I quicken my gait and climb over the passenger door and into the car without bothering to open it.

"I will not let—"

"Shut the fuck up, Trace." I rest my head back on the seat and close my eyes. "I don't want to hear it."

I keep my eyes shut during the short drive from the shelter to the casino. The silence is volatile, building and darkening like a thunderstorm.

I'll drop his ass off and go to my sister's. Because going home to a house of broken memories sounds even less appealing than hanging out with a cantankerous casino owner.

I know I'm impulsive with money and men and pretty much everything, but why does Trace care how I live my life? How could he possibly be offended by anyone donating money to a good cause?

Maybe I shouldn't give him this time to gather his thoughts. His unspoken judgment charges the air around me, strengthening, galvanizing. When he pulls into the underground garage, the noise from the wind dies and he opens his mouth.

"You live in a shit hole, drive a shit car, and wear…"

Opening my eyes, I twist in the seat to face him. "Go ahead. Finish that sentence."

His eyes are stark beneath the overhead lights. He swerves the car into a reserved spot beside a sleek gray sports car and shuts off the engine.

"You wear sandals," he says to the windshield, "from the clearance aisle in a drugstore. You need money desperately, yet you give it away like it's nothing."

"If I embarrass you, get your pretentious ass out of my car and go back to your fancy penthouse where you never spend a night alone." My toes curl in the discount flip-flops, and my heart pounds at the base of my throat. "Fire me or don't fire me, but stop casting judgment on my life."

His eyebrows pinch together. "You don't embarrass me."

He opens the driver's door and unfolds his tall body from the car. There's no one else in the vicinity, and very few cars fill the parking spaces. We must be in a private level of the garage.

He shuts the door and grips the ledge, facing me. "With the money you'll be earning, you can live more comfortably. Unless you continue to hand it all out."

"I *am* comfortable. I like my shit hole and shit car and my drugstore sandals. It's just stuff." I release the seatbelt and bend forward with my elbows on my thighs. "You know what makes me happy, Trace? People. Relationships. Connections." I tip my head to look at him. "Have you ever been in love?"

"No." He scrapes out a tired breath.

"I didn't think so. That's why I let your cruelty roll

off me so easily. I don't condone your insults. It's just..."
I sigh and pull the hair tie from the windblown mess on
my head. "I pity you, Trace."

"*You* pity *me*?" Straightening his spine, he puts his
hands on his hips and watches me finger comb my hair.

"I really do. All the money in the world won't buy
the best kind of happiness."

He grips the edge of the door and leans in, eyes
like blue blades. "And where is your happiness now,
Danni?"

My heart lurches with a hollow achy thud. I lower
my head, lower my hands on my lap, and squeeze the
engagement ring.

"He left me," I whisper. "Then he died."

Unbidden, a brew of misery pushes against my
senses, forming wool in my ears and blackening the
edges of my vision. Trace fades from my periphery, but
his footsteps are there, circling the rear of the car. He
removes his jacket from the trunk. Then the passenger
door opens, and an outstretched hand appears beneath
my face.

"Come on," he says quietly, softly.

I stare at the hand, fully aware of the
unpredictability that comes with it. Cruel words and
passionate kisses. Outrageous paychecks and mercurial
moods. Scowls and laughter. Silence and banter. Who
knows what he'll deliver next?

He's well-versed in calloused expressions, but his
indifference is skin deep. If Trace Savoy wasn't affected
by me, he wouldn't be standing here now, offering me his
hand.

I clasp his fingers and allow him to pull me out of

the car, toward the exit, and inside the elevator. As we ascend, he tucks me against his body with my cheek on his chest. It feels good. So deeply, inviolably, wonderfully good.

"I'm sorry." He cups the back of my head. "For your loss. And for the way I talk to you. I'm not a nice man."

My throat tightens at the unexpected apology. Maybe there's hope for him yet.

"The former isn't your fault," I say, "and we can work on the latter."

"You're remarkably optimistic." He props his chin on my head.

"Ever heard the saying, *an optimist laughs to forget, and a pessimist forgets to laugh?*"

"No, but it sounds like it was written by a realist."

The elevator dings, and when the doors open, I expect to hear the beeping din of hundreds of slot machines. But it's silent. As I lift my head, he leads me out and into a huge unfamiliar room.

"Where are we?" I glimpse an open kitchen to the left and a dining area to the right. Beyond the humongous sitting room straight ahead, a wall of glass brings the St. Louis skyline indoors. "This is your penthouse?"

"Correct." He leaves me teetering in the entrance, tosses his jacket over a chair, and veers into the kitchen.

"I thought you were going to show me the restaurant."

I shouldn't be here. I mean, I *want* to be here. My interest in seeing his private space ranks right up there with my desire to see him naked. But my current frame of mind is on the fragile side of messy. I'm already imagining the countless women he's paraded in and out of this bachelor pad.

And what a pad. It's like something out of a Marvel Hero movie, with an industrial warehouse feel, exposed pipes, brick columns, and raw wood beams. Very rugged and masculine but also trendy in a way only money can buy.

"It's been a long day." He walks out of the open kitchen with two Bud Lights. "I'll show you the restaurant another time."

"This is…really nice." I linger near the elevator, unsure why he brought me here.

"Thank you." He lowers onto a buttery brown couch near the two-story windows and sets the beers on a large vintage trunk that serves as an ottoman. Then he reclines, spreads his legs the way a man does when he's relaxed, and crooks a finger at me. "Come here."

I move my feet, taking in every detail of the penthouse. Most surfaces have a cement or stainless steel finish. Copper fixtures hang from the loft ceilings, and little silver rivets run like stitching along the walls.

With all the metallic pipes, concrete, and structural joints shining through, the space should feel cold and uninviting. But it's not. The furniture is dark and chunky and plush. Richly colored rugs cover the wide-plank ebony flooring. Thick drapes frame the multistory wall of windows in sections. Jesus, those curtains must be forty-feet long.

There's a lot of brick—the walls, the fireplace, the base of the massive kitchen island. Overhead, skylights glow with sunlight between the splintery wood beams. And like his office, there are no photos or personal keepsakes. His parents are dead, yet there isn't a sign of their life together displayed anywhere in this room. Maybe I'm the only one who needs a shrine of pictures to cope with grief?

"Do you have siblings?" I approach the couch, stopping a few feet in front of him, locked in eye contact.

"I'm an only child."

Is that why he's so rigid? He never learned how to share or play with others?

His black pants are starched to crispness, even after squeezing in and out of the Midget. Who irons his clothes? A butler? A maid? Whatever woman slept over the night before?

Stop it, Danni.

"Sit." He pats the cushion beside him.

"If you talk to me like a dog, I might crawl onto your lap and lick your face."

He holds his arms out, as if welcoming my threat.

Baffling, volatile man.

I'm reminded of our scorching kiss and how much I already miss the feel of his velvety lips. But the cold shoulder I received immediately after he stuck his tongue down my throat prompts me to choose the spot beside him.

"I didn't take you for a Bud Light guy." I reach for the beer.

"I'm not." He sips from his bottle and makes a face. "But you like it."

How did he—? Oh, right. I was drinking beer the first night he came to my house.

His attention to detail is uncanny. And creepy. And kind of endearing.

"You stocked your fridge," I say, running a hand

through my tangled hair, "knowing I'd come here?"

"Yes." A devious flicker dances in his eyes.

Before I can question him further, the elevator dings.

Three servers bustle out, dressed in suits and carrying trays of domed platters. I stand, and Trace joins me.

"People can come and go," I whisper, "right into your penthouse?"

"I can lock the elevator with the push of a button." He moves toward the kitchen. "I hope you like Moroccan cuisine."

"I do." Suspicion narrows my gaze. "When did you order food?"

"At the homeless shelter, when you sent me outside."

The servers leave as quietly and quickly as they arrived, and I recognize one of them from Bissara.

When the elevator shuts, I turn to Trace. "This is the fine dining cuisine you'll be serving in the new restaurant?"

"Yes. A few samples of the dishes." He extends an arm toward the platters. "Dig in. You haven't eaten all day."

The rich scent of spices permeates the room, an infusion of lemon, cinnamon, ginger, and cloves. My mouth waters as we pile our plates with *zaalouk*, couscous, beef, lamb, anchovy, and unleavened pan-fried bread.

I follow him back to the couch, balancing the heavy dish in my hands. "I think I need a bigger plate."

"Or a bigger stomach."

"Oh, no. I'll eat all of this. Watch and learn."

I moan and hum throughout the meal without a single decipherable word. Fuck me, it's good. Better than good. The old Bissara wouldn't have been able to compete with this.

When the last crumb is scraped from my plate, I lean back and attempt to untangle the knots in my hair. Nothing's taming this shit without a brush.

"Did you hire a new chef?" I ask.

"I brought in a New York chef to design the cuisine and teach the existing chef how to prepare it."

"Wow. That's...really nice of you. I'm sure the Bissara chef was relieved to keep his job."

"He kept his job because he works for next to nothing. I'm running a business, Danni, and I make decisions based on profit. Not emotion. You'll do well to remember that."

"Of course." I grit my teeth. "I almost thought of you as human for a second. My bad."

I move to collect the dirty plates, but he beats me to it, stacking them and carrying them to the kitchen. I stay on the couch as he makes a phone call, his timbre too low to make out what he's saying.

He tilts the mouthpiece away from his chin and catches my gaze from across the room. "You left the prescription in the car. Do you need it brought up?"

"No, it's not for me."

Virginia won't run out of her arthritis pills for a few days. Besides, I need to leave soon. Playing house with Trace Savoy is wreaking havoc on my already confused brain.

"That'll be all," he says into the phone, ends the call, and returns to the couch.

"Thanks for dinner." I stand, tugging on the short hem of my cut-offs. "I'm gonna head out."

"Stay." He leans back on the couch, staring up at me.

"Why?"

"Watch a movie with me."

That's the last thing I expected him to say. This day just gets weirder and weirder.

"What movie?" I chew the inside of my cheek.

I shouldn't stay. Any second, something coarse and horrible will vomit from his sexy mouth, and I'll regret sticking around.

He grabs the remote, and the screen on the wall powers on. "Dirty Dancing."

My pulse spikes. "Why did you suggest that one?"

"You have the movie poster framed in your bedroom."

Oh. *Duh.* "Isn't it the best movie ever?"

His thumb moves over the remote, his attention on the TV. "I've never seen it."

"No way." I press a hand against my heart as excitement percolates through my blood. "How in the ever-loving world is that possible?"

"It's a wonder I've made it this far without the experience," he says dryly.

"No shit." I trip over his legs in my hurry to climb onto the couch beside him. "Prepare to be blown away."

And just like that, I'm committed to spending the next hour and forty minutes with Trace Dirty-Dancing-Virgin Savoy.

As he rents the movie, the elevator chimes again. What now?

He hands me the remote and crosses the room to greet whomever steps off the lift. I can't see around his tall frame, so I crane my neck and lean.

The same three servers sweep through the kitchen, gathering the platters and dirty dishes. But they're not alone. Someone stands on the other side of Trace. When he shifts, long slender legs come into view. A form-fitting skirt suit encases a curvy body. Dark brown hair falls around slender shoulders. Golden skin glows on a face I'm not thrilled to see.

Marlo Vogt hands him a black gift bag, and as they exchange words too quiet for my ears, her fingers slip around his waist, resting on his hip with familiarity.

My stomach cramps, but I can't look away. Because I'm a fucking masochist.

In five-inch heels, she's only an inch or so shorter than him. They look like they belong together. Dressed to the nines. Elegant postures. Perfectly coiffed. Beautiful. I want to gag.

She doesn't spare me a glance as she returns to the lift with the servers and vanishes from sight.

Trace taps a digital panel on the brick wall. Locking the elevator? Then he joins me on the couch and sets the gift bag on the floor. "Do you want another beer? Mint tea? Coff—?"

"Why am *I* here and not her?" My voice is louder than I intended, drilling, accusing, demanding.

His heated gaze touches my eyes, my throat, and lower, scanning the length of my stiffening body. "I enjoy looking at you."

I stare at him blankly. He doesn't want to have sex with me. He thinks I'm messy. But he enjoys looking at me?

"I don't know what to say to that." I laugh raggedly, uneasily.

"Don't say anything." He starts the movie, and the intro plays to the backdrop of *Be My Baby*.

He settles in, propping his shiny shoes on the trunk and stretching an arm along the back of the couch behind me. I'm not ready to let go of the conversation he just swept under the rug, but I'm drawn to the TV screen compulsively, addictively, absorbed in the movie that defines me.

Scene by scene, I inch toward the edge of the cushion, leaning, bouncing, reciting the words by rote. Yeah, I'm one of those.

Then comes one of my favorites parts, when Baby carries a watermelon and watches Johnny Castle get PG-13 dirty on the dance floor for the first time. I vibrate with the need to jump up and shake my ass through those exact steps.

"You know how to do that?" Trace's voice shatters my trance.

I startle, twisting to look at him. "What?"

"Can you dance like that?" He nods at the bodies writhing and bumping on the screen.

"Yeah," I whisper wistfully, turning back to the movie. Boy, can I ever.

ten
three years ago

My lungs heave. The muscles in my legs burn, and perspiration clings to my nape. But I can't stop smiling as Nikolai flings me away, spins me back in, and slams me against his damp chest.

His smile's as huge as mine, because holy shit, we nailed the routine. In one month, we're going to rock the St. Louis Microfest, taking the main stage with our modern compilation of Dirty Dancing dance scenes.

The acoustics in my studio thunder with the music and the pound of our feet. He wraps an arm around my hips, the other hanging loosely at his side as he jackhammers against me, the fluid thrusts of his pelvis rivaling that of Patrick Swayze. I arch back, hang my head upside down, and XXX grind with the undulation of his ripped body. Then he snaps me back to his chest.

Now for the hard part. With a determined breath, I propel myself upward, lifting my torso and hips while pushing against him. Midway through the jump, I turn myself into a balanced, steel-stiff form. He takes it from there, leveraging my momentum, lifting me above his head, and locking his elbows.

Whew! Excitement fizzes through me as I plant my knees on his shoulders, grip the folds of my pink skirt, and slap the gauzy material wildly around my waist in rhythm with the music.

The crotch of my leotard writhes inches from his face, but that's not what this is about. He's grinning up at me, suspending my weight and mouthing the words to *Talk Dirty* by Jason Derulo.

I'm so consumed in the dance and the music, I don't hear Cole walk in. I don't feel him until his arm hooks around my waist and rips me from Nikolai's shoulders. I don't see him until his fist flies past me and collides with the other man's nose.

Blood spurts across Nikolai's bare chest, and he stumbles back, colliding with the mirror and cupping his face.

"Cole!" The wind whooshes from my lungs, and my knees lock in horror. "What have you done?"

Expression tight and eyes aglow with black fire, he rears back for another punch, hellbent on putting my dance partner through the wall.

My legs propel me forward, and I hurl myself in the path of his strike. I narrowly miss four knuckles in the face as he redirects his fist into the mirror behind Nikolai.

Glass shatters, and Nikolai's arms come around me, hauling us away from the detonation of testosterone and fury.

I slap the power button on the sound system, plunging the room into a haze of panting, wheezing breaths.

Cole steps toward us, hands flexing at his sides and the cords in his neck stretched taut. "What the fuck — ?"

"Don't come any closer!" I thrust a finger at him and swivel toward Nikolai.

Oh God, blood trails from his bent nose, the cartilage twisted and swelling rapidly. I grab a towel and hold it up to catch the bleeding.

"I'm leaving in two weeks!" Cole shouts behind me. "Is this what you're going to be doing while I'm gone?"

"Dancing with my dance partner?" I whirl around, voice rising. "Yes, Cole. You better fucking believe that's exactly what I'll be doing."

Cole and I fell in love so easily, naturally, perfectly. But I'd be lying if I said our relationship has always been easy. His temper is explosive, his jealousy obnoxious and turbulent on the best days.

"Where's your ring?" He glares at my left hand with murderous accusation.

Shit, I forgot to put it back on. "Bathroom counter. I took it off to wax my — "

"Don't *ever* take it off!" His roar echoes off the walls.

"Stop yelling at me!" I scream back.

"I can't do this." He paces through the room, threading his fingers through his hair and locking them together on his head. "I can't be halfway across the world thinking about you rubbing your pussy all over another man."

"I warned you. The morning we met, I said no jealousy. This is my job. You told me you could deal with it."

"I also said I was hotheaded, and you told me you could handle *that*."

He's right. I *can* handle it. But…

"Nikolai didn't sign up for this." I step to the side and place a hand on my friend's chest. "*Un*-fuck this up, and I mean, fix it right. I want groveling, Cole."

"Danni, don't." Nikolai glares at me over the bloody towel against his nose.

"I want bowing and scraping and heartfelt apologies," I say to Cole. "If Nik leaves here without forgiving you, you'll be leaving with him."

I walk toward the kitchen and pour a glass of wine as their footsteps trudge into the bathroom. A moment later, Cole's voice rumbles through the house.

"I don't like you."

Christ. I pinch the bridge of my nose and release a heavy breath.

"I get that." Nikolai's Trinidadian accent sings through his pained voice. "But just because I fucked your girl in college— Ow! Fuck! You don't have to press so hard."

Cabinets slam. The faucet turns on and off. Then Cole's hoarse timbre fills the silence. "I'm sorry."

More silence.

"I'm struggling with…" Cole rasps out a sigh, and something thumps against the bathroom wall. "It's killing me to leave her, and I'm going mad with worry.

But there's no excuse for taking it out on you. I don't like you, but I do trust you. Because if you put your dick anywhere near—"

"That's a threat," I shout from the kitchen. "Not an apology."

"You know," he shouts back, "I eased up on that punch at the last second. His nose isn't broken, so there's nothing to forgive."

I roll my eyes and leave them to it. Making my way to the front of the house, I recline on the couch and wait.

Fifteen minutes later, they emerge from the bathroom, both shirtless and sullen.

"Well?" I look at Nikolai expectantly.

"He loves you." Nikolai prods a finger around his nose, his silver eyes squinting in pain.

My chest pinches. "Yeah, but—"

"He's scared, *hoss*. Fucking terrified he's going to lose you while he's gone." Nikolai rubs the back of his blond head, the corner of his mouth lifting in a small smile. "He and I won't ever be buddies, but I'm gonna cut him some slack. He's sorry. I forgive him. And my face doesn't look so bad after he cleaned it up."

His nose is swollen but seems a lot straighter in the light.

I turn my attention to Cole, where he stands a few feet away, hands on his hips and unblinking eyes fixed on my lips. He looks wrecked, desolate, and all I want to do is curl my body around him and give him back his smile.

"Since Cole won't be here when we dance at Microfest," Nikolai says, lugging the strap of his duffel over his shoulder, "we're going to perform the routine for him tomorrow. A private viewing."

"Is that right?" I ask.

A muscle bounces in Cole's cheek, his gaze still locked on my mouth.

With his chest bare, his unease is evident in the bunched ridges of his abs. The tattoos, whiskered jaw, broad shoulders—everything about him is ruggedly intimidating. I should give Nikolai kudos for not cowering.

"He wants to see how hard we've worked." Nikolai walks backward to the front door. "And how fucking awesome we are, because hot damn, we own that routine." He holds a fist in the air and opens the door.

"All right, Nik." I laugh. "See you tomorrow."

When the door shuts behind him, Cole lifts his eyes to mine.

The fire, the wind, the mystical energy that defines the connection between us sparks, inflames, fueling itself and pulling us together. He gravitates toward me, our gazes consumed with each other.

Lowering to his knees before me, he wraps his arms around my waist and buries his face in my lap. "I'm so incredibly sorry, baby."

I weave my fingers through his unruly brown hair. "I'm sorry, too."

He lifts his head. "For what?"

"This." I reach down and squeeze his nuts.

He hisses and jerks backward, but I follow him to the floor, landing atop his chest and tightening my clamp on his balls.

"That's the last time you'll ever hurt one of my friends." My lips brush against his, softening my words.

"Got it." He grunts in discomfort, and his warm

Cole-scented breath fans my face.

Lying on his back with his arms out to the sides, he doesn't buck me off, doesn't try to dislodge my grip from between his legs. But he overpowers me in other ways. With his shirtless chest, low-slung jeans, and swelling cock jerking against my hand. Add the five o'clock shadow on his jaw and the heated look in his eyes and I don't stand a chance.

My bones turn to dough. My insides tingle, and my fingers loosen around his sac. The anger and regret from moments ago dissipates, replaced by something more fundamental. Stronger. *Us.*

"You're so fucking beautiful." He lifts his hands, cupping them around my face. "I can't stand the thought of another man touching you, looking at you, fantasizing about you."

"You're the only one I see, Cole." I rest my brow against his and speak each word into a languorous kiss. "You're the only one when you're here. When you're not here. For the next year. Forever."

Briefly closing his eyes, he slips a hand into his pocket and holds out my ring. "If you never take it off again, I'll be the happiest man on the planet."

"It'll stay." I slide on the silver band and curl my fingers around it. "I promise."

"Good. Now what about that other ring?" He paws through the gauzy layers of my dance skirt, his hands becoming rougher, more urgent in his hunt.

"You tell me." I adjust my position on top of him, straddling his hips and gathering the material around my waist.

He proposed two weeks ago, and the day after, he

took me to get my labium pierced. The procedure was done by a beautiful woman, of course. Probably one of his old fuck buddies, but I didn't ask. The past is what the past is. And the future? I'll deal with that when it comes.

It's the present that I hug close—his wide shoulders, to be exact, as he sits up and takes my mouth.

His arms are my orbit, encircling my body. His eyes are my center of gravity, righting me in perfect balance. And his fingers are my eight wonders of the world as they sink between my legs and make my vocal chords scream his name in awe.

Then, with the crotch of my leotard shoved to the side, he slides me down his hard cock.

"Danni," he growls, his fingers burrowing into my hip bones. "You feel so damn good."

His muscles shake, and I tighten my hold on him, latching our mouths together, our kisses desperate, frenzied, and weighted with torment.

Enduring a year without him will be a special kind of hell. But it has an expiration date.

One year.

It's just a blip in the span of forever.

eleven

present

"Danni."

The growl of Trace's voice snaps me back to the present, and I swallow around the knot in my throat. *Stupid girl.* This is neither the time nor the place to get bowled over by the past. Especially not after our strange day of errands and kissing and hanging out in his penthouse.

I straighten on the couch and stretch my neck. The movie's paused, and the intensity of his gaze presses against my skin.

"What's wrong with you?" His tone is soft, but there's an edge to it. Concern? Aggravation? Who knows?

"I should go."

"And miss the best movie ever?"

I swivel to look at him, catching a rare glow of warmth in his blue eyes. "You're enjoying Dirty Dancing?"

"I am." He tips his head down, studying me from beneath blond brows. "It has depth. Like you."

My lips part on a stalled breath. Was that a compliment?

He touches my chin, nudging it upward to close my mouth. Then he presses play on the remote and stretches back on the couch. I mirror his pose, letting my head fall back and tranquility settle in.

Beyond the windows, the sun has fled, leaving smears of deep purple across the sky. It's getting late, but no part of me wants to move. My eyelids feel heavy, and the couch is so warm and comfy. The breathing heater beside me makes me want to stay forever.

Doesn't take long before I lose the fight against sleep.

When I wake, the credits roll on the screen, and my cheek rests on soft twill over steel. Not just my cheek. My arms and legs hug a warm pillar of muscle.

I move only my gaze, following the length of our bodies, down, down, to our feet. His are covered in black socks and propped on the arm of the couch. Mine hook around his calves, so pale and small against his dark slacks.

My knee is bent over his thigh, inches from the soft bulge between his legs. My arm drapes across his chest, my other tucked beneath his shoulder. My neck goes taut, but it's not our positions that alarm me. It's the knuckle running along my side, over my hip, and back up. Down and up, down and up, he's *stroking* me.

And I like it.

I love it.

So fucking much.

I close my eyes and will myself to fall back to sleep. I want to stay here, wrapped in this gorgeous paradox of a man, and pretend he wants that, too.

"I know you're awake." His voice reverberates in his chest.

Dammit.

I shift against him, rest my chin on his sternum, and fall into the crystal blue of his gaze. "I missed the end of the movie."

He brushes a stray hair from my face. "I know why you like it so much."

I beam. "It's a job requirement."

He doesn't move to untangle us, seemingly waiting for me to climb off. I doubt he does much snuggling with women, not even with the ones he doesn't want to fuck.

Rising on my knees, I instantly miss the warmth of his body. So much so my fingernails stab my palms as I slide off the couch.

Rain spatters the floor-to-ceiling windows, and the black sky rotates with even blacker clouds, veiling the twinkle of the cityscape.

The rain isn't ideal since the top is down on the Midget, and it's a bitch to put up. I groan at the task ahead and scan the floor for my flip-flops. When did I take them off?

"I have to put the top up on my—"

"You're not going anywhere tonight," he says

matter-of-factly.

"What? Why not?"

"It's raining and dark. You're tired, and I don't have to be anywhere."

But where would I sleep? Turning, I scan the warehouse-sized penthouse. The kitchen and dining area opens into the monstrous sitting room. There's a hall that leads to... A bedroom? Multiple bedrooms?

I head in that direction, veer into the dimly lighted corridor, and poke my head in the first doorway.

A workout room the size of my house stretches toward an exterior glass wall. Beyond the windows is a rooftop pool, the illuminated blue water rippling beneath the rain.

"Rich people," I mumble, "have all the things."

"Indeed." His arrogant self-assertion breathes against my nape.

I continue down the hall, pausing at the only other doorway. His bedroom.

He slips past me and sets the gift bag on a tall bureau. I want to know what's in that bag, but it came from Marlo. If their relationship is at a gift-giving level, I'd rather not know.

Why does it matter? Trace is a job, not a lover or boyfriend or even a friend.

Except I'm standing on the threshold of his bedroom, thinking about the possibility of sleeping in his huge king-of-the-casino-sized bed.

The exposed brick walls bring the warehouse ambiance into this space, with large picture windows, a private balcony, and a bird's-eye view of the Mississippi River. The charcoal bedding plays off the elegant use of red in the pinstriped furniture gathered around a fireplace and wall-mounted TV screen. It's masculine and industrial. Modern and cozy.

"Is this the only bedroom?" I lean a shoulder against the door jamb.

He nods. "I'll sleep on the couch."

"How many women do you say that to?"

His head drops, and his hands fall to his hips, as if he's annoyed by my question.

I can't figure him out.

He disappears into a closet and returns a moment later with a white collared shirt. "You can wear this to bed."

It's a beautiful herringbone shirt, with a split yoke between the shoulder blades and perfectly aligned white stripes. I can't imagine what it cost, and he wants me to sleep in it?

I pull the buttons through the holes. "I never agreed to stay."

He wings up a brow.

Yeah, it was a stupid thing to say. We both know I'm not going anywhere.

"You can dress in the bathroom." He flicks a finger at the double-wide doorway to the en suite.

"I'm a dancer. We change clothes anywhere and everywhere."

"Suit yourself." He steps back into the closet and closes the door partway, blocking my view.

Man, he's a hard nut to crack.

Speaking of nuts, what am I doing? Should I seduce him? Ignore him? Play with him? Play *hard to get* with him? I'm so out of practice, I don't know where to begin. But I do know what I want.

Him.

Preferably on top, but I'll take him behind, beneath, and upside down. I'm flexible like that.

I strip my clothes and undergarments, pull on his shirt, and button the front up to my breasts, leaving the neck wide around my chest. Then I roll up the ten-feet-too-long sleeves and let the collar slide off my shoulder. But not before I sniff the fabric and shiver a little.

The closet door swings open, and swear to God, the man who emerges transports me into the era of Viking kings and barbarian battles.

Tall, lean, and bare-chested, he moves with graceful intensity toward the bed. Brawn ripples across his back as he pulls down the bedding. Textured blond hair falls rebelliously over his brow as he picks up the clothes I left on the floor. His navy pajama pants hang so low on his sculpted hips I have to swallow the drool pooling in my mouth.

"What?" His head cocks.

He knows *what.*

"You...uh..." Good God, I'm stammering. Dizzy. Pulsing between my legs. "Gimme a minute. This is a lot to take in."

He gives me the same full-body perusal, his eyes glittering with unguardedness. An air of casualness. All pomp and circumstance discarded with the suit. Yet standing there all chiseled and confident, he looks more formidable than ever.

"You make use of that workout room, huh?" I circle his strong stance, devouring the cuts of muscle and golden dusting of hair on his forearms and below his navel.

He pinches the pressed collar that hangs off my

shoulder and slides it toward my neck, causing the other side to fall. "I should've given you a bigger shirt."

A laugh escapes me. "The angry scowler suddenly makes jokes when he puts on pajamas? Is that your superpower?"

"That's not a superpower." His lips twitch for a fraction of a second before they return to their natural downward bow.

"It could be. Lure unsuspecting women into your bedroom with your cryptic glare. Out come the pajamas and bam! Laughter and mayhem. Like the Joker."

"You're crazy." He shakes his head, studying me intently.

"It can't be helped. So what's next?" I hop onto the mattress and hang my legs over the side. "What does a slumber party with Trace Savoy entail?"

His snorts a soundless breath.

I don't date. I fuck. Which means I'm never alone at night.

My nostrils flare. "What does *this* slumber party entail?"

He rubs the underside of his jaw and turns toward the gift bag on the bureau. I lean forward as he removes... A bamboo paddle brush?

My mind takes a fast trip to Naughtyville, and my backside tingles in memory of Cole's darker desires. "You could redden an ass with that."

Trace's fingers clench around the brush handle, his expression smoldering.

I flutter my eyelashes. "Just throwing that out there."

"The brush is for the knots in your hair."

"Lame."

Or so I thought. The moment he crawls onto the bed and nudges me onto my belly, I realize something monumental is about to happen.

He reclines beside me, braced on an elbow with our bodies aligned. "Look the other way."

I turn my head and hug the pillow beneath it as wonderment buzzes in my belly.

His fingers run through my waist-length hair, gathering the heavy strands down my back. When the wide brush replaces his hands, I can't stop the sigh from billowing my lips.

He starts at the ends and works his way up gently, affectionately, taking care around the tangles like he knows what he's doing.

"Thank you," I mumble happily. "This is really nice."

"You're welcome."

It's the weirdest, most amazing feeling. I've never had man brush my hair. Especially not a pompous, well-to-do suit. Hell, I struggle to imagine him combing his own hair. Wealthy men with chauffeurs don't do this. Serial killers do. The kind that *rubs the lotion on its skin.*

"Are you going to chop me up into little pieces when you're finished?"

"Your mind is a scary place."

"Sometimes. Have you ever done this before?"

The brush pauses mid-stroke. Then he resumes with careful strokes. "No."

Big steps for Stodgy Savoy. Good for him.

"What else can you do with those hands?" I ask.

"I'm not answering that."

"Chicken."

He goes still. So fucking quiet and still. Then slowly, methodically, he sets the brush down on the mattress in my line of sight.

Worry tingles up my spine. I'm in for it now.

He wraps my hair around his fist, and with an eye-watering yank, he cranes my neck at an uncomfortable angle.

"Stop taunting me." His mouth touches my ear, the gentle caress at odds with his tone. "You won't like the consequence."

"I *want* the consequence. Show me, Trace."

His breath rushes out, harsh and ragged, and his hand tightens, stinging pain through the roots along my scalp. I squirm against his grip, hating and loving the anticipation.

"No." He releases me, tempers his breaths, and calmly picks up the brush.

"Disappointing." I wilt in defeat on the mattress.

"Get used to it."

"No need." I shift to my side, facing away from him. "I'm not going to pursue someone who doesn't want me."

I've gone without sex for three years, and now I'm starving for it. Trace triggered something inside me, something that awakened my libido. But there are a lot of men out there. Plenty of hard long dicks who would be more than willing to give me a night to remember.

So for the next twenty minutes, I simply savor the pleasure of the brush sliding through my hair rhythmically, hypnotically. He continues to stroke long after the tangles are smoothed out, his breaths steady and composed, rasping in sync with his hand.

I must've drifted off, because when I open my eyes, the brush lays on the mattress and his warm body presses against my back.

His breathing is no longer measured. It's erratic and shallow. And his hand… He's rubbing my bare thigh beneath the shirt. I'm not wearing panties, and each time his fingers creep upward, I ache to raise my leg so he can rub where I need him the most.

This is madness. What game is he playing?

The free-spirited, Bohemian half of my soul urges me to roll with it. What's life without a little adventure?

But the broken half, the half that remembers what it feels like to love and lose, cringes in fear beneath every furtive caress of his hand. Furtive, because I'm certain he'll stop touching me if I move.

That can only mean one thing. He's hiding his feelings from me.

He said he's never been in love, but maybe something or someone in his life made him distrustful and wary. Maybe it's just his nature, hence the stiff upper-lip.

Or maybe I intimidate him?

Now that's funny.

His fingers trail upward, following the curve of my hip over the shirt. When he reaches my elbow, he ghosts his touch along my arm, stretching toward my hand where it rests on the bed. He feathers his fingers over mine, circling, lingering. Then he bumps against the engagement band, and his breath stops.

He yanks his arm away, slips quietly off the bed, and pads toward the exit behind me.

I crane my neck and watch him leave with his hands stabbing through his hair and tension tightening his shoulders.

Something just happened, and it had everything to do with the ring on my finger. On my right hand!

I roll to my back and stare at the exposed beams in the vaulted ceiling. If I go after him and press him to talk, he'll recoil with hateful, chest-thumping blather. Or he'll turn into a statue and give me useless one-word answers — which is worse.

Wrapping the blankets around me, I try to sink back into sleep, but my brain won't shut off.

Why does he care about a piece of jewelry on my right hand?

Because that ring symbolizes everything. The life I loved. The man I lost. The happiness I'll never get back.

If my engagement to Cole is such a point of contention for Trace, why doesn't he ask about it? Why doesn't he ask how Cole died or why I still wear the ring?

The missing answers leave me wide awake. Confused. Flipping and flopping. Anxious. Huffing and puffing.

Screw it. I throw off the covers and find Trace in the sitting room. Perched on one end of the couch, he's bent forward with elbows on spread knees, sipping an amber drink from a crystal tumbler. A bottle sits on the trunk in front of him. *Scotch.*

I stop within arm's reach and put my hands on my hips. Then I lower them, because it feels confrontational.

With his head tilted down, he lifts only his eyes and suspends me there, in the full force of his gaze.

He says nothing. I say nothing. We're rocking the communication.

I release a sigh and lower to sit on the trunk, facing

him.

"What goes through your mind when you see this?" I hold out my right hand, and the silver band glints in the lamp light.

He takes a sip of the scotch, swallows. "Your fiancé could've splurged a little and at least bought you a diamond."

My cheeks inflame, and the sharp rise of anger burns the backs of my eyes. "Diamonds are synonymous with greed and slavery and murder. No one had to die for my ring." I drag in a serrated breath. "Cole gave me exactly what I wanted."

"Except a marriage."

I flinch, and my fingers ball into fists. "Why would you say something so cold and heartless?"

"It's the truth."

"A truth I live with every second of every day," I whisper, on the verge of tears. "The reminder is merciless and unnecessary."

I don't need this. The more time I spend with him, the more I feel like a mat he uses to scrape the shit off his shoes. I stand on unsteady legs and stride toward the hall to change my clothes. This is me, being strong and mighty. *Roar.*

Until his voice drifts across the room.

"You're the kind of woman a man marries."

My feet stick to the floor, my heart thundering for more. More to that declaration. It sounds like a compliment, but coming from him, it could be anything.

I need to let it go, get dressed, and get the hell out of Dodge. But I know what will happen. I'll stew on his statement, wondering if he meant this or that or... *Fuck!* I want answers.

He hasn't moved, his chest still angled over his knees, his hand curled around his scotch.

"Explain what you mean." I retrace my steps, pausing a few feet away from the man responsible for my flighty state of mind. "Why am I the kind of woman a man marries?"

"You're empathetic." He meets my eyes. "The donation at the shelter. The arthritis prescription for who the hell knows? Your abhorrence of the diamond industry. Most women don't even think about the blood shed for diamonds. They just want the ring—the one with the biggest price tag." He swallows the last gulp of scotch and stares into the empty glass. "That kind of empathy translates into compassion, support, and encouragement toward your partner."

My heart thuds, and my brain short-circuits. I'm not a religious person, but I feel the strong need to pray about this to whomever is listening.

"You're intellectually challenging," he says. "Straight-forward, honest, and genuine—all of which trumps shallow beauty. A physical relationship is…nice." His lips form a sinful smirk and settle back into a frown. "But when a man meets a woman he can hold meaningful conversation with, he won't tire of her. Ever."

My mouth gapes, and I snap it shut. How do I process this? What the hell do I say? Thank you? Fuck you? My God, I've never met a more complicated, confusing man.

"To top it off, you're…aesthetically pleasing." His eyes roam over me, making me shiver. Then he grabs the bottle of scotch and refills his tumbler. "You take care of your body, which means you'll take care of his."

His. Some unnamed man who isn't Trace.

"I'd bet my casino," he says, "there isn't a woman in the world more beautiful than you. I should know. I've been surrounded by beautiful women most of my life."

"That's enough." I cross my arms over my chest, trembling with the need to cry or laugh or lose my fucking mind. "Why are you telling me this?"

"A man doesn't fuck you without wanting more. Without wanting the long haul. But I'm not looking for forever. I'm not going to date you or fuck you or marry you." He drinks from the tumbler, rolls the scotch around in his mouth. "It's just not in the cards for us, sweetheart."

His flippancy is needles dragging beneath my skin.

"I don't understand," I say.

"You're in love with another man."

And there it is. I straighten my spine, an attempt to belie the quiver in my chin. "He's gone. He's…not coming back."

"Tell that to your heart. It missed the memo."

Is that true? I've come so far in the last two years. I can go days, sometimes a week, without breaking down. And I can talk about him now. About his life. His death.

But I can't remove his ring.

My fingers clench around it, and Trace zeroes in on the reflex.

I try to put myself in his position. If he was hung up with another woman, a woman he'd lost years ago, it would raise red flags. Maybe I'd admire his beauty from afar, but I wouldn't pursue. Wouldn't get attached.

"So that's it." The weight of resignation pushes down on my shoulders.

He wants me here because he likes to look at me.

And brush my hair. And he thinks I'm interesting to talk to. I like to look at him, too, and I'd happily brush his hair. But talking to him is like walking along the rim of a volcano. Sometimes he's quiet and tolerable. Sometimes he spews cruelty and ugliness.

My gaze drifts to the elevator. I don't care if it's three in the morning and pouring down rain. "I need to—"

"You're not leaving," he says sternly. "It's the middle of the night."

That's fine, because if I'm going to continue to work here, we need to have another conversation. One that addresses the way he speaks to me.

I circle the trunk and sit on the couch a couple of feet from him, tucking my legs beneath me. "For a classy, top-notch executive, your manners leave a lot to be desired."

He reclines back, balancing the tumbler on his thigh, his chest bare and eyes focused on me.

"The size of your bank account doesn't make you classy," I say. "It's the dignity you carry yourself with and the respect you show to others. If you have an ugly attitude and belittle those around you, it doesn't matter who designs your suits or how posh your penthouse is. None of it matters." I harden my voice and give him firm eye contact. "If you want me to work with you and hang out with you, *respect* me. Respect my intelligence, and most of all, respect my feelings."

He watches me for a moment, his pupils large and expression slack. "Do you put this much effort in everything you do?"

"In the things that are important, yes."

"That's remarkable. And rare." Sincerity scratches through his voice. He sets the tumbler on the trunk, twists the cap closed on the bottle of scotch. Then he laces his fingers together between his spread knees and stares at his hands. "You strive for greatness without calculation or awareness that you're doing it. That's empowering. It inspires me to be a better version of myself."

His praise tightens my chest and pulls my brows together. It makes me uncomfortable, but I'll take it any day over his hurtful comments.

He lifts an arm along the back of the couch, beckoning me to slide beneath it. I shouldn't give in to my desperate need for affection, not with this man. But a voice in the back of my mind urges me to live in the moment.

As I scoot across the cushions and rest my cheek on his chest, another inner voice whispers, *How is this different than dating?*

"Are you tired?" He grabs the remote and absently runs his fingers through my tangle-free hair.

"Wide awake."

"Want to watch Dirty Dancing?"

I nod, and ten minutes into the movie, I tumble into sleep, fantasizing about dancing dirty with Trace Savoy.

twelve
present

"Don't get me wrong. The cuisine is superb." A distinguished man with silver hair and a sharp suit corners me in the back of Trace's restaurant. "But *Chermoula* mackerel isn't the only thing I'm interested in eating tonight."

I hear the come-on loud and clear. The man is old enough to be my father, and he's staring at my chiffon belly dance skirt like he wants to tear through it. With his dick.

It's closing time, and no one's around to witness the confrontation. I'm tempted to head butt his leering look into next week. But I'm an employee here, and I take my job seriously.

"Thank you," I say. "I'll pass your feedback along to the owner."

Speak of the devil. Here he comes, storming through the dining room in all his scowling glory. It's after midnight, and Trace looks like a million bucks, all freshly starched and vibrating with energy in his charcoal suit. I just finished eight hours of dancing and feel like death slapped in glitter.

It's been three months since I spent the night in Trace's penthouse, and I haven't been back since. Not because he hasn't invited me. It's confusing. The sexual tension that ignites the air whenever we're together isn't one-sided. It stretches and fires between us with no relief, no resolution, no budging.

I said I wouldn't pursue him, and I've had plenty of distractions to stop me from accepting his invitations. Five weeks ago, Nikolai and I nailed our Samba performance at the Fourth of July celebration at the Arch. I've also been juggling dance lessons at home and the shelter in between the evenings I work here.

The schedule is killing me, and after a lot of internal debating, I've decided to transfer my dance students to Nikolai. He teaches at another school and needs the income more than I do. I can always take the students back, if and when this casino gig goes south.

As Trace charges around the empty tables, I cast him a cease-and-desist order with my eyes. He slows his roll, hovering at a distance behind the creepy restaurant patron.

"Do you do private dances?" The man's tongue slithers like a dying slug along his bottom lip. "I'll pay handsomely for the lap variety."

one *is a promise*

Bile creeps up my throat. Do I look like an exotic dancer?

My cherry-red half-circle skirt wraps low on my hips and attaches to a metallic gold mini underskirt. Chunky glass rhinestones and beaded appliques fringe the hardshell bra, red panel draped around one hip, and matching satin upper-arm bands. The belly dance costume is feminine and artistic. Certainly not designed for a lap dance.

I lift my chin and meet his beady eyes. "Do you miss the warm wet center of your mother's loins?"

So much for taking my job seriously.

"My mother's *what*?" His face pinches, deepening the pucker of wrinkles on his brow.

"Her loins. You spent nine months there. I assume that's why you're staring at mine with pathetic longing."

His shoulders snap back, and his gaze darts toward the exit. "You don't need to be nasty."

"Don't I? You just asked me for a lap dance."

"Excuse me," he mumbles, slipping away and walking out of the restaurant.

Servers flutter around the tables, collecting dishes and making a wide berth around the mountain of bristling power glaring at me.

"What are you looking at?" I anchor my hands on my hips.

Trace glances over his shoulder, as if I couldn't possibly be addressing *him*.

"I'm talking to you," I say. "The man with the eternal scowl."

Clasping his hands behind him, he prowls toward me. "Interesting tactic there. He'll never look at his mother the same way again."

"Oh, please. All the creepers have mommy issues. That was a free therapy session. Maybe I should start charging."

"Stay with me tonight. We can watch a movie and—"

"Nope." Dear God, I want to. *Iwantto-Iwantto-Iwantto.*

I hustle out of the restaurant before I change my mind.

But he's right on my heels, nipping and growling. "Why not?"

"I have plans." *With a jug of wine and a vibrator named Dimples.*

It's a five-second walk to my dressing room, where I slip in and close the door on his sexy scowl. Except his shoe prevents it from shutting. Then his hand.

"You're avoiding me." He barges in.

"I'm avoiding cuddles on your couch and long brush strokes in your bed."

"Why?" He shuts the door behind him and crosses his arms.

Why, he asks? Why, oh why? Because I'm horny, and when I'm around him, I want to strip him, lick him, and fuck the frown off his gorgeous face.

"I'm attracted to you." I walk into the luxurious bathroom he designed just for me. "That attraction makes me want the things you are very clearly withholding."

As he follows me in, I reach behind me to unhook the beaded bra. The rainfall shower head with recessed body jets is heaven, so I always shower here before heading home. Besides, removing my clothes is a sure way to make him disappear.

Except he doesn't leave.

Brushing my fingers away, he swiftly releases the row of hook and eye closures.

My heart races, and my hand flies to my chest, holding the cups in place. "Trace."

"Danni." He shifts closer, closer, until his necktie brushes my spine, his palms cup my bare shoulders, and his forehead rests against the back of my head. "Come upstairs with me."

That sounds like an invitation for more than a movie. Then again, I tend to have an overactive imagination, and it shoots straight out of my mouth.

"I'm hungry, Trace."

"I'll feed you."

"Will you feed me what we both want?"

His hands clench on my shoulders, and his breaths quicken. He's thinking it, wanting it, even if he won't admit it out loud.

In a moment of insanity, I loosen my grip on the bra and let it fall to the floor. My nipples harden against the cool air, and my breaths catch the tempo of his, growing louder, shorter, ragged with desire.

Standing behind me, he can't see my breasts, but if he lowers his hands just a few inches, he could hold them, play with them. God help me, it's been so long since I've been touched there I have to bite down on my tongue to stop myself from begging.

"I shouldn't be here," he whispers.

If he's trying to convince himself, it doesn't work because his hands are already moving over my body. One sweeps across my upper chest, and the other caresses a path around my hip to flatten against my abs.

My breasts feel heavy, tingling for attention, but he ignores them. With his arms folded around me, he holds my back to his chest as his mouth lowers, feathers along my neck, pressing harder, growing rougher, until he's kissing, sucking, and greedily biting my skin.

Every lick and scrape of teeth shoots a current of pleasure between my legs. I let my head fall to the side, giving him better access. The hand on my stomach splays wider, dipping, sinking beneath crystals and satin to stroke the trimmed hair on my mound.

Oh, Jesus. Please don't stop.

I melt against his chest, my hands falling back to the hard bricks of his ass and digging into the fabric of his slacks. We're both panting, shaking, grinding together as he reaches deeper between my legs, sliding over the wet waxed flesh of my folds.

His engorged cock prods my backside, and my knees weaken. Stars blot my vision, and the pound of my heart roars in my ears. If his long confident fingers plunge inside me, I'm done for. I'll come instantly, and the whole casino will hear me. But I don't care. I need this. I need *him*.

He rolls his hips against my ass aggressively, frantically, simulating sex. I bask in the claiming, in the heat of his harsh exhales on my neck, the fingers tracing my slit, and the massive body curled around mine. Teeth graze my shoulder, and his panting strengthens into a deep groan.

Until he bumps against the ring on my labium.

His breaths cut off, and his entire body goes still.

"What's wrong?" Dread knots in my stomach, suffocating the flames of my arousal.

His hands leave my body, and he steps back,

taking all the air with him. The same reaction he had when he touched the ring on my finger three months ago.

"It's just a piercing." I'm frozen with hope. Hope that he'll snap out of it and finish what he started.

Oppressive silence pushes against my back. I cross an arm over my nude chest and fight to keep my shoulders from hunching. Then I shift to face him.

With a hand on the wall supporting his slumped posture, he holds his other hand beneath his nose, as if smelling me on his fingers.

"What just happened?" My voice is low, hoarse.

His gaze lifts, locking on mine as his hand balls into a fist and drops to his side.

"A lapse in judgment. Forgive me." He stands taller, blanking his expression. "I made a mistake."

My airway constricts, and chills crash through me. I feel injured, insulted, but the pain is minuscule. I've endured worse. *Survived* worse. Nothing compares to burying my heart in a grave of ashes, and my body seems to recognize this. My limbs go numb. My chest lifts, and the tingling pressure behind my eyes evaporates.

"Good night, Trace," I say softly and swivel toward the shower to adjust the faucet.

The door clicks shut behind me, plunging me into the cold familiarity of loneliness.

I don't come out until I've washed away the sweat, makeup, and glitter...and the resentment.

Maybe I'm too forgiving, but in my mind, there's nothing to absolve. For a standoffish, reserved man, he's been straight-up with me. He's attracted to my body, but he doesn't want the messy relationship. Yes, he had a weak moment. So did I. And he shut it down before it went too far. Before he hurt me. Deep down, I admire his restraint.

Adding to my clemency is my conversation with Father Rick at the homeless shelter earlier this week. I donate most of my income and while dropping off a check, Rick mentioned The Regal Arch Casino has been matching my gifts to a ratio of 3:1. For every dollar I donate, Trace has been giving three dollars on the sly. Maybe he saw an opportunistic tax write-off. But after all his huffing and puffing about giving my money away, he jumps on the bandwagon? What is he up to?

When I emerge from the bathroom, the dressing room is empty and quiet. But he left something behind. An envelope, propped against a can of hairspray on the dressing table.

I pull on a casual strapless dress, slide on some flip-flops, and open the envelope. Inside is a concert ticket, and as I read the print, my heart slams against my ribs.

Presenting Beyoncé at America's Center & The Dome

It's a single ticket for tomorrow night in a luxury suite. I've seen my favorite artist live once, and it'd been from the nose-bleed section. But to watch her from a premium seat? In a private suite? Holy fucking shit, I'm going to explode.

I bound out of the dressing room in a frenzy of excitement, taking the long way through the gaming area to look for Trace. He might've left me feeling unsteady and frustrated, but it doesn't overshadow how grateful I am for the ticket. The need to say thank you in-person has me scanning all his usual spots — the restaurant, gaming tables, two of the three bars, the lobby.

Then I spot him twenty feet away, tucked in the

corner of the third bar with a pretty brunette on his lap. He's staring right at me.

My strides careen to a stop, and the concert ticket crumples in my hand.

I wish I was one of those people who can shield their emotions. I want to give him a smile, maybe even a small wave, and continue on like there isn't an invisible band around my ribs, crushing my chest.

Be cool, Danni. Don't overreact.

The muscles in my face ignore my demands. They contort, bunch, and turn cold, expressing everything I don't want him to see.

Humiliation.

Hurt.

Regret.

Had I accepted his invitation tonight, that woman wouldn't be running her hands through his hair, rubbing her double-D tits against him, or whispering in his ear. He wouldn't be across the room, staring at me with dispassion deadening his eyes.

Rejecting his offer to go upstairs meant I'd be alone tonight. But the same isn't true for him. And that's the sucker punch that blurs my vision and turns my feet toward the elevator.

It's a long walk across a short distance as I fight back the damnable tears in my eyes. Holding my chin up and gait casual, I feel like everyone's staring. But they're not. No one glances away from the beeping, flashing slot machines. No one cares.

That's good. I'm just the resident dancer, tired and anxious to get home after a long night of entertaining.

If I'm honest, my reaction isn't rational. For the

past three months, I've watched women hang all over Trace. Watched his hand rest on their lower backs. Watched his eyes glimmer when he talks with them, drinks with them at the bar. He's a player. We're not together, not exclusive, not anything. Even though it felt like *something* only fifteen minutes ago.

I guess that's the dig. Feeling the full brunt of his arousal in the bathroom, knowing he left worked up and fully aroused, and seeing the woman who will be enjoying the release of his sexual tension.

The woman he'll be taking to his bed tonight. Instead of me.

For a moment, I consider stopping by a bar on my way home and picking a man for the night. It would be so easy. I did it too many times to count before I met Cole.

Except one-night-stands lost their appeal after I discovered what it feels like to be adored, worshiped, and loved by a man who holds my heart.

I won't ever go back to grunting and groping in the dark with a passive man.

Maybe that's a lie. Maybe that's exactly what my future holds. But not tonight. I haven't reached that level of desperation.

By the time I arrive at my car, my eyes are dry and my hands are no longer trembling. I stare at the crumpled concert ticket, warring between ripping it up and straightening out the creases.

My excitement about going is squashed, but do I really want to be a petty brat about it? He gave me a gift, not a promise to be my boyfriend.

Before I lose my nerve, I type out a quick text.

one *is a promise*

Me: Thank you for the concert ticket.

Seconds later, a text buzzes my phone.

Trace: I'll pick you up at 7PM.

He's going with me? I should've guessed as much. Maybe he'll bring the brunette who's currently on his lap. Make it a threesome.

A whimper escapes my throat, and I drop my forehead against the steering wheel. Why in the fresh hell do I care?

Because I'm stupid.

And lonely.

And I might be falling for him.

Startled by the direction of my thoughts, I lift my head and press a hand against my racing heart as a violent mix of emotions roils in my gut.

I'm falling for Trace.

thirteen
three years ago

Time's run out, and it's an incendiary feeling, leaching the strength from my body and burning the air in my lungs.

A taxi cab idles in the driveway, glinting in the dim glow of dawn, waiting to take Cole away from me.

For an entire year.

Before the sun rose, in the early hours between dreams and reality, I woke with him moving inside me, with a promise on his breath. Through every long drugging stroke of his cock, he stared into my eyes and vowed that he'll return. That he'll marry me. That he'll always love me.

His promise for forever.

It was goodbye in the rawest, most pleasurable, most harrowing sense of the word.

Now we stand on the front porch, tightly wrapped in each other—our arms, our thoughts, our hearts refusing to let go. Every part of us tangles and melds together. One soul. One future. Distance be damned.

He cups my face and kisses me, his tongue rubbing against mine, our breaths fusing tenderly, passionately. But the heartache is overpowering, striking against my breastbone and shooting pain to the deepest reaches of my being.

Staring into his eyes, I seek, interlock, and connect with him on a soulful level. Like it's the first time I'm seeing him.

Or the last.

I feel like I'm losing him. We've only known each other ten months, and he's going to be gone a year. Will our newborn love withstand this separation? What if he finds someone else? An exotic beauty to pass his lonely nights with?

"Let me transfer my income into your account," he says at my ear.

"No."

We've been over this. He wants to pay my living expenses and cover the wedding deposits while he's gone. I want to put all our money together when he returns. When we're married. My way makes more sense.

"So fucking stubborn." He kisses me tenderly. "I don't know how I'm going to survive a year without you." His lips whisper against mine. "I won't do this again."

"Again?" My pulse jolts. I've been so focused on

getting through the next year, I hadn't considered there would be more deployments after this one.

"No." His hands flex against my jaw. "This is my last job. I'm quitting when I get back."

"Quit *now*." Hope rushes through me. "Don't go. You can find a new job and—"

"Shh, baby." He rests his lips against my hair, holding my cheek against his pounding chest. "I'm under contract for the rest of the year. But when I return, I won't renew."

My shoulders sink, and the cab driver lays on the horn. We both tense.

I hug him harder, my sinuses flaring against the assault of tears. But I refuse to cry. Not yet. This is hard enough for him. I won't make him leave a sobbing, miserable wreck of a woman.

"Call me when you arrive at the al-Bashrah oil terminal."

"I'll try, Danni, but we went over this."

My fingers sink against his back as my worry for his safety courses and spikes anew.

Americans live in converted cargo containers at one end of the oil platform. Their meals are delivered from the main ship. Access to a satellite phone is limited, and Internet is spotty. It could be months before I hear from him.

At least I don't have to share air time with his family. His mother left when he was a child, and he hasn't spoken to his drunk of a father in years. I'm his only phone call, as well as his next-of-kin in case of an emergency.

The taxi driver honks again, smacking the horn in

rapid succession.

"By the grace of God, give them a minute," Virginia shouts from her open window next door.

Cole smiles down at me, popping those dimples, and I commit every detail of him to memory. The soft scruff on his jaw, the deep chocolate of his eyes, the snake tattoo that coils around his strong neck, and his proud posture clad in black leather and denim.

"Say it again." I kiss his full lips.

"I promise to return to you."

"In one year, Cole." I wrap my arms around his shoulders, blinking back the burning ache in my eyes. "I'll be waiting at the altar."

"My beautiful bride. My Mrs. Hartman. It's all I'll think about." He untangles himself from my hug and steps back. "Keep the doors locked."

"Yeah." I glance back at the deadbolt he installed. "Okay."

"I love you," he whispers softly, achingly.

"I love you." I fade into his adoring gaze, barely holding myself together.

The moment he turns away, the tears spill over. I swipe at them, but there's too many coming too fast. By the time he's in the cab, my face is drenched and my vision is blurred.

As the car shrinks and disappears in the distance, I force myself to stand taller, stronger.

He'll be home in a year.

I have a year to plan a wedding.

Most girls dream about the cake, the flowers, the dress. This girl dreams about choreographing the first dance, and it's going to be the biggest production in the history of wedding dances.

one is a promise

My heart feels like a trampled, miserable pile of shit at my feet, but I have a sure way to channel the pain. For the next twelve months, Beyoncé will help me through it.

The lyrics to *XO* swirl through my head, and I see a crowded reception hall with Cole and me at the center. Him, holding me in his arms, rocking his sexy ass to the beat. Me, sliding through Lambada Zouk steps with flowing body waves, hair flicks, and sensual footwork. Together, we're smiling, twirling, lost in the intimacy of our eye contact.

No one's going to out-dance us at our own wedding.

fourteen
present

The roar of thousands of concert-goers echoes through the dome. The lights, the music, the energy of Beyoncé's dancers pulls me into the moment, gripping my hips like a lover's hands and leading me through the rhythm.

I harbored doubts on my way here, sitting beside Trace in the back of his fancy sedan and squirming in the uncomfortable silence.

Spending time with him, being casual with him, pretending like he didn't spend the prior evening with another woman—all of it twists me up and turns me inside out. But now that I'm here, I intend to enjoy the experience to its fullest.

We have the suite to ourselves, and Trace keeps his distance. Reclined in the back row of the balcony seats, he rests an ankle on a knee, a hand against his jaw, and watches me in that way he does. Intently. Unnervingly. Compulsively.

I haven't asked about the brunette, and he's made no attempt to explain his actions. Why would he? We're not a couple. Are we even friends?

Standing in the front row of the closest balcony to the stage, I hold onto the railing and shake my ass to the thumping beats. Over the years, I've created dance routines to all of Beyoncé's songs, and while I don't have a lot of space to work with, I make use of every square inch.

But every time I glance back at my audience of one, it takes a few moments to catch my breath. That isn't the look a man gives a woman he doesn't want. His gaze trails over me like a blistering fire that melts through my skin and sizzles in my blood. It's the kind of look that brings two bodies into complete union, a wild uncontrollable fusion of kissing, licking, and fucking.

If he were to step behind me and lift my dress, would I try to escape? Would I fight him? Withhold my desire? Or would I let him use me until we were both exhausted, limp, and satiated? Then could I let him go, to return to his women and un-messy lifestyle?

I must be falling for him, because I couldn't live with being one of his flings in a rotation of bed partners.

So as the concert continues, I block out the heat of his gaze and dance for myself, possessed by the vocals, controlled by the rhythm, completely immersed in my element.

Until the one song I hoped Beyoncé wouldn't sing

echoes through the dome.

The song I passionately, painstakingly choreographed for a year.

For a first dance that never happened.

Her beautiful voice belts the lyrics, knocking the wind from my lungs. I teeter in the heels and recover quickly, locking my knees, grounding myself in the here and now.

I can't dance to this. I don't even want to hear it. But I will *not* break down.

Behind me, the suite is stocked with enough food and liquor to entertain twenty people. I head up the stairs, brushing a hand casually over Trace's broad shoulder as I pass.

"Want a drink?" My smile is strained, forced. Maybe he won't notice.

He shakes his head, squinting at me.

I keep moving, focused on the ice chest filled with beer. Rummaging through the amber bottles, I find a Bud Light and pop off the cap.

Warm fingers touch my spine, bared by the open back of my dress. "You don't like this song?"

I hate it. I love it. I nod my head and guzzle the beer.

He lifts the bottle from my fingers and sets it aside. "What's wrong?"

I hum a conflicted noise and set my gaze on the beer. "We can go whenever. Or stay. Whatever you want."

"I asked you a question." He grips my chin, forcing my eyes to his.

"It's messy." The tiered fringe on my ivory mini

dress quivers violently, broadcasting my discomfort.

"If I didn't want to know, I wouldn't have asked."

I ease my chin out of his grip and cross my arms. It's a defensive posture, but I don't feel safe with him. Not with my feelings.

He stands a foot taller than me, hands at his sides, shoulders back, and frown firmly in place. So confident, intimidating, and sexier than he has the right to be. He's a curse, a blessing, and a second chance, like the black walls of desolation collapsing to reveal a glimpse of light. Being near him shakes me to the very roots of my soul.

He's wearing another charcoal suit, sans the tie. A few buttons open at the neck. If I hadn't seen his pajamas with my own eyes, I would've imagined him sleeping in a suit.

"Do you own a pair of jeans?" I ask.

His scowl deepens. "Answer my question, and I'll answer yours."

"All right." I reach around him for the beer and swallow a zealous gulp to flush the knot in my throat. "Cole was overseas for a year, and I spent that time planning our wedding, specifically our first dance."

"To this song."

"Yep." I lift the beer to finish it off.

He intercepts it and pours it out. Then his arm comes around me, pulling my chest against his.

"I own four pairs of jeans." His mouth moves against the top of my head, his breath fanning my hair. "Listen." A pause of silence. "The song's over."

"Yeah." I gaze up into his soft blue eyes, my hands falling on the placket of his white shirt.

"Are there any other songs you don't want to hear?" he murmurs.

I shake my head.

"Then we'll stay till the end." He leads me back to the balcony, down to the front row, and closes in behind me at the railing.

His hands rest on my hips, and his brow lowers to the back of my head. Maybe he wants to stare down the length of my nude back to watch my ass move. Maybe he simply wants to keep me close.

Either way, it takes several songs before I loosen up enough to dance again, and when I do, I limit my movements to a gentle sway, remaining right where I am. Because I love the feel of his hands on me. Because his breath on my nape gives me comfort. Because the heat of his body reminds me what it feels like to be intimate with a man.

I thought I lost my one chance to experience this — the elusive, all-consuming high that can only be found in a romantic connection.

Maybe I just needed time.

Or the right person.

When he walks me to my front door, it's after one in the morning. The August humidity lingers in the air, and a blanket of silence stretches over the moon-soaked street.

He reaches for my hand, holding it between us. "I had a nice evening."

"Same. Thank you for taking me."

As I pull away, I realize he's not holding my hand. He's gripping the ring on my finger, pinching it as if he wants to yank it off.

My chest tightens, and my brows pull together.

If you never take it off again, I'll be the happiest man on the planet.

Cole broke his promise to me. He's gone. I'm not beholden to the promise I made to him.

I straighten my fingers and slowly inch my hand back, away from the ring. But as the band slides over the first knuckle, Trace lets go.

My gaze jumps to his, but he's already turning, striding back to the car where his driver waits.

Teasing and dodging. Connecting and missing. I swing right, and he steps left. I'm over the ballad of Trace Savoy.

"Hey, Trace?"

He pauses, glances over his shoulder.

"I just wanted to warn you." I cock a hip.

"Yes?" He shifts to face me fully, hands clasped behind his back.

"I ordered this thing online called Her Ultimate Decoder, and it'll be here tomorrow."

"Okay," he says slowly.

"It's guaranteed to decipher confusing cryptic men. Hundreds of five-star ratings on Amazon support the claim." I fold my arms across my chest. "Your evasive maneuvers are about to be exposed. Any last words?"

The shadows might be playing tricks on me, but I swear there's a grin on his face.

He drops his head, shakes it slightly, then turns away with an unmistakable smile in his voice. "See you tomorrow night, my tiny dancer."

fifteen
present

The next morning, my sister wakes me at the ungodly hour of nine o'clock with my niece and her husband, David, in tow. I mentioned the previous day that the brakes on the Midget are screeching, and now she's here to meddle… I mean, fix it. Or rather, make David fix it.

With the car up on jacks in the driveway, he stretches on his back beneath it, grunting and clanking tools. Angel squats in the flowerbed, stabbing Rollie Pollie pillbugs with a stick, while Bree and I drink coffee on the loveseat under the old oak tree.

Bree knows every quarrelsome detail of my time spent with Trace Savoy. After catching her up on the concert, I'm anxious to hear her thoughts. But the slaughter going on behind me makes my skin crawl.

"Tell her to stop doing that," I say to Bree.

"Angel, leave the bugs alone."

The hem of my niece's cute sundress drags through the dirt as she drives the stick down over and over, chanting, "Die. Die. Die."

"They're just bugs." Bree tilts her head, studying her daughter. "That's normal behavior, right?"

A first-grade teacher is asking *me*—someone who's never around children—what I consider normal?

When Angel was born, I thought it was adorable that Bree named her after our family name, Angelo. But if I knew then what I know now, I would've given her The Book of Baby Names: The Demonology Edition.

"Yeah, there's nothing frightening about her at all," I say dryly.

Bree slumps back on the seat. "Okay, so when you called Trace out last night for being confusing and cryptic, what did he do?"

"He shook his head and walked away, smiling."

"The smile is new. Sounds like progress."

"Progress? I thought you were against me getting involved with him." I lift my coffee mug and find it empty. *Damn.*

"Jesus, Danni. You blew past *involved* when you stayed the night at his penthouse."

I open my mouth to argue, but she sticks a finger in the air.

"Hold that thought. We need more coffee." She grabs my cup and darts into the house.

Footsteps approach behind me, and I turn, staring into the large brown eyes of a demon.

Angel brushes a wayward hair back toward her pigtails and smiles a toothy fiendish non-smile. "I'm going to eat your head."

"That sounds...complicated."

"I'm going to put it on a stick and roast it and eat it with a fork." She swishes the dress around her knees.

"If you eat my head, we won't be able to have these creepy conversations." I shudder.

She lifts a shoulder. "I'll find other heads to talk to."

Where does she come up with this shit?

I raise my voice toward the car. "Are you hearing this, David?"

"A little busy," he yells back.

Yeah, but I know he's listening, and that's what I call *denial.*

Angel skips away, humming Hell's version of *A-Tisket, A-Tasket.* I love that kid, but sweet lord have mercy, she scares the crap out of me.

"What's that look for?" Bree steps out of the house and hands me a warm mug.

"I've changed my mind. There's something really disturbing about your child."

She blows on her coffee. "She's just going through a phase."

Is demon possession a phase?

"So." Bree regards me, as if revving up for a scolding. "You don't think you're involved with this man?"

"I didn't say that. I'm just not going to pursue a relationship with him."

"Why not?"

"He doesn't want one, not with anyone. Least of all with me." My stomach hardens. "He sleeps around —

"You don't know that."

"I see him with women, Bree. And he said he never spends a night alone."

"He told you that…like three months ago." She props an elbow on the back of the loveseat, her sharp gray eyes looking straight through mine. "I think he's waiting for you."

"That's ridiculous. Waiting for what?"

Her gaze drops to my engagement ring, and her voice softens. "For you to get over Cole."

My throat goes dry, and I twist the band on my finger. "It's been on my right hand since I met Trace."

"Okay. But can you take it off?" She gives me a small, encouraging smile. "From what you've said, it seems to bother him."

Without letting myself think about it, I work the ring off my finger and slip it into the pocket of my jeans. "There's your answer."

My heart thunders painfully, but after a few measured breaths, all is quiet.

"How are we doing?" She rests a hand on my forearm.

I resent the concern in her eyes. It reminds me of that godawful part of my life, the months that followed Cole's funeral, when she repeatedly dug me out of the alcohol-induced abyss I numbed myself in. Which is why I'm also so fucking thankful for her. Every damn day.

"I'm good, Bree. But I think you're off-base about Trace. He's not waiting for anything. I mean, it's not like he's competing for my attention. Cole's dead, and I'm here, single and available."

"You're single. But you're not available."

"That makes no sense."

She eyes the mug of coffee in my hand. "Hold out your cup."

"Why?"

"Just do it." She guides my fingers to the handle and adjusts the position of the mug over a patch of grass. "Imagine that the cup is you, and the coffee is all your love for Cole."

The mug is full, sloshing over the sides as I hold it in place. "This is stupid."

"Shut up and pay attention." She stands over me and lifts her mug, which is equally full. "My cup represents Trace, and all the love he wants to give you."

I snort. "As if."

She ignores me and proceeds to pour her coffee into mine. As it flows over the sides and into the grass, she continues pouring, her expression taut with concentration.

"You just wasted all that coffee," I say. "Maybe you should stick with teaching first graders."

"I swear, *Danielle*." She fists her hands on her hips, the empty mug dangling from her fingers. "Sometimes you're denser than a first grader."

"I'm not dense, *Gabrielle*. I get it. My cup runneth over because it's half-full of shit." I grin, knowing full well that's not what she's insinuating. "I need a bigger cup."

"Wrong." She plops down beside me. "I was trying to demonstrate an old Chinese Zen saying. You can't fit Trace's love into the love you already possess. It's supposed to ask the question…" She meets my eyes. "Do you have the right cup full?"

"Apparently, I don't." With a sigh, I stare at the mug. "So I empty my cup."

"Empty the cup," she echoes.

"But it's also filled with my love for you and the demon—"

"Don't call her that."

"The *angel* and mom and dad—"

"Nope. That's a different cup. This is the man cup."

For the love of God. My head hurts. "What if I'm in a polyamorous relationship?"

"Do you want that?"

"Well, no." I can't even hold onto one man. "But—"

"Empty the damn cup."

I do it to make her happy, dumping delicious java all over the grass.

Emptying the metaphorical cup, however, will be much harder than flicking my wrist.

"I'll go get us more coffee." I stand, needing a moment to regroup.

"Danni," David calls from beneath the car. "Come here."

"I'll get the coffee." Bree takes my mug.

"What's the verdict?" I step beside his supine position on the ground.

Clothed in athletic gear, he's recently acquired a dad bod, with the requisite *extra* around the middle. But he's still a good-looking guy, especially for a high-school math teacher and soccer coach.

He doesn't move his head from beneath the undercarriage. "When was the last time you had your brakes replaced?"

"Umm..."

He rolls out on a scooter thing and stares up at me with grease smeared across his brow. "Did Cole do it?"

I nod.

"So at least three years ago." He sits up and blots a towel over his swarthy face. "As hard as you ride the brakes, I'm not surprised they're already grinding metal on metal."

Shit. I blow out a breath. "What does that mean?"

"It means your car doesn't leave this driveway until I have time to replace the brakes."

"I can have it towed—"

"It'll take longer." He collects his tools and climbs to his feet. "I can do it tomorrow night."

"Are you sure? I'll pay you."

He laughs. "Your sister would castrate me if I took your money."

It's clear who wears the pants in their family, but who am I to judge? They're in love, and I'm enviously happy for them.

After they leave, I change into a mini dance skirt and strappy crop top. Then I head into the dance studio and send Trace a text.

Me: I need a favor

My phone rings within seconds, displaying his name on the screen.

"Did you miss my voice?" I set it on speaker, on the floor, and bend at the waist, warming up to work on a new routine.

"Is everything okay?"

I melt at the worry rumbling through the phone. "Brakes are shot on my car. Can I get a ride to and from work tonight?"

His relieved exhale makes me smile. Stretching my arms over my head, I study my form in the mirror.

"Yes, of course. I'll send my driver." He pauses, breathing softly through the silence. "Is that all?"

Not even close. I want to talk to him. Share my feelings, my thoughts, my desires. I *want* to empty my cup.

Lowering to the floor, I arch in the Cow Stretch to warm up my tummy muscles. "What are you doing today?"

"Running a multi-million-dollar empire."

"What's that involve? Snapping fingers and counting dead presidents?"

"Dead presidents?"

"Money." I roll into a neck-stretching back bend. "You know, Jackson, Grant, Benjamin—"

"Benjamin Franklin wasn't a president."

"Then why is he on the hundred-dollar bill?"

The phone vibrates with his chuckle. "What are you doing today?"

"I'm practicing a new belly dance routine. Wanna hear the song?"

"I'd love to."

A smile lifts my cheeks. "Hang on."

I leap over the phone on the floor and power on the sound system. Keeping the volume low enough to hear him, I move back to the phone. A moment later, *Criminal* by Britney Spears streams through the speakers.

"Talk me through the movements," he says. "So I can visualize it."

one *is a promise*

Warm energy fizzes through my veins. "The dance begins with just my hips." I move them, watching my reflection in the mirror. "I'm sweeping through soft figure-eight motions."

He listens without interruption as I speak through every twitch, head toss, and hip thrust.

I love his interest in my dancing. He might be moody and layered with mixed signals, but there's something underneath it all, something behind the stuffy suits that calls to me, awakens me, makes my heart flutter like a baby bird.

The first and last time I felt anything like this, it was instantaneous and explosive, spinning and colliding and welding Cole and I together under the force of our own gravity.

With Trace, it's different. More like seeds. Two hearty seeds that weather drought and neglect and tribulation, all the while sprouting roots — roots that grow toward each other, building a foundation, stretching, and blooming, not two but one single stalk, straight through the cracks in a hostile landscape.

We'll either grow into something beautiful.

Or we won't.

The song winds to a close, and his voice echoes behind me, *in stereo*. "Play it again. I want to watch this time."

I spin and find him leaning in the doorway, his phone and a set of keys dangling from his hand.

Today's suit is navy, with a light blue shirt and black tie. His tailored slacks fit so well my gaze is drawn to them, to the way they cup and mold to his groin. He's so insanely, incredibly sexy and masculine it takes a great deal of effort to look away.

I wish I'd worn something nicer or at least brushed my hair. That's what he does to me. Makes me want to tear through my closet, try on ten outfits, take a shower, put on makeup, hairspray and tease and hairspray some more. Because at some point in the last four months, this man helped me move past a broken promise and gave me a reason to try again.

I feel him watching me, and when I look up, my heartbeat ricochets in my chest. With his chin tilted down and hands resting in his pockets, his gaze roams along my bare legs, traces my hips, pauses on my chest. My nipples harden, my breasts unbound beneath the loose crop top. I think he likes what I'm wearing, given the way his lips part to accommodate the rush of his breath.

His attention drops to my hand—my naked finger—and his jaw flexes. "You took off the ring."

"Yeah." I clear my throat, feeling awkward. "Did you break the speed limit getting here?"

He continues to stare at my hand, a turbulence of emotions descending upon his features. Then he blinks, smooths out his expression, and lifts his head. "I drive a fast car."

I don't know what to make of his reaction to the ring, so I slip around him and step outside, shielding my eyes against the setting sun.

Parked behind the Midget is a sexy luxury sports car with charcoal metallic paint. Fat tires give it a wide stance, and the convertible top, black leather interior, and rear bumper spoiler all scream, *Pay attention to me.* It looks pricey, and I bet the inside smells like him—rich, dark, manly. I can totally see him driving…whatever it is.

"What is that?" I ask.

He makes a sound of disbelief. "A Maserati GranTurismo."

"It's like a fancier, forty-years-newer version of my car. Look, they're the same height."

"Except mine's a lot longer. Sleeker. More powerful." He punctuates every word with a heated growl.

"Are we still talking about cars?"

"You tell me."

Our eyes meet and hold for several seconds before I glance away.

"Better check yourself, Trace. You're dangerously close to flirting."

"I came early to watch you practice." He turns back into the house, vanishing inside.

He said he was sending his driver, but never mind that. He's *four* hours early. That's a lot of time to spend with a man who ties me up in knots.

But I want him to tie me up. And kiss me and love me and never release me.

I take a calming breath. I'm just going to let this run its own course. I won't fight it. Won't deny it. Won't push it. But I might tease it a little. If he wants me to practice in front of him, I'll give him a show.

Inside, I set *Criminal* on repeat and take my position before him. He found a folding chair and reclines on it, legs spread, fingers laced together on his flat stomach. Then, without a twitch or a word, he watches me dance. A god on his throne, immaculate power and authority, straight-faced and unmoved.

Until I dance closer, more erotically, putting everything I have into the roll of my abs and hips. I inch so close I'm swaying in the *V* of his legs, moving my arms to the rhythm and stirring the air around his tense posture.

He shifts on the chair, licks his lips.

Then he touches me. A knuckle against my inner thigh. The backs of his fingers beneath the short hem of my flowing skirt. By the time the song cycles three times, both of his hands are on me, curved around my thighs and edging toward my backside, which is bared by a thong.

Suspended in eye contact, lost in the pressure of his fingers, I give up on the choreography and free fall into improvisation. My hands drop to his shoulders, digging into the fabric and muscles beneath.

The slouch of his body begs me to dance on him. While I'm not a stripper, I know my way around a lap, having spent a year playing kinky games with Cole. I also know that the build-up, the sexy tease, is crucial.

As the song restarts, I perch my butt in the air, pushing my chest closer to Trace's slack face. Then I nudge back on his shoulders, using his body to gracefully stand straight and step back.

Lips parted and smile playful, I strut around him, tilting my hips up and down and running my hands along my body. He doesn't take his eyes off me, twisting on the seat to watch me dance behind him.

With my feet positioned behind his chair, I touch his jaw, nudging him to look forward. Then I gently lower my chest toward the back of his head, moving my body downward and twisting my hips to the beat.

Now would be a good time to take a step back and talk myself out of whatever this is. But every nerve ending below my waist rages at the thought. Instead, I reach around him and boldly graze my fingers along the thick shape of his cock through the slacks.

Hard and long, he jerks against my hand, and his head falls back. "Danni."

Sliding upward, I explore the chiseled expanse of his abs and run my nose along his neck. "You smell hungry, Trace."

His chest heaves, and one leg stretches out, scraping his shoe along the floor. "Come here."

A hand curls around my wrist, and I let him pull me around the chair. When I return to his front, I give him my back, writhing sensually, tauntingly between his knees.

"You have a great ass. Not big. Not small." His voice is hoarse, raw, lacking its usual eloquence as he caresses my backside. "It's a perfect shape that looks incredible on your body."

Emboldened by the compliment, I slowly lower onto his lap with my back to him, grinding gently and shivering against the hard press of his erection. His hands slide to my thighs and move upward beneath the skirt, settling on my hips.

"Your skin feels like silk," he breathes raggedly at my ear. "And the dips here…" His thumbs stroke my waist. "I dream about these curves and the way you move them. You're built for sex." He touches his mouth to my neck, groaning. "Christ, I'm so fucking hard."

Quivers race along my inner thighs, and my core tightens, pulsates, driving my movements to the music. I lean back and press my backside into his lap, my shoulders against his chest, and wrap an arm around his neck.

"You always smell like Nag Champa." With his hands beneath my skirt, one sinks between my legs, over the thong. The other lifts, slipping under my shirt to cup a bare breast. "Such a sexy, potent, exotic scent. It lingered on my sheets for a week after you left."

"Your maid didn't wash them?" I moan against the tweak of his fingers on my nipple.

"I wouldn't allow it. Not until I couldn't smell you anymore."

My chest flutters.

Who am I kidding? There's a damn butterfly migration taking off inside me. His confession is just so…unexpected. So is the hand caressing the soaked crotch of my thong.

He's rock hard beneath me. I'm dripping wet. Why are we still talking?

I remind myself he was with another woman two nights ago. Hell, he could've spent the night with another woman after dropping me off at the concert.

Miserable thoughts. But my body doesn't seem to care. His touch feels too good, and I'm so fucking worked up my pussy throbs with its own heartbeat.

"I love your tits." He squeezes my flesh. "Perfectly round, sitting up high on your chest and driving me insane every goddamn day." His finger circles around the bud. "I bet these perfect little nipples are pink."

"See for yourself."

"Turn around."

I'm not fully standing before he spins me to face him, pulls me onto his lap, and guides my legs to straddle the spread of his.

"So damn beautiful." He cups my face, seemingly hypnotized by whatever he sees there.

I look him in the eye and give him a sweet subtle grin, communicating that I know how entranced he is.

His attention lowers to my chest, and his hands follow, lifting the hem of my shirt with slow, agonizing patience. Cool air brushes my nipples. Then his gaze.

"Pink." His expression intensifies, lighting me on fire.

He grips my ass and shifts me up his chest to nuzzle my breasts. I use my hands to squeeze what little I have around his face. His breaths become shallow, and his teeth graze my skin. When he swirls his tongue around a nipple, my head falls back, my fingers clutching his shoulders for support.

But he has me, his arms holding me tight as he lowers me onto the rigid cock trapped within his slacks. He rocks his hips upward, groaning, his hands roaming everywhere — my thighs, my breasts, my neck, always returning to knead my butt.

I slide my face along the side of his until I reach his ear. Then I draw the lobe between my lips and suck.

It sets him off, his hands plunging into my hair and his tongue sweeping into my mouth.

"You're so fucking hot." He growls into the kiss, the fingers in my hair wrenching my head back for a deeper angle. "You make me crazy."

I know the feeling. All reason has abandoned me in the powerful arms of desire. I want him, need him, and none of this is rational. But I'm caught in the rapid rhythm of his breaths, the flex of his body, and the expert strokes of his tongue.

With my legs hooked around the back of the chair, my skirt rides up to my hips. I gently grind against him, rocking up and down, like I'm riding a bull in slow-motion. The wetness between my legs will no doubt leave a stain on his slacks, and the thought makes me grin against his lips.

The song loops again, and he eases back but not away. "I can't do this anymore."

A fist of dread clenches inside me. "Can't do what?"

"I can't keep pretending you aren't the first thought in my head when I wake and the reason I can't fall asleep at night."

I stare at him in shock.

Eyes hooded, mouth parted, he cradles my face and touches our foreheads together. "I lied to you."

My heart skips. "What do you mean?"

"I want you, Danni."

Oh. "That's not exactly a secret." I press my weight down on his erection.

"It's more than that. I've wanted you since the moment I saw you." His fingers tighten against my jaw. "I want *all* of you."

sixteen

present

"You want *all* of me?" My pulse accelerates, and my voice cracks on a fragile breath. "What does that mean?"

"Just when I think I can't possibly want you more," Trace says roughly, heatedly, "this hunger, this gut-deep *need* I feel for you consumes me until I can't imagine a future without you in it."

My mouth dries, and the room spins around me, tipping me off balance.

"I don't understand. All this time…" I slide off his lap and back out of his hold on my neck. I don't know what this is, but something's off. "You said you wouldn't fuck me. You didn't want the *mess*. Why would you lie?"

I shove my hair away from my face. "Why are you telling me this now?"

He bends forward, dropping his head, and bracing his forearms on his knees. "This isn't about sex."

"Really," I drawl, incredulous.

"Okay, yes, sex is... I want to be inside you. Desperately." His eyes burn into mine. "But that's not all."

I cross my arms over my chest.

"I need to know, Danni." Scraping a hand through his hair, he releases a breath. "If Cole was in this room right now, where would I fall? Would you shove me aside to get to him?"

"What kind of question is that?" Blood pumps hard and fast through my veins. "You wouldn't be here, because I would've never left him."

"But he left you, and *I* am here. What if we were both here? Who would you choose?"

"That's not fair!" A chill sweeps over me as I pace through the room and power off the sound system. "Way to buzz kill my libido, by the way. You're like your own cockblock."

"Answer the question." His glare doesn't waver.

"There is no answer. Because one, Cole's dead. And two...he's fucking *dead.* Why are we even talking about this?"

"Am I your second choice?" His tone is angry and confrontational, but the creases around his eyes and the uncertainty in those blue depths halt my feet.

Is the right cup full?

If Cole were here, there wouldn't be a choice. He's my forever.

Was.

He *was* my forever.

Empty the cup.

"You're not a choice." I take a step toward Trace, and another, softening my expression. "You're my second *chance*."

"Not good enough."

I suck in a sharp breath. "Too bad. I'm not making a choice that doesn't exist."

"It exists to *me*." He stands and charges into the kitchen. "I won't live in his shadow."

"His shadow?" I chase after him, voice rising. "What are you talking about?"

He grabs a water bottle from the fridge and shoves it into my hand. "You can't love me, because you're trapped in another life with another man."

Love him? Why did he go there? Why now? And I am *not* trapped!

"That's not true!" I scream, slamming the water down on the counter. "I lost someone I loved. I miss him desperately, but I'm moving on. I am!" My breaths wheeze as I fight to rein in my temper. "What do you want from me?"

He reaches toward my face and slips his fingers beneath the hair hanging near my eyes. Without touching my skin, he slowly, tenderly, slides the strands back to expose my distressed expression.

"I need to know if you're mine or his." He lowers his hand, scrutinizing every twitch on my face.

What have I done to make him so fixated on Cole? Is it the shrine of photos in my bedroom? The motorcycle in the dining room? The ring I only just took off this morning?

They're keepsakes. Memories. Fundamental pieces of my life. I would *never* be with someone who asks me to give that up.

Except… If I turned the tables, if I walked into his penthouse filled with physical reminders of another woman, I wouldn't like it. My heart sinks. I'd lose my fucking mind.

I uncap the water bottle and drink, calming my sprinting pulse. "What about the woman on your lap two nights ago?"

"What about her?" He steps out of the kitchen and pauses in the hallway with his back to me.

"Were you thinking about how you *can't possibly want me more* while you fucked her?"

Silence vibrates from his rigid posture.

Why is he just standing there? He can turn left toward the bedrooms. Or he can walk his sexy ass through the dining room and out the front door. Instead, he pivots right and grips the one doorknob in the house that I avoid.

"What's behind this door, Danni?" He twists the glass knob, unable to open it.

I try to keep my voice casual, but it scratches. "The basement."

He lifts his hand and tests the padlock I installed two years ago. "Where's the key?"

My stomach knots. I pass that door countless times every day. I don't look at it. Don't think about it. I certainly don't want to open it. Everything Cole left behind—his personal things, our wedding, the life we lost—is on the other side.

I retreat into the kitchen and chug the rest of the water.

"That's what I thought," he says quietly behind me.

Tremors grip my limbs, and my throat seals up. I feel myself crumbling, and I hate it.

Trace slides around me, and for a second, I think he might hug me. I hope, I want, I *ache* for his arms to hold me.

"I need to think." His keys jingle as he removes them from his pocket.

He's leaving.

"Don't go." I grit my teeth at the pleading sound of my voice.

"I'll send my driver to pick you up for work." His mask falls into place, vanishing all emotion into oblivion.

Turning, he calmly strides through the dance studio, toward the back door. Always walking away. Always so fucking remote.

Anger quivers through my body, curling my lip. "Are you sure you don't want to look around some more? See if you can find a personality that doesn't suck?"

His detached gaze connects with mine as he steps outside. I follow, flexing my hands with the need to strangle him. His direct eye contact only pisses me off more. He sees how upset I am, and he's unmoved. Climbing into his car without a care in the world.

"Fine. Go." I shove my hands on my hips. "I was saving myself anyway. For Mark the siding guy. Remember him? Turns out the foreveraloner has a foot-long boner. And he's not afraid to use it!"

What a childish thing to say. But the fury reddening Trace's face? *Worth it!*

He slams the door, throws the car in reverse, and burns rubber out of the neighborhood.

Choking on fumes of frustration, I trudge back inside and stand before the mirrors. What does he see when he looks at me? A defeated, trapped, eternally grief-stricken woman?

Blonde hair hangs in waves around my face and down my chest. My cheeks glow with a pink flush, my lips swollen and parted. And my gray eyes are bright, unblinking, and full of yearning.

I look like I'm in love.

Because I am.

I'm in love with Trace Savoy.

"You get off on your own pain, don't you?" I ask my reflection. "Love could bring you more agony. Are you willing to risk that again?"

The woman in the mirror doesn't have the answers, but as my temper cools, it becomes easier to break down my confrontation with Trace. For the next couple of hours, I lie on my bed with a framed photo of Cole and me in front of a Christmas tree. Our first and only Christmas together.

He was in and out of my life in ten months. An infinitesimal amount of time for such a lasting impact. His love branded me, left its mark beneath my skin, like swirling colors of ink. I don't need pictures or an engagement ring to be reminded of the euphoria, the fuzzy whirling dream state that swallowed us in those ten months. I feel his absence in my blood, in my thoughts, every day.

Because love doesn't end with death. It doesn't shrivel and disintegrate with the ashes. It hovers, follows, *haunts* the living.

But after months of missteps and drunken pity parties, I learned how to cope with it. I learned how to breathe again. And in the past four months, I rediscovered my smile in a man who scowls through every emotion.

As much as I bitch about Trace being cryptic and impersonal, I'm magnetically drawn to his confidence, his strength. He challenges me, pushes me, and I need that. Because I'm not without shortcomings.

He wanted to see the basement. I should've showed it to him. Hell, I should've cleared out the space a long time ago. But he didn't ask me to do that. He didn't ask me to get rid of anything, not even the seven-hundred pounds of steel and chrome sitting in the dining room.

Cole might've been my favorite smile, but once I discovered the emotional depth in Trace's scowl, I realized I love it more than any smile. Cole's charming, animated personality won me over instantly. Contrarily, Trace's strict, reserved nature makes me appreciate how deeply sensitive he is beneath the suit.

All Trace wanted was reassurance that my heart didn't belong to another man, and I didn't give him that. If anything, I reinforced his doubts.

I really fucked this up.

But I have a plan to unfucktify it, and by *plan*, I mean a slight chance of success based mainly on hope.

He wants *all* of me? That's what I'll give him — the honest, barefaced, take-a-leap-of-faith answer to his question. Because he was right. I have a choice to make. A decision between the past and the future.

I choose the future. I choose Trace. And tonight,

I'm going to tell him I love him.

When his driver picks me up for my three o'clock shift, my stomach twists into knots. I recognize this feeling, this vulnerability. I'm opening myself up, letting Trace in. He could make me blissfully happy. Or he could crush me beneath his shiny shoe.

At the casino, I let the restaurant staff know that I'm leaving early tonight. In the four months I've worked here, I've never taken time off. But waiting until midnight to talk to Trace is out of the question.

For five hours, I dance on the stage, wrapped in the moving beam of light. Every table in the dining area is filled, and the usual crowd gathers outside the glass walls. Some are just passing by and pause to watch me before meandering on. Others linger through several songs, their eyes fixated on the swing of my hips, hypnotized.

My dancing has a similar effect on Trace. He watches me every night, if only for a few minutes as he passes through the dining room or from afar when he makes his rounds on the casino floor. But I haven't spotted him once tonight. Neither in the restaurant nor the gaming area. By the time eight o'clock rolls around, my mind is a spinning tunnel of doubt.

"She's incredible," a man says from one of the tables as I slip off the stage. "Unbelievably beautiful."

"I come here just to see her," another man replies from across the aisle.

I slip by several more compliments and dodge two propositions on my way out. Down the hall, I duck into my dressing room and spend the next hour showering, spritzing, and primping. Then I step back from the full-length mirror and scrutinize the result.

A silver strapless dress hugs my body from chest to upper thighs. The color makes my gray eyes look metallic and glitters against the gold in my hair. Matching stilettos complete the outfit. No panties or bra — I'm optimistic like that.

Frosted lip gloss, cheek blush, and smoky eyeshadow defines my face, and my hair ripples in voluminous beach waves around my arms.

I look pretty hot, but not overly made up. I also look like I'm seconds from hurling, but I can live with the nerves. What I can't live with is chickening out.

"Go get him, Danni." I square my shoulders and head out onto the gaming floor.

A small wristlet holding my phone and cash swings from my hand as I walk from one end of the casino to the other. Trace has been missing all night, but the cameras in the ceiling remind me that he might be watching me on his laptop.

I add a sexy sway to my hips on my way to his private elevator. When I started working here, he gave me a passcode to access the offices on the 30th floor. I've never tried to enter his residence alone. I assume he's in his office, but I push the button for the penthouse on impulse.

The *31* illuminates, and my breath catches. As the elevator begins its climb to the top floor, I consider pressing *30* and stopping by his office first. But curiosity holds me immobile.

Why is his penthouse unlocked? He's either there or the passcode he gave me unlocks it. I've had that code for four months.

I've wanted you since the moment I saw you.

Excitement buzzes through my veins, eradicating any lingering nerves. I love this man and his perplexing, mysterious ways. I love him, and I can't wait to tell him. And kiss him. And… Holy shit, I'm totally getting laid tonight.

When the elevator opens on the penthouse floor, my thighs clench, and my blood hums wildly. I step out and breeze past the kitchen, dining room, and living room, searching, craning my neck, and starting to sweat. There's no sign of him, and the silence is unnerving.

I enter the hallway, and the end is illuminated by the light in his bedroom. Maybe he's in the shower. Maybe he's waiting for me in bed, naked, and fully erect.

Grinning like a fool, I quicken my gait. The click of my heels sound my approach, but that's not the only thing I hear as I reach the open door.

Heavy breaths.

A low moan.

My heart freezes in my chest, and I stumble on the threshold.

The bed is perfectly made and vacant, but I know he's in here, and he's not alone.

Sharp pain ignites behind my eyes as I follow the panting sounds to the sitting area by the fireplace.

Bent over the arm of the couch is a woman with long dark hair, her face pressed against the cushion and her hips skyward, held in place by the man standing behind her.

The man I chose.

The one I love.

Agony stabs my chest, ripping the air from my lungs and shaking my knees violently. I grip the door jamb to keep myself upright, frozen in horror, nauseous beneath waves and waves of horrendous pain.

He's arched over her, his chest covering her back and his trousers around his thighs. They're angled toward the door, both wearing suits, with her skirt ruched to her waist. I can't see his dick, but it's clear he's buried inside her. He's not thrusting, not moving. Because he's staring right at me.

I thought he was detached before...

It's like I'm looking at someone else. There's no expression on his face. Nothing. No scowl. No hint of lust. Just...emptiness.

How could he do this? Everything he said was lies. He's just a player. A liar. And I fucking fell for it. Hard.

I cover my mouth as heaving breaths break free from my lungs.

The woman stirs, wriggling her hips against him as she lifts her head and brushes the hair from her face.

The flawless face of Marlo Vogt.

Her eyes find mine, and she gasps. Her complexion pales. She reaches back to shove at him, her other arm yanking her skirt down. Embarrassed.

Not as embarrassed as I am. My skin burns with humiliation, disgust, and anguish.

I hurt so badly blackness dots my vision and strangles my throat. My feet stumble backward, carrying me ungracefully into the hall, turning, and running toward the elevator.

I feel like my insides are tearing, separating, and bleeding out. Like I'm grieving.

Like the day that destroyed my world in the most irrevocable way.

seventeen
two years ago

"He's retiring when he gets home." I twirl around Bree in the dance studio, sliding seamlessly through the steps I've been practicing for the past year. It's my coping mechanism. I might be falling apart inside, but I keep moving, keep dancing. "I just need to be patient."

And trust him. I trust Cole more than anyone on the planet.

"I don't understand why he couldn't retire before he left." Bree crosses her arms and stares at the ceiling. "It's the silence that concerns me the most." She sighs. "Danni, you must be asking yourself… What if he doesn't show up for the wedding? It's only a week away."

I lose my footing, but she doesn't notice. Her eyes are closed, as if that could hide the worry on her face.

"Can you at least try to move through his steps?" I grip her shoulders and wait for her gaze to find mine. "I want our first dance to be perfect."

"I'm not the one who needs to practice. Even if he showed up today, how will he learn this routine in a week?"

He was supposed to be home a month ago. Something's happened. I feel it like a gaping jagged hole in my gut, but I refuse to examine it. I can't. I need to focus on the wedding. It's the only thing keeping me from crumbling.

"Let's run through the song again." I walk toward the sound system.

"No." She blocks my path and places her hands on my face. "I've been humoring this...this cloud of hope you're floating on long enough. We're at *T* minus six days, and your groom is nowhere to be found. You haven't heard from him in months—"

"Four months." I turn away and walk toward the wedding dress hanging in the corner. "Four months, ten days, twenty-two hours."

That's the last time I received an email from him. Over the past year, we talked on the phone five times. Short calls. The connection was horrible with a frustrating delay. But he sounded well, if not tired. We exchanged several emails in the first few months. Then they became more sporadic, with longer and longer stretches between his responses. Until nothing at all.

"He promised me he'll be back in time." I run a hand over the white tulle skirt of the dress. "We talked about the wedding in every message. He picked the date." My voice thins. "He said he could learn the dance in a month." *And make me orgasm in awe of his skills.*

My chest squeezes painfully. Why is he a month late?

Every day away from him is an eternity in hell. But the last four months of silence, not hearing a word, not knowing if he's okay is like a poison, dripping into my organs, spreading toxins of doubt, and making me ask all the questions Bree has finally worked up the nerve to voice.

Why didn't he say *fuck it* and break the employment contract?

Why did he leave me?

Why hasn't he emailed me?

What if he doesn't show up for the wedding?

What if he never comes back?

When he stopped emailing, I called the government building downtown. No one would connect me with his department. They wouldn't even acknowledge his employment there. When his one year came and went, I waited a week before I showed up at the building. The armed guards wouldn't talk to me, wouldn't ring his boss — whoever that is — and they definitely wouldn't let me inside.

I have no way to reach him.

No way to ease this soul-gutting desolation.

I straighten my spine with the reminder of his promise. He loves me, and he'll do everything within his power to return to me.

For the next two hours, Bree and I chill on the couch in the front room, sharing a bottle of wine. She's been spending more time with me recently, her concern for my mental state growing more blatant with each visit.

"I need to go, Danni." She glances at her phone. "Or the family won't eat."

"Thanks for coming." I stand and follow her to the door. "You don't have to, but I really appreciate the company."

"I know you do." She hugs me, breathing into my hair, "I love you."

"Love you, too."

She opens the door and falters. "Oh, sorry. Umm..."

"Danni Angelo?" A middle-aged man in a dark suit looks past Bree to gaze unerringly at me.

"Yes?" I step next to Bree. "That's me."

"I'm Robert Wright." He clasps his hands in front of him.

His expression's warm, friendly, but there's a trace of something else in his eyes. Intelligence? Rigidness? I can't put my finger on it, because there's no emotion there at all.

"As a representative of GAO, U.S. Government Accountability Office, I'd like to speak to you about your fiancé, Cole Hartman." His nose twitches with a soft sniff. "May I come in?"

A simple update on Cole's whereabouts could've been done over the phone. A house visit brings ugly news. The most vicious kind of news.

My stomach caves in, and Bree grabs my hand, clutching tightly.

"Yes, come in." I move on numb legs as the hole in my gut fills with harrowing dread.

"Can we sit?" He gestures at the couch, already lowering in the chair that sits perpendicular.

Bree and I perch side by side, and I clutch her hand like a lifeline. A lump of ice lodges in my throat, freezing my voice and shredding my breaths. Time stands still.

"There's no easy way to say this, Miss Angelo." His eye contact is firm, his face composed. "There was an accident at the..."

A low keening sound crawls from deep inside me, and blinding pain bursts behind my eyes.

Bree wraps her arms around me, her voice thready. "At the oil terminal?"

"Yes, the oil terminal. An explosion killed several contractors." He sits taller, adjusts the drape of his tie. "I'm sorry, Miss Angelo. Cole didn't make it."

I blink rapidly as his words sink in and suffocate the life from me. An uncontrollable, sobbing meltdown works its way to the surface, but I deny it, swallowing over and over to clear my voice.

"When?" I ask hollowly, barely a whisper. "When did it happen?"

"Four months ago. His remains were exhumed from the wreckage, returned to the States, and identified." As Robert stands, he seems to make an effort to soften his voice. "His body was cremated and his financial assets will be transferred to you, per his request. Someone from our office will be in contact to help you make funeral arrangements."

Bree untangles her hand from mine, crying quietly as she walks him to the door. They exchange words, details about the death, contact information, but I can't make sense of it over the ringing in my ears and the brutal shaking through my body.

That's when the wailing starts. Like a spout

busting loose, the pain shoots from my vocal cords and doubles me over. I don't hear the door shut, don't feel the couch beneath me, don't taste the tears flooding my face. The agony is all-consuming, crippling my body, twisting me into something unrecognizable, and spiraling me into a shapeless, hopeless place.

Bree's arms come around me, and that's where they stay. She holds me through the funeral. Through the burial of his ashes on my wedding day. Through Mom and Dad's visit from Florida. She doesn't leave my side until summer ends and school begins, and she's forced to return to work.

I heard once that hardship brings the true nature of a person to light. If that's true, I'm a deeply angry woman, seething with hatred and resentment. The rage is powerful and incapacitating, like a beast roaring and pacing inside me and pointing blame.

He left me.

He broke his promise.

He lied.

He's not coming back.

As the bitterness threatens to smother me, I welcome it. I climb into the darkness, lugging a bottle of hard alcohol with me. When the booze doesn't numb, I break things. Like the mirror I just shattered with an empty fifth of whiskey.

Two months after Cole's funeral, I lie on my back on the floor of the dance studio, stinking to high heaven and staring at the broken image of my reflection. I look like a monster with jagged teeth protruding out of my sunken, miserable face.

I'm drunk. I haven't showered since…whenever. I closed my dance school indefinitely. I canceled life, my future, everything.

I've been okay with checking out. Until now —
staring at my splintered self in the mirror. I don't
recognize the woman reflected back at me. She's
hideously sad and pathetic and weak. I hate her, because
she's not who I thought I was.

My inebriated brain sparks with life, and I sit up,
swaying with disorientation.

Fighting hurts. Living without Cole hurts. But
nothing's as painful as hanging onto the broken pieces of
a dream. Doesn't matter what I choose — stay here or
move forward — he's gone. Giving up on life won't bring
him back.

After several failed attempts, I climb to my feet and
stagger toward the shower. Every step is small and
laborious, but I focus on putting one foot in front of the
other. I focus straight ahead and allow myself a grain of
hope.

Hope that one day I'll look back and appreciate the
distance I covered.

eighteen
present

Acid hits the back of my throat, and my gag reflex kicks in. I cover my mouth and slam a hand against the elevator call button in Trace's penthouse. He didn't follow me out of the bedroom, but that doesn't mean he won't.

Please, open. Please, open.

I made it this far without surrendering to the impending meltdown. I just need to get through the casino, outside, and into a taxi cab. Then I can cry.

Voices drift from the hall, and my shoulders climb around my ears.

Her hair spread over the couch. His hips pressed against

her ass.

I don't want an apology or an excuse or worse…the sight of his ironclad indifference. I just need to get the fuck out of here.

The elevator opens, and I scramble in, punching the ground floor and holding my breath as it closes.

Her skirt around her waist. His hands — those masculine fingers I so desperately wanted on my body — gripping her hips.

I don't release my breath on the ride down. If I do, the tears will come. They're already trembling behind my eyes, simmering, burning, threatening to explode.

The elevator opens on the lobby level, and I forge into the crowded gaming area. Hunched over, shoulders curled forward, I feel like I'm holding in all the parts that hurt. Protecting them. As much as I want to stand straight, I can't unlock my posture, can't seem to draw enough air.

When I step outside, my phone buzzes in the wristlet hanging from my arm. I peek at the screen, see an incoming call from Trace, and power it off.

"Do you need a cab, ma'am?" The hotel's bellhop tips his head toward me.

"Yes. Thank you." I clutch my throat, hating the creak in my voice.

He leads me to the curb where a taxi waits, and I'm grateful for the cloak of warm night air. Tears are already streaming down my cheeks, and my entire body shivers persistently, uncontrollably.

On the ride home, I wrap my arms around myself and rest my forehead against the window, lost in my miserable thoughts. After everything Trace said at my house, why would he stick his dick in another woman? Was he so absorbed in her he didn't know I entered his penthouse? He didn't look surprised, guilty, or pissed. His face was utterly blank. It's as if he knew I was coming and wanted me to find him with her.

Why? If he cared about me, why would he so viciously hurt me?

I wipe at the river of moisture on my cheeks and try to calm my sniveling. God, I've made a mess of my life. How did I go from loving one man to loving another? I didn't even date in between them, didn't shop around and weigh my options. I just...

Fell madly, sickeningly, desperately in love.

Again.

I love two men, and I lost them both.

A sob rips free, abrading my throat and vibrating my bones. It's an angry, gutted sound that echoes through the cab. The driver's probably staring at me, but I don't care, because goddammit, this fucking hurts. I swore Trace couldn't hurt me, that I couldn't be devastated like this again. How could he do this?

I give myself five more minutes of wheezing, shoulder-shaking tears. Then I bottle that shit up and stuff it way down deep. I prefer to let the darkness devour me when no one's watching, when I'm alone and armed with liquor.

The cab starts and stops with the heavy downtown traffic. Up ahead, the brightly lit bars on Washington Avenue illuminate the street for several blocks. It's a scene I used to thrive in before Cole—the clubs, the dancing, the men. Maybe I should go back to that. Find myself again.

The thought of dancing and flirting makes my stomach cramp. I just want to go home and drown in a bottle of grain alcohol.

Don't do it, Danni. You've come so far.

Before my brain catches up, I lean forward and find the driver's eyes in the rearview mirror. "I changed my mind. Drop me off up there at 14th and Washington."

While Trace is spending the night with another woman, he has the satisfaction of knowing I'm not with someone else. Well, fuck that, and fuck being alone. I'm angry enough, fucking revengeful enough to finally put an end to three years of celibacy.

Using the selfie camera on my phone as a mirror, I wipe away the runny smudges of makeup and smear on lip gloss. Then I pay the driver and step out onto the sidewalk crammed with barhoppers.

Everything inside me feels cold and hollow. I'm not in the right mindset for this. I don't want to be anywhere near here. But the image of Trace and Marlo together collapses my chest and moves my feet toward the entrance of the closest bar.

Adjusting my strapless dress, I curve my mouth into a casual smile. As I enter the bar—one of many I used to frequent—the boom of deep bass rattles my chest. Huddles of men and women turn their eyes in my direction, grinning and staring and making my skin itch with discomfort.

There are four types of men who peruse the club scene for sex. The wingman—the married guy looking to hook up his shy single buddy. The wolf packs—the group of rowdy boys who gain confidence in numbers. The slurring drunk—the guy who imbibed enough liquor before he arrived to numb his sorrows and build his courage. The lone cowboy—the one who comes alone and doesn't drink because he knows he won't be leaving alone.

It's the latter that I seek out as I scan the crowd of singles, club dancers, and trendy loft-apartment dwellers. I'm not halfway around the circular bar before I find him.

Perched on the far side of the bar, a man with short dark hair and a collared shirt follows me with his gaze. A glass of water sits in front of him, a hand resting beside it, his other loosely curled beneath his chin. He's attractive in a wonderfully average way. There's no stuffy suit, no visible tattoos or black leather. He's casual, relaxed, and looks nothing like the two men who broke my heart.

I squeeze through the shoulder-to-shoulder bodies and steal an empty seat at the bar, directly across from him. He doesn't take his eyes off me, his mouth crooking up at the corner. He's cuter than I first thought, with a youthful face and bright eyes. I'd put him in his late thirties. Old enough to know what he's doing.

I order a water and tip the bartender. Then I watch the man who watches me, all the while giving myself a pep talk. When he comes over here—and he will—I need to go through with this. Rip off the chastity belt. Break the dry spell. Move on with my life.

As he finishes his water and stands, I get a glimpse of narrow hips in relaxed denim. Without looking away, he prowls around the bar, sidestepping flocks of laughing people and heading straight for me.

My smile hangs on by a thread as I turn my neck, holding his gaze. He's not intimidating enough. Not tall enough. Not sexy, cocky, or scowly enough.

He's not Trace.

My jaw flexes. Trace is with Marlo, touching her, pleasuring her, and giving her a cock I've never even seen. I hope it was worth it, because tomorrow, he'll be looking for another foolish girl to dance on his stage.

The man with the dark hair and firm eye contact slides in beside me. He doesn't speak, but his smile is warm, welcoming. Definitely interested.

I stretch my spine to lean toward his face, speaking over the music. "Anyone ever tell you that you look like Paul Rudd?"

"Yeah." He huffs. "All the time."

"Does that annoy you?"

"Depends." He bends closer, his chest brushing my shoulder and his mouth at my ear. "Do you think Paul Rudd is attractive?"

"Yes."

"Then it doesn't annoy me."

My energy for this is nonexistent. I'm not in the mood to talk or flirt or connect on any level but one. There's a game that's supposed to be played here, but if I'm reading him right, he won't be offended if I forgo a few steps.

"Do you want to take me home?" I ask.

"Yes." His throat bobs.

"I don't want an overnight or a call in the morning. I had a really bad day, and I just want to forget about it for a couple of hours. Can you handle that?"

"Absolutely."

"I live about ten minutes away. Can we skip the build-up and—"

"Let's get out of here." He grabs my hand, helps me off the stool, and leads me out of the bar.

On the way to his car, we exchange names—*his is Jason*—talk about the humid weather, and keep it light and impersonal. He owns a Honda Civic fastback, and he drives it *fast*, his hands relaxed on the wheel and his foot never leaving the gas.

The heated looks he casts in my direction tell me he's ready to fuck. The hard bulge in his jeans confirms it.

My body's not warmed up, not even close, and I need it to be. If he fucks as fast as he drives, he'll be in and out before I orgasm. I experienced too many of those in my club scene days.

With my address programmed into the navigation system, the screen shows nine minutes until we arrive. Nine minutes to make him come. If I can take his edge off, maybe he'll take his time with me when we get to my house.

Unbuckling my seatbelt, I touch him with my hands and lips, stroking him everywhere, quickening his breaths and making him moan. Then I release his erection from his jeans and wrap my lips around him.

He jerks and grunts and tastes like fabric softener. It's just a blow job, like any other one-night-stand. A job for me and a blow for him, which he does within sixty seconds, shooting his load down my throat.

I straighten in the seat and wipe my mouth, tensing against a sudden wave of nausea. I didn't expect to be aroused by that, but the twisting, coiling sensation in my stomach shouldn't be there. I need to do this. I need to have sex. What the fuck is wrong with me?

Tears prick my eyes, and I blink them back, forcing all thoughts of Trace out of my mind.

"Why did you do that?" Jason asks through heavy breaths.

"I'm hoping you'll return the favor." My voice is even, despite the bile crawling up my chest.

"I will." He grips my bare thigh, his fingers slinking beneath the hem of my dress. "Jesus, I came so hard I'm still shaking. That was the best head I've ever had."

"The sex will be even better." *I hope, for my sake.*

He pulls into my driveway and twists in the seat, looking out the back window. "A car just parked on your curb. I think it's a…Maserati?"

nineteen

present

No, no, no. My entire body stiffens, and my hands ball into fists. He wouldn't dare show up at my house. Why would he? He has 2,994,463 women in the state of Missouri to manipulate, use, and fuck.

But as I crane my neck and squint at the street, there he is, Trace Womanizer Savoy, rolling out of his Maserati and heading this way.

In a burst of rage, I explode from Jason's car and charge toward him. "This is private property, you selfish, narcissistic prick! Get back in your car and go unfuck your fucked-up self!"

"You…" His voice crackles the air as his eyes spear

the man behind me. "Leave."

"I don't want any trouble." Jason approaches my side, hands up in a calming gesture. "She wants you to go and—"

"I won't tell you again." Trace erases the distance between us, his gait thundering with authority, shoulders squared, and arms relaxed at his sides.

"Why are you doing this?" My hands clench and shake with the need to inflict unholy violence. "Haven't you hurt me enough?"

He slams to a stop a few feet away, his abs contracting inward, as if I punched him. Then he straightens his spine and hardens his eyes. "We need to talk."

"I don't care what you think we need to do. I want you out of my fucking sight!" I turn and storm toward the back door. "Come on, Jason."

"Look, Danni," Jason says through an exhale, "I don't want to get in between whatever this is."

My teeth crash together as I swing around and gape at him.

Standing on the side of the house, he's locked in some sort of stare-down with Trace. If this is a battle of egos, Jason's losing spectacularly. As Trace steps forward, Jason stumbles back, shoulders drooping and gaze diverting to the side.

Christ, I really know how to pick 'em. But I'm not ready to give up. "Jason, I don't have any business with that man. Are you coming?"

"I...um..."

He's not coming, because he already *came.* In my mouth.

The blow job in the car was stupid, stupid, stupid.

He got his release, and now he has zero incentive to stick around. Clearly, I'm not worth *getting in between whatever this is.*

My neck tenses to the point of pain as I march over and whisper harshly in his ear. "I gave you the best head you've ever had. You just lost your chance to find out what else I can do."

"You what?" Trace's low, deadly growl pounds a warning in my ears.

I have two seconds to lean back before his fist disperses the air and slams into Jason's face.

"What the—" Jason falls against the bumper of his car, holding his jaw. "Goddammit!"

I gasp, teetering in my heels. The way Trace struck, so swiftly, with such terrifying composure, it's like he didn't move at all. It was just a snap of his arm, out and back, without a grunt or hitch in his breath.

"Why did you do that?" I glare at him with awe and horror.

"He's still here." Trace shifts his icy eyes to me. "You sucked his dick?"

"Did Marlo suck your dick?"

"No."

"You poor thing. Is that why you're here? Hoping I'll fall on my knees and let you fuck my face because I'm too naive to clue in on how fucking sick you are?"

Jason's car door slams shut, and the engine turns over. I don't blame him for getting the hell out of Crazytown, but the tears well up anyway, searing my sinuses with rejection and humiliation.

As he throws it in reverse, I check my wristlet to make sure I didn't leave anything in his car. Then he drives away without so much as a glance in my direction.

"Well done, Trace." I dig out my house key with trembling fingers. "I commend you on your ability to chase another man from my home. That wasn't predictable at all." Turning away, I head toward the back door with my middle finger in the air. "Consider this my two-weeks notice."

I don't hear footsteps behind me as I unlock the deadbolt, and for a stupid moment, I think he's still standing where I left him.

Until my scalp tingles. I hurriedly shove the door open. Too late.

A hand covers my mouth, an arm hooks around my waist, and my feet lose purchase with the ground. The wristlet falls to the floor as I kick and swing my elbows, pulse spiking, chest heaving, my screams frantic and muffled.

He hauls me deeper into the dance studio, kicks the door shut, and releases me.

"Why did you—?" He swipes a hand over his mouth, eyes forged with steel. "Why did you put your mouth on him?"

I stagger forward, righting my balance in the heels as fury powers through me.

Arms out and teeth bared, I shove at his chest and keep shoving. "Get out of my house!"

He slips around me and paces to the other side of the dance room.

"Answer the question." His tone is so still and icy it lifts the hairs on my nape.

"Fuck you!" I yank off a stiletto and chuck at him.

He catches it easily and flings it aside. Then he shrugs out of his suit jacket, tosses it, too, and prowls toward me.

I back up, because holy fuck, he's angry. The flush in his face, the crazed look in that glare, the hard line of his lips—he's unraveling, losing his precious control, and I'm backed into a fucking corner.

My breaths quicken, and my muscles go rigid. I don't think he'll physically hurt me, but I didn't think he'd fuck another woman, either. My judgment is total shit.

Pressing my back against a mirror, I remove the other stiletto and hold it like a weapon. "Don't come any closer."

His gait doesn't slow, and in two strides, he's on me, his hand like a vise around my wrist and his chest hard against mine. "Tell me why you were with that motherfucker."

Tears are already coursing down my face. I can't break his hold, can't escape the strength of his body bearing down on me. All I have is my voice and the devastation attached to it.

"I haven't had sex in three years." The bitter words scrape from my throat, seething with self-loathing. "I was *finally* ready, and you…you…"

He didn't cheat on me, because we weren't together. But it feels so much like betrayal my shoulders curl in and my chest collapses beneath a thousand doubts. I should've told him how I felt about him, that he made me want to try harder, be stronger, smile more. I should've told him I loved him.

My face contorts with unbearable pain, and the shoe falls from my shaking hand. "You stuck your dick in her, and I picked up a guy at a bar. Because that's what broken people do."

His nostrils go wide. "If all you want is sex..."

He pulls the knot loose on his tie and yanks it off. Then his hand goes to his belt, tearing at the buckle.

"No!" I shove at his chest, digging my shoulder blades against the mirror behind me. "No, no, no, you're not—"

He grips my throat and squeezes. "Don't say that word again, unless you mean it."

I clutch the shackle of his hand and stare up at him with watery eyes. He's not cutting my airway. Not really hurting me, either. But I can't move, and my lips won't form the word I'm mentally chanting. *NoNoNoNoNo...*

His belt slides free, and the sound of it dropping against the floor shoots a ripple of warmth through my core. My skin heats. My nipples harden, and my pulse goes wild.

He's going to fuck me, and I can't let him. Only an hour ago, he was inside another woman. He doesn't want me, doesn't respect me, doesn't give a shit about me. This is just a power trip to feed his childish, self-serving ego.

I raise my chin and force my gaze to the raging depths of his. When his mouth parts, I drive a knee into his groin. He grunts, and the hand on my throat loosens just enough for me to twist away. But I only make it two steps.

He slams against my back, and we stumble, our hands flying out to brace our collision against the wall. But we're still moving, his weight pushing down on me, deliberately sending us to the floor.

I land face down with his body on top of me and his arm around my waist, buffering the fall. I try to pull my knees beneath me to scramble away, but he holds tight to my hips, his free hand clutched around the back of my thigh. Then he yanks up the hem of my mini dress.

Cool air brushes against my bare bottom right before his palm slams down, igniting my skin with fire.

"Fucking...God, fuck!" My arms and legs give out beneath the shocking pain, and my wail echoes through the room. "Why—?"

He spanks me again and again, and the sound of his hand slapping flesh punctuates the ungodly burn. The arm beneath my hips suspends me over his lap, giving him leverage to pommel my ass relentlessly.

I struggle and scream, but after a few seconds, it starts to feel forced, like I'm making myself fight it, deny it, hate it. Only I don't hate it. With every strike, the pain dissolves into languorous curls of heat. It seeps through my pleasure centers, soothing, stroking, and coaxing my inner muscles into a spasm of need.

In a swift shift of his weight, he rolls on top me, his chest smothering my back and his hand beneath my hips, between my legs, sinking into my soaked pussy.

A gasp fills my lungs, the stretch of his fingers excruciatingly perfect. I don't want this. I don't. I can't...

"Goddamn, you're soaked." He grips the ring on my labium and tugs it. "Such a kinky, filthy girl."

"Not for you." I kick and writhe, my voice gritty, clawing from the deepest, darkest places inside me. *"Never."*

Except my body betrays me, drenching his plunging fingers, clamping down on the invasion, and quivering for release.

I buck my hips and arch my spine, knocking him off long enough to escape on hands and knees. Before I make it to my feet, fingers capture my ankle and flip me over. With a powerful yank, he drags me across the floor on my back and wrenches my thighs apart.

Without panties, I'm wide open and exposed for his greedy gaze. I struggle to get free, but he's stronger, bigger, his hands impossible to dislodge as he spreads my legs wider.

His gaze meets mine, and I know the instant something shifts inside him. His anger's still present, but it's eclipsed by raw, unhinged hunger.

"Don't," I whisper, trembling.

Lightning flashes behind his eyes. Then he hoists my lower body off the floor and buries his face between my legs.

My hands plunge into his hair, pushing, pulling, and ripping at the strands. Desire wars with disgust. Anguish begets pleasure, and I'm lost beneath the diabolical swirl of his tongue, torn between wanting him and hating him, aching for relief and despising myself for it.

I need him. I want to hurt him. I yank his mouth against my pussy. Then I shove him away, crying, spitting, "I fucking hate you."

He licks a path up my slit, breathes deeply against my mound, and looks directly in my eyes. "I love you."

Bullshit. He's sick and twisted, and so am I.

As he returns to my center, lapping at my clit and sucking on my piercing, I want nothing more than to come on his tongue. I'm crazed in my need for it, and sweet God, it's gathering, rising, curling my toes, and bowing my back.

I should tell him to stop, but I can't. I want— "Oh God, oh fuck, I'm coming."

The orgasm crashes through me, shaking my limbs and shredding my voice as I moan and pant, my eyes fixed on his, frozen in shock. His mouth continues to grind against me, forcing me to ride his tongue harder, faster, extending the unendurable pleasure.

But as the bliss begins to taper and aftershocks twitch through my nerves, regret sinks in. He just fucked Marlo Vogt, and I let him lick me to climax. He's no good for me, his intent manipulative, his desire poisonous.

"Get off me." A sob rips from my throat, and I dig my heels against the floor, attempting to slide away.

He stays with me, crawling between my legs and covering my mouth with his. As his tongue sweeps the tang of my arousal across my lips, I can't stop thinking about his betrayal and my need to hurt him as badly as he hurt me.

I break the kiss, pushing against him as I sneer. "Can you taste his come? When I sucked him off in the car, I swallowed every drop."

His agonized roar rattles the walls, and his fist slams against floor beside my head. Arched over me, he holds himself up, his arms shaking with the force of his rage.

Then breath by breath, he reels it in.

Stillness settles through his muscles, and his eyes soften into molten blue glass.

My heart stops and restarts, galloping into a frenzied tempo. He's so damn gorgeous. So potently masculine and intimidating I sink my teeth into my lip to stifle my plea to be fucked.

Don't give in. Don't give in.

I swing my fists and kick out a leg, hitting air. But

my traitorous body wants, wants, wants. My pussy throbs and heats as he wedges his hips between my thighs and swats away my punching strikes.

"Say it, Danni." His hooded gaze dips, taking in the length of my body, the spread of my legs, the heave of my chest, and the pulse in my throat. It's a slow-burning perusal, full of sin and venom and *promise*. "Tell me *no*, if you don't want this."

The room fades away, and my brain malfunctions. Everything narrows to the rugged angles of his face and the intensity sharpening his cheekbones. For a man who can't be controlled, he's completely possessed by the grip of his desire.

I'm right there with him, consumed by the same suffocating fire. There's only one way to quench this need, and it isn't the word *no*.

I try to say it anyway, attempt to make my lips form the sane response, but that's not what tumbles out. "I need you."

"You have no idea how long I wanted to hear that." He reaches for his fly, his other hand tangling in my hair and angling my head back to hold my gaze. "I love you so damn much."

The sound of his zipper echoes in my ears, and I whimper.

Why can't I fight this? I can't stop my hands from reaching between us, fumbling over his in my urgency to pull him out.

He fits his cock at my entrance and looks me in the eyes. A swallow sticks in the back of my throat, and I grip his shoulders, trembling, panting. *Please.*

He thrusts, and we groan together, trembling as one in our relief. Burying himself as deeply as possible, he stretches me, fills me up, and makes me burn.

Then he fucks me, grunting like a feral caveman and hissing past clenched teeth. He's a hurricane of fury and aggression, slamming his cock rapidly, violently, and punishing my mouth with deep bruising kisses.

God help me, I forgot what this feels like, the exquisite sensation of being taken, dominated, and fucked into mindless oblivion. It's been three years. Three of the longest years of my life, and what a way to break the fast.

In that stunned moment, my mind blocks out how I got here, too absorbed by the cock stroking inside me, the tongue in my mouth, and the hands sweeping over my body. We're longing and lust, sweat and muscle, skin on skin, two beasts in a mating dance, panting, clawing at clothes, and stabbing nails into flesh.

I rip open his shirt, pinging buttons across the floor. With a labored grunt, he tears it off his arms and flings it. There's an undershirt beneath, baring bulges of biceps and pumped veins over muscle. I want to see more of him, but he attacks my dress, pounds his hips, and tears my strapless bodice down the center.

Breathing heavily and gnashing his teeth, he ravages my breast. His lips are firm and forceful, sucking my skin and leaving his mark. Then he starts to bite. Hard.

Panic rises, shattering my hungry trance. I shove his mouth from my nipple and thrash beneath him.

His eyes flash to mine, and he growls a low, combative noise.

"So damn feisty." His thrusts quicken, hammering with urgency. "God, yes... Yes..." He doesn't look away, his moans gravelly and hoarse. "You feel unbelievable. Fucking heaven."

It shouldn't feel this good. I should be repulsed and fighting him off. He fucking spanked me! How did I let this happen?

I grip his ass to stop his movements, but the muscles flex harder against my palms with each drive of his hips.

He's a frenzy of testosterone, pounding into me like a lust-fueled piston. His eyes never leave mine, watching me, worshiping me with that ice-blue stare as his long fingers slide between us and clamp onto my clit.

My spine arches off the floor, and my legs shake against a flood of intoxicating pleasure.

"That's it." He circles and rubs my bundle of nerves, spiraling me toward the crest. "You're going to come now."

His other hand wraps around my throat, and that does it. The heart-pounding pressure against my airway ignites fireworks across my vision and shoves me into a climax so explosive I feel like I'm shattering into a million pieces.

"There's my girl." His thrusts lose rhythm, jerking and deepening. "Sexiest thing I've ever seen."

My head falls back as I catch my breath, panting and moaning beneath the erratic stab of his hips. His hand slides from my throat to my face and pulls my mouth to his. Then he kisses me.

This kiss is different, lacking the usual hostility. It's affectionate and tender, full of soul-stirring languish. I melt against his lips, feeding, sipping, falling into the gentle slide, the roaming strokes, and the ecstasy of love.

I love him, but I don't forgive him. And as he

comes, I see it all in his eyes — his pain and pleasure, remorse and devotion, heartache and passion. He said he loves me, too, but he ruined it.

"Danni." He chokes, groaning deeply, gutturally, his entire body shaking as he grinds against me and pants through his release.

As he comes down, his forehead drops to mine, and he holds me, nuzzles my neck, his hands caressing my face.

The urge to curl in on myself shakes my shoulders. What have I done? What am I going to do now? I can't be with him. I can't love him.

When he lifts his head, his expression's dazed, shocked, like he can't believe he's here, that he did this, with *me*.

He looks spooked.

My chest clenches as he pulls out and tucks himself away. I never saw his cock. He didn't even take off his slacks, and now he's avoiding my eyes.

"Trace?" I pull the ruined dress around my nudity, reaching for something, *anything* to say. "I don't know what to do. I can't…" *Can't be alone right now.* "We should talk."

With his back to me, he collects his clothes from the floor. Then he stands there, facing away. No chin raised in victory. No whispered apologies. Just a distant man, sullied with the come of two women. And, in the dissonance of my breaking heart, his silence.

His hand clenches at his side and releases. A jagged breath, and he strides out the door.

My insides cave in, beaten and bruised. As much as I want to call out to him and beg him to stay, I won't.

I'm not his girl.

The door shuts behind him, and the hollow sound of desertion ricochets through me. I roll toward the mirrored wall, tucking my knees to my chest. Pressure builds in my head, and the stupid tears spring up with a vengeance.

I've never felt so used, so...*thrown away*. But I'm just as much to blame. I could've said *no*.

I wanted sex tonight, and now that I've broken that crippling dry spell, I feel worse. Because intimacy is what I desperately crave—intimacy with a man who loves me.

For a poignant moment, Trace gave me a glimpse of that. Then he took it away.

I don't even want to think about our lack of protection. I have an IUD, but what about disease? Did he use a condom with Marlo?

Nausea roils in my stomach. He fucked her...an hour before he had sex with me. Maybe he's on his way back to her now. To hold her in his bed. To love her the way I ache to be loved.

Cole would've never done this to me. He was nothing if not faithful and one-hundred-percent devoted.

Waves of pain smash into my chest, and I slam a fist against the floor, pounding it as I cry ugly, self-loathing sobs. "I miss you, Cole. I miss you so much."

Before he died, he ripped out my heart and held it between us, dripping with the blood of dreams. Old anger surges to the surface, cracking my ribs and burning up my skin. He shouldn't have left me. He put his job first and destroyed everything we had.

I need a drink. A lot of drinks. It's the only way to numb the pain and forget.

Blinking through blurred vision, I find my

reflection in the busted hole in the mirror. My splintered, pitiful, broken face stares back, judging me.

Are you giving up, you pathetic bitch?

I'm comfortable here, lying on the floor in a pool of regret. I've grown addicted to sadness. It's familiar, reliable, *effortless.*

I know that's resignation talking. Giving up is a whole lot easier than fighting through the scar tissue. There are so many things holding me down, suffocating my will to breathe.

I need a purpose. A reason to contribute in this unfair world.

I have that, don't I? I have passion — dancing, family, neighbors, the homeless shelter. That's where I'm needed.

Love isn't a choice. Nor is life. We connect, or we don't connect. We live, and we die. There is no forever. The real fight is in making the best of it, making a difference, and appreciating the small glimmers of happiness.

I stretch out an arm and trace the cracks in the mirror. The last time I stared at my broken reflection was the night I moved my life with Cole into the basement. I just hauled it all down there, left it where it fell, and locked the door. It had been such a big step then.

Tonight, I need to finish it.

Forcing myself to stand, I shed the tattered scraps of the dress and remove my phone from the wristlet on the floor. Then I set my playlist to *Dancing On My Own* by Calum Scott.

Trembling, I pull on a camisole and boyshorts. Choking, I collect the key and my engagement ring.

Weeping, I stand at the basement door as Calum Scott serenades the ruins of my heart.

With a deep breath, I unlock the door, turn on the lights, and descend into the fumes of damp concrete and Cole Hartman.

When he moved in, he took over the unfinished basement, filling it with tools, motorcycle parts, weight-lifting equipment, and other manly stuff. The scent of engine oil lingers in the air. Punk rock posters cover the walls. His old futon sits beside multiple workbenches.

Then there are the things I moved down two years ago. His clothes, cologne, watches, CDs, wedding decor, boxes of photos and keepsakes I collected during our ten months together. But the sight of the white dress crumpled on the floor is what releases the floodgates.

My eyes drown in tears as I move my feet toward the gown. My fingers travel over the dusty tulle and beaded bodice. It would've been a beautiful wedding. Our marriage would've been as epic as our love.

My ribcage quakes with the force of my heartache as I gather the dress and hug it to my chest.

I don't know when I finally uncurl my fingers and set the gown aside. I move in a fog of turmoil, opening the empty boxes Bree gave me, digging through piles of Cole's shirts, sniffing each one, and crying harder.

Then I start packing.

twenty

present

The next morning, I wake on Cole's futon in the basement to the sound of footsteps creaking the floorboards overhead. My brain slowly rouses, my eyes swollen and itchy. I shiver and pull the scratchy blanket over my shoulders.

No, not a blanket. I slept with my fucking wedding dress.

The intruder breaches the basement door, and the stairs groan beneath the tread of feet. Multiple feet. Maybe it's Bree and David.

What time is it? I sit up and grab my phone. *6:05 AM*

Groaning, I rub my head. The only person who would wake me at this hour is my next-door neighbor, which means I left my door unlocked. Again.

Her feet come into view on the stairs, squeezed into compression hosiery and shuffling in house slippers with the aid of her cane. I move to help her down the steps, but the second pair of shoes freezes me on the edge of the futon.

Shiny black loafers. Charcoal slacks. Long powerful legs…

My pulse sprints, and my fingernails dig into my palms. Trace has some nerve showing back up here.

When they reach the last stair, Virginia lifts her cane and pokes the end into his back, nudging him forward.

"Does this belong to you?" she asks.

He's still wearing the white t-shirt from last night, untucked and wrinkled. Same slacks and shoes. He didn't go home last night?

Head down and hands shoved into his pockets, he lifts only his eyes. Bruised eyes. Add to that his drawn expression and unruly blond hair, and I struggle to process his appearance.

He looks terrible.

"No." My throat tightens, and I cross my arms. "He doesn't belong to me."

"Well…" Virginia huffs. "I found him sleeping in a car in your driveway." She lowers the cane and smacks it against the backs of his legs. "He said he knows you. Filled my head with all kinds of nonsense, like how you took his heart and he doesn't want it back."

My jaw sets. "Give me a break."

His shoulders heave as he takes a ragged breath,

his gaze submersed in regret. "Danni…"

"Don't." My nerves prickle, and I pull the wedding dress tight against my lap.

Virginia gives him a glowering once-over. "The good Lord has no mercy for lying, skirt-sniffing hounds like yourself."

"Danni, please…" He runs a jerky hand through his hair and stuffs it back in his pocket. "I need to —"

"How dare you bring your sexual urges to Danni's door." Virginia whacks him again. "If Cole were here — God bless his soul — he'd run you over with his bike until you stopped breathing."

Funny how she snubbed Cole every day he lived here, and now that he's gone, she can't stop singing his praises.

I fidget with the tulle skirt of the dress and look around the basement. I made huge progress last night. Everything is packed in boxes by the stairs. Except the wedding gown. I couldn't let go of it. But I feel stronger this morning. Grounded. Ready to take on Trace Savoy.

"It's fine, Virginia." I stand and set the dress aside. "I'll handle him."

"I know you will." She leans against her cane. "When you're finished, I have a bulb burnt out in the washroom. Can't reach the damn thing."

"I'll be over a little later." I walk toward her to assist her up the stairs.

She waves me off, grunting a perturbed sound. "I can walk just fine by myself."

I hold my breath as she hobbles up the steps. Then she shuffles through the kitchen and shuts the back door.

With a slow exhale, I walk past Trace and perch on

the futon. "You've been here all night?"

"I left." He scratches the stubble on his jaw, stalks toward the futon, and sits on the other end with the wedding gown between us. "I didn't make it a block before I turned back."

"You slept in the driveway? In your car?" I narrow my eyes. "Why?"

"I thought it would be best if we both slept off our anger."

I itch and burn beneath his stark gaze. He looks dejected, but his appearance does nothing to diminish his intensity. If anything, his eyes are more penetrating than ever, probing and pressing and making me squirm. It's maddening how deeply he affects me, even now, after everything he did.

"Say what you're going to say." I flex my hands on my lap. "Then please, just…leave me in peace."

He shifts, leaning closer, expression hard and determined. "I didn't have sex with Marlo."

I suck in a breath, my heart pounding with hope. And denial. "Don't insult my intelligence, Trace."

"Swear to God, Danni." A muscle bounces in his jaw. "I knew you quit work early and intended to confront me. I knew the instant you accessed the penthouse."

"I didn't leave work early to confront you!" I leap from the futon and stand over him, shaking. "I was coming to give myself to you. All of me!"

"I know that now." He bends forward and laces his fingers behind his lowered head. "I saw you in that dress, and I knew. I knew I fucked up spectacularly. I knew I would spend the rest of my life trying to make it right."

"Except you didn't make it right. You punched my

date, fucked me like a deranged animal, and left. You left me on the floor like discarded trash."

His hands tighten on his nape, and his chest heaves. "I came here last night to apologize, to throw myself at your feet. Then I saw you with him, heard what you did with him." His breathing grows louder, harsher. "I fucking lost it." He lowers his arms, flexes his hands between his spread legs. "It's no excuse, and I can't tell you how sorry I am." He releases a self-depreciating laugh. "I'm not good at this. Christ, I'm a fucking nightmare. I know this, but I'm trying." His eyes, tormented and bloodshot, find mine. "I want to be the man who deserves you."

My breath leaves me, and my shoulders sag. "If you knew I was coming to find you after work, why were you with her? I saw you fucking her, Trace. She was naked from the waist down and *moaning*."

"Marlo works for me, and she'll do any damn thing I tell her to do. Including touching herself while I watch."

My teeth slam together.

"I didn't watch," he says quickly, furiously. "I wasn't even hard."

"You're a real piece of work." I pace away, trying to make sense of his words. "If you wanted a relationship with me, why sabotage it by fucking another woman?"

"I didn't fuck her!" He shouts then lowers his voice. "I have cameras in my room. The video feed is recorded. I can prove it. Hell, you can watch the last four months of footage. You're the only woman who's been in my bed."

"I don't believe you." Even though my foolish heart feels like it's floating out my chest. "You told me you never sleep alone."

"That was the first day we spent together, and it was true at the time." He frowns and rubs his forehead. "I haven't been with a woman since we met."

I'm too emotionally drained for this. He's messing with my head and breaking down my resolve.

"What about the woman on your lap at the casino?" I stand taller, bracing my fists on my hips. "Or the dozens of others I see you flirting and drinking with?"

"Last night, with you, was the first time I had sex in four months."

"Whether or not that's true, you wanted me to believe you fucked Marlo. It doesn't make sense."

"When I was here yesterday, I wanted you to choose me. I needed you to say it." He slouches on the cushion, dropping his head back and staring at the rafters. "I left here thinking I was nothing more than a rebound, a way for you to bounce back from the only man you'll ever love." He glances at the wedding dress beside him and closes his eyes. "When you left work early, I assumed you would seek me out to give your two-weeks notice."

He couldn't have been more wrong. I lower onto the futon and massage my temples. I need coffee.

"I'm accustomed to getting exactly what I want." He looks me in the eyes. "But with you, I'm at a complete loss of control. The feelings you stir in me, the goddamn pain I felt yesterday when I thought you didn't want me… I wasn't prepared for this. Jesus, Danni, I've never put myself in such a powerless, vulnerable position."

"Sounds like love," I say softly.

He stares at me, with something akin to

desperation in his eyes.

"Love isn't a choice, you know." I finger the fabric of the wedding dress. "You can't control it. It just…happens, and you better hold on for dear life, because you never know when you'll lose it."

"I shouldn't have demanded you make a choice." A pained smirk twists his lips, there and gone in a blink. "But I did, and your non-answer was incapacitating. I was hurt, wounded…"

"So you set up the thing with Marlo to hurt me back."

He nods. "I'm a jealous, vindictive son of a bitch."

I scoop up the dress and walk to one of the boxes by the stairs — the box that holds the engagement ring. Then I pack the gown away, folding and tucking and keeping my hands busy while I think.

Any trust I had with Trace is broken. It would take a long time to reach a healthy place with him. That's if we're both willing to put maximum effort into some kind of future together.

"What are you doing?" he asks.

"Moving on." I close the box, straighten to my full height, and stare down at my progress.

He rises from the futon, his eyes softening as he approaches me. "The gravity of that statement isn't lost on me."

My brows furrow, and I hold still, waiting for him to continue.

"If anything happened to you…" He stands behind me and places a hand on my shoulder, guiding me to lean back against his chest. "If I lost you, if you *died*, I'm not sure I would be able to move on."

I draw in a frayed breath, shivering at the heat of his body against my back. "Relationships don't always hurt like this. When it's good, it's the best feeling in the world. Those are the moments to fight for."

His mouth lowers, exhaling a warm sigh against my neck, as if my words give him hope for us.

"We're stuck, Trace. Stuck in a toxic cycle of poisonous mistrust, jealousy, misunderstandings, and closed-off emotions. None of that works in a lasting relationship."

He wraps his arms around my waist and rests his brow against my temple. "Please, don't give up on me."

"I don't know what I'm going to do, but I won't give in. We have so much shit to wade through, first of which is your relationship with Marlo."

He spins me around and cups my face. "I've never had sex with her."

Trust. Broken.

I grip his muscled forearm. "I want to see the video footage from last night."

"My laptop's in the car." He grabs my hand and leads me up the stairs.

twenty-one
present

My thoughts lump together in a jumbled mess as I follow Trace out of the basement. Maybe he didn't fuck Marlo. Maybe my feelings for him haven't been completely demolished. But that doesn't make him any less of a manipulative bastard.

At the top of the stairs, he closes the door and fidgets with the padlock. "Why did you keep this locked?"

"It leads somewhere that no longer exists."

He rests his lips against the top of my head for a silent moment. Then his hand catches mine and leads me away.

In the kitchen, he turns on the coffee maker and rummages through my cabinets while making a phone call.

"I'll do this." I nudge him to the side and grab the coffee beans.

"Yes," he says into the phone and walks to the fridge. "Miss Angelo and I won't be back to work until Friday. Make the appropriate arrangements."

What? Friday is…four days away. I whirl around, glaring at his back as he digs out packages of eggs and bacon.

"Send someone to Miss Angelo's house with an overnight bag for the week." He turns and gives me an uncomfortable smile. "Jeans and t-shirts."

I lean against the counter and fold my arms. "What are you doing?"

"That'll be all." He stares at the floor for a second and pulls in a breath. "Marlo, wait." His hand goes to the back of his neck. "I'm sorry about last night. I used you. It was wrong and—" He closes his eyes, listening for several seconds. "Understood."

He disconnects the call and meets my waiting gaze. "Marlo turned in her two-weeks after you left last night."

I don't blame her for quitting and can't help but feel selfish relief. "She could sue you for sexual harassment."

"She took the severance package, which required her to sign a release that frees me from potential lawsuits."

"Lucky you."

I drum my fingers on the counter as unease chews holes in my stomach. I'm not comfortable with his treatment of her. Maybe I should let it go, but that's not my style.

"You think it's okay to treat women like that?" I straighten my spine, meeting his glare head-on. "I mean, she worked for you, and you told her to masturbate for you in some disgusting game that had nothing to do with her. That's not okay."

He slides his hands in his pockets, stares at the floor, and releases a breath. "Marlo isn't what she seems."

"What do you mean?"

"She didn't just want to hook up." He looks up at me, his eyebrows gathering. "She's infatuated with me to the point of delusion. I found her, not once but three times, naked on the desk in my office."

"What? When?"

"It started around the time I hired you. I removed her security access and fired her."

"Then why was she still working for you?"

"She brought in a team of lawyers, threatening sexual harassment — of which she had absolutely no grounds."

"With all your money, you couldn't fight that?"

"I could." He scratches his jaw. "But I chose to teach her a lesson."

"By watching her masturbate?"

"By waiting for the right moment to record her touching herself willfully, consensually, in my bedroom."

Oh. "You showed her the video footage?"

"Yes, right after you left. She didn't hesitate to drop her threats against me and take the severance." He narrows his eyes. "I told you I'm a vindictive son of a bitch."

He could've sued *her* for sexual harassment. He could've destroyed her career, her livelihood. Instead, he apologized for using her and paid her to quit.

He calls himself vindictive, but his actions hint at compassion. *In a depraved, fucked up way.* But still, it's compassion, and it warms me from the inside out.

I blow out a breath. "What's with the overnight bag?"

"We're stuck in a toxic cycle, and I'm committed to resolving that."

"It can't be fixed in four days."

"I know that, but I'm not leaving your side. I assume you'd rather be anywhere but the penthouse. We can spend the week here. Or in Hawaii, Paris, Australia…"

He's lost his ever-loving mind.

I prepare the coffee, forcing myself to think about this logically. I don't know if I should spend the day with him, let alone a week on the other side of the world. "I'm not going anywhere with you."

"We'll stay here then." Stepping behind me, he touches his brow to the back of my head. "I won't leave you, Danni. Ever."

My heart latches onto those words while my brain screams, *Lies, lies, lies.*

He grips my hip and pulls my backside tight against him. "You're not quitting the casino."

The command in his tone raises my hackles, but there's no sense in denying it.

"I'll stay," I say. "Until you fuck up again."

"I won't." He steps back. "Where are your light bulbs?"

I point toward the hall. "Closet. Why?"

"I'll be right back."

As I pour our coffees and start the bacon, the front door opens and shuts. I angle toward the kitchen window and watch Trace stride next door to Virginia's house, carrying a light bulb.

I smile, thinking about how much hell she's going to give him. If he wants to win her over, he'll have to do a lot more than change her lights. But it's a good start.

If he wants to win me over, well... He can start by proving he's worth the risk. He needs to convince me to think of him in terms of *regardless* and *in spite of* and *anyway*. Because right now, he's a huge fucking *if*.

He returns as I start cracking eggs in the bacon grease.

"How did it go?" I ask.

"She's a stubborn woman."

"That bad, huh?" I laugh.

"I have bruises on my legs from that damn cane." He grabs the spatula from my hand and sets his open laptop on the counter. "The video is loaded. Just push play."

As he finishes the eggs, I climb onto the counter and move the device to my lap. The video begins when he and Marlo enter his bedroom. There's no audio, but I sense the awkwardness between them. He doesn't look at her, his mouth moving and finger pointing absently at the couch where I found them. On screen, Marlo touches her throat, tracking his pacing steps with infatuation in her eyes.

"Jesus." My mouth dries. "She really wanted you."

The spatula in his hand pauses. "The attraction wasn't mutual."

Maybe not, but it's still painful to see him move behind her on the video, to watch her lift her skirt and touch herself for him. He doesn't look down, his attention flicking between his watch and the door. His slacks are lowered, but his underwear stays on. With her face buried in the cushion and her hand working between her legs, she doesn't seem to notice he didn't take his cock out.

Thirty seconds into the recording, I walk in. He doesn't grip her hips until that exact moment.

He wanted to hurt me, and the impact is written all over my face on the screen.

I've seen enough. My hands tremble as I close the laptop and set it aside.

He slides the skillet off the burner and steps between my legs. Torment contorts his expression, and his arms fold around me. With a hand gripping my nape, the other bites into my spine, holding me so tight I feel the remorse coiling his muscles.

"I love you." His mouth presses against my shoulder. "I love you so much it terrifies me."

"I'm scared, too." I let myself hug him back, thawing in the exquisite warmth of his embrace. "One day at a time, okay?"

He exhales heavily. "Okay."

We eat side by side on the couch in the front room, sipping our coffee and lost in our thoughts.

He finishes first and leans back, watching me. "You don't have a TV in here or your bedroom. But there's a nice one in the basement."

"It was Cole's."

"But it works?"

"Yep." I collect our plates and walk to the kitchen.

He trails behind me. "I don't understand why it's in the basement."

I set the dishes in the sink and brace my hands on the counter. "I moved all of his things down there."

"Except the Harley."

"If I could roll it down the stairs, I would have." I smile, and it feels like a grimace. "Seeing his stuff every day wasn't helping my grieving process. I had a rough few months after he died. Kind of lost myself there for a while."

Rather than offering condolences or useless words, he gives me exactly what I need. Framing my face in his huge hands, he rests his lips against my forehead. I slip my arms around his waist, and we stay like that until the doorbell rings.

He greets his driver at the door and collects his overnight bag. Then, with his hand in mine, he leads me to the bathroom. "Shower and a nap. Sound good?"

Sounds perfect. I only slept a couple of hours last night, and I doubt he slept at all in his sports car.

In the bathroom, he wedges into the tiny walkway between the sink and tub. Does he intend for us to shower together? My belly flutters at the thought, which is ridiculous after what we did together last night. But I haven't seen him nude from the waist down.

He grips the back of his t-shirt and yanks it over his head. His hands fall to his pants, releasing the fly and shoving them off with his shoes and socks. Then he turns to me, wearing tight black briefs and nothing else.

All that flawless skin and sculpted muscle makes my mouth water and my insides throb. His beauty is the stuff of legends, and he exudes the kind of vibrating power one would find amid a Viking siege.

Every mythical god began with a story, based on a person and a series of events. I wouldn't be surprised if the Norse divinities of war, beauty, and sexuality began in Trace's family tree. He's so damn gorgeous and tall and insanely intense I can't stop myself from trembling.

And it's my turn to remove my clothes. I'm not a shy person, not even a little, but stripping while he watches suddenly feels like I'm stepping off a plank.

"You're nervous." He touches a finger beneath my chin, lifting my face.

My nipples tighten, and I bite my lip.

All drama and heartache aside, I'm undeniably attracted to him. I went so long without sex, and now that I've been with him, it's like all these dormant cravings have been jarred loose. We had angry sex—hateful, bitter, pound-me-into-the-floor sex, and it was mind-blowing. I can't stop wondering what other kinds of sex would be like with him. Gentle, playful, kinky… Jesus, after the spanking and choking, I know he's a kinky bastard.

I might not be able to forgive his heartlessness, but I can't ignore this snarling, relentless hunger he's unleashed in me.

"I'm just going to wash you." He runs a hand through my hair, his voice soft and scratchy. "Okay?"

"Okay." I slowly release a breath.

He slides the shower curtain back and stares at the tiny green tub with wide eyes.

"You had that exact expression when you drove my Midget," I say.

"I imagine Cole experienced the same claustrophobic horror when he saw this green coffin."

A swallow sticks in my throat. "You don't have to do that."

"Do what?"

"Include him. Talk about him."

"Yes, I do. He's part of you, and I don't want you to ever close off that part, or any part, of yourself from me. If you need to talk about him, I want to be the one you come to."

He's trying, and gratitude tingles through my limbs. But there are some things I won't share, like how many times Cole followed me into that tub and fucked me against every square inch.

"But I require something from you," Trace says. "If and when you forgive me, I need you to make room for me" — he taps my chest — "here. Understood?"

"Yes." My heart pounds, devouring his words and the vulnerability in his eyes.

I reach for the hem of my camisole, but he brushes my hands away and lifts the top over my head. Then he slides off my boyshorts, his fingers caressing my skin with tenderness.

Any nervousness I felt about being nude is muted the instant he removes his boxer briefs. A different sensation grips my body as I take in the glorious shape of his. Appreciation, amazement, desire — all of it expands my chest with a heavy intake of air.

The strength and definition packed into his shoulders and arms, the grooved washboard of abs, and the heavy cock hanging hard and long between powerful legs makes me weak in the knees. I reach out and brace an arm on the wall.

Chin angled down, he raises a brow. "Get in the

shower, Danni."

I move my feet, and he follows me in. Then he takes over, lathering his hands and massaging my neck, my toes, and everywhere in between. He's thorough, gentle, and sinfully seductive.

He cleans my hair and turns me toward the wall, gliding soapy fingers over my breasts and between my legs. I drop my head back on his shoulder, not even trying to muffle my moans.

"You're making it impossible to keep my word." He slides his lips down my neck, his breaths hot and hungry. "You and your tight little body." He slams a palm against my ass then rubs the hurt with wicked pressure. "I want to do things to you. Things that should be illegal."

I spin in the circle of his arms and grip his face. His lips part, and his eyes search mine. Then he kisses me—a deep breathless kiss, full of fire and need. Tongues tangling, hands grasping, we fall against the shower wall, locked in a frenzy of desire.

His swollen cock presses against my belly, and I curl my fingers around it, stroking up and down and wrenching a choked groan from his throat.

"I said I was just going to wash you." His hands plunge through my hair, and he rocks his hips, sliding his length in my grip.

"You washed me. Now you need to put your massive cock inside me."

"Danni." His hand covers mine around his girth, halting my movements. "I want more than sex with you."

I slide my free hand through his hair, marveling at how the thick wet strands fall perfectly tousled over my fingers. "We're spending the next four days together?"

"If I don't make any more mistakes," he says, brushing a kiss against my wrist, "we're spending the rest of our lives together."

My heart hiccups. "If you're staying here, we're going to have sex. Does it matter if it's now or a week from now?"

"I can't believe I'm saying this, but yes, it matters." He steps back and grabs the shampoo. "I know what I want, and your heart isn't there...yet." His biceps contract as he lathers his hair. "I will not trade long-term desires for short-term impulses."

His voice is rough, his scowl formidable. It's obvious how difficult it is for him to refuse me. His short-term impulse looks painfully engorged between his legs.

I back off, keeping my caresses chaste as I help him soap up. Ten minutes later, we lie in bed, naked, legs entangled. His body wraps around my back, spooning me from behind, with his thigh wedged between mine. He's still hard, but he doesn't grind against me. He seems content to just hold me. In the bed I shared with Cole.

The thought is unwanted, but I can't block it out. Cole bought this bed for me when he moved in — the wrought iron headboard, foam mattress, gray linen bedding. His scent lingered in this room for months after he left.

"Tell me about him," Trace says quietly.

Can he read my thoughts? I crane my neck and find his gaze on the picture frames across the room.

"I should probably put those away." My hand fists in the sheets.

"Don't do it for me." He pries my fingers from the bedding and entwines them with his. "I intend to make myself at home in the house you shared with him. I'm going to make love to you in the bed I assume he once slept in. If I can't handle seeing a picture of him, our relationship is doomed."

My ribcage stretches with cautious happiness, and I tighten my hand around his. "You really want to hear about him?"

"Please."

I start with how we met then share highlights of the ten months we spent together. His design and construction of the dance studio, the road trips on his motorcycle, his hatred for Nikolai. Trace doesn't speak or tense up, and his arms stay around me, cradling, comforting.

My voice chafes my throat as I explain Cole's job, the reason he left, and the explosion that took his life.

"You sound angry," Trace says. "You can't blame him for —"

"He chose his job."

"Sounds like he didn't have a choice, Danni."

"You're right." With a sigh, I shift in his arms to face him. "I hold onto the anger like a crutch. It's just…it's easier. So let me have it, okay?"

"I'm finding that I'll let you have whatever you want." He kisses my lips.

"Is that right?" I reach down and wrap my fingers around his thick erection.

"Except that." Groaning, he moves my hand from his cock to his back. "Tell me about your family."

"You want me to talk about my parents while you have a hard-on?"

"I want you to talk about them," he says, tucking me closer against his chest, "to get rid of the hard-on."

one *is a promise*

We chat for hours about everything and nothing. Family and work. Likes and dislikes. We stay away from conversations about the past or the future, satisfied to simply immerse ourselves in the present.

I don't know when we fall asleep, but I wake to a startled gasp in the doorway of the bedroom.

"Shit!" Bree spins away, shouting into the hallway. "Everyone outside!"

Footsteps sound through the kitchen, presumably David and Angel making a swift exit.

Trace lies on his back beside me, unabashedly nude with an arm bent behind his head. His lips aren't smiling, but the glimmer in his sleepy eyes is unmistakable. The man has no shame.

"I'm confiscating your key," I say to Bree's back and sit up.

"You can have it." She blindly tosses the keyring toward the dresser and sends it flying to the floor. "Mr. Savoy...uh, Trace...I'm sorry I saw your...um..."

"Cock?" I pull the sheet over his hips and against my chest. "We're covered now. You can turn around."

A flush sweeps up her neck as she faces us, and her gaze lands on his bulge beneath the thin cover. "I didn't stare. It's like...I saw it and looked away really quick. I'm not even sure that I actually saw that much. Maybe just a—"

"You're rambling and staring." I grin and place a hand on his chiseled chest. "Trace, this is my sister, Bree."

He holds the sheet in place and rises to the edge of the mattress with his hand out. "It's a pleasure to meet you."

"Oh, umm..." She stares at his hand for a beat

before shaking it. "The pleasure's all mine." Her eyes widen, and her cheeks turn bright red. "That's not what I meant. I mean, it *is* a pleasure, but not that kind of pleasure—"

"Bree." I snap my fingers.

"Hmm?"

"Give us a minute?"

"Right." She grabs the door and shuts it behind her.

Trace yanks off the covers and climbs over me, guiding me to lie back while nuzzling my neck. "She's..."

"Awkward?"

"I was going to say delightful. But yes, definitely awkward."

"She deals with first-graders all day, not gorgeous naked men." I splay my hands over his muscled backside and squeeze. "Though, I'll admit I've never seen her that nervous. I think you intimidate her."

"She's hot for me." He peppers a trail of kisses along my collarbone.

"She is not." I push at his jaw, trying not to laugh at the tickling scrape of his whiskers.

"She couldn't stop eying my *massive cock*." He echoes my earlier compliment with a smile.

I'd say that's the last time I'll ever inflate his ego, but I'd be lying. Because that smile... it's a shockingly sexy curve on his lips, stretching his cheeks, lighting up his face, and making me light-headed.

"You should smile more often." I trail a finger along his mouth. "This is potent stuff right here."

He parts his lips and bites my finger hard enough to make me gasp. Chuckling, he kisses a path from the ticklish spot beneath my ear, across my throat, to nibble the other ear.

I squirm beneath the wicked stimulation. "They're waiting on me."

"Do they always stop in unannounced?"

"Yeah, but I kind of knew they were coming and forgot. David's here to fix my brakes."

"Then I better get out there and help." He slides off the bed and strides toward his overnight bag, the muscles in his perfect ass flexing with each step.

"You know how to work on cars?"

"I used to be an auto mechanic."

"Really?"

"No." He snorts arrogantly. "But anyone with a dick knows how to change brakes."

Ten minutes later, I recline on the loveseat outside with Bree, sipping on a Bud Light.

"I saw the fancy car in your driveway." She stares at Trace where he crouches beside David and the MG Midget. "I assumed you were doing ballroom lessons with one of your rich clients."

"I don't do that anymore."

"I know, but I never imagined I'd walk in and find you in bed with…*that*." She gulps. "I'm so jealous of you right now."

I follow her gaze to the blond, blue-eyed tower of hard muscle in my driveway. He stares down at a greasy part he pulled off my car, leaning his weight to one hip and working those jeans like they were designed for a Viking.

The t-shirt is white, fitted across his shoulders, and showcasing the ridges of definition beneath. He's the epitome of well-honed beauty, the kind that dilutes my brain cells and fucks my common sense into quivering mush.

Even Angel is captivated by him. She hasn't left his side since we stepped outside. When she tips her scowl up at him, he scowls down at her, and they connect on some devious, calculating level I don't understand.

She was only a year old when Cole left, so Trace is the first man I've introduced to her. Watching them interact is surprisingly enjoyable. In fact, seeing him with my family spreads a comfortable warmth through my chest.

If I'm not careful, I'm going to fall into a swirling, consuming abyss with this man. A frightening thought, because I don't trust him. I can't.

"Don't get too excited, Bree." I keep my voice too low for his ears. "We have a lot to work through."

"What do you mean?"

As the guys change the brakes out of hearing range, I recap everything that happened after she left yesterday morning — the lap dance, the argument that followed, the drama with Marlo then Jason, the angry sex, and his plan to spend the week with me.

"You packed up the basement?" She touches her throat, eyes watering.

"Yeah."

"You emptied the cup!"

Oh my God. "You're so damn cheesy."

"Cheddar is cheesy. I'm sentimental." She tackles me in a hug. "I'm so very proud of you." Leaning back, she holds tight to my hands. "You have to forgive him."

"What?" My neck stiffens, and I pull away. "No, I'm not—"

"He's helping you. Can't you see that?"

I see a gorgeous asshole with a fine ass clad in denim, his muscles bunching and flexing as he bends under the car.

"I don't mean with the car. He's helping you move on." She lowers her voice. "Besides, with a Johnson like his—"

"Please don't call it a Johnson."

"—I'd forgive anything that man did."

"You would not." I stretch my toes, tracing the design on the brick pavers. "Seeing him with Marlo really hurt me."

"Because you hurt him."

"I didn't do it deliberately. That's the difference. He's vicious."

"He's in love, and you know firsthand that love makes people desperate and crazy." Her attention drifts to the man in question, and she licks her lips.

"You just want me to keep him around so you can ogle him."

"Totally."

"Not helpful." I droop against the back of the loveseat. "I'm trying to be smart about this."

She mirrors my posture, casting me a side-long smile. "You love him."

"So?" I lift a shoulder.

"You always said there's no real choice in love."

"I never thought I'd fall in love twice," I whisper.

"Everyone deserves a second chance."

Her double-meaning settles through me.

He deserves a second chance, and so do I.

twenty-two

present

Trace makes me wait three weeks for sex. I know tonight's the night, because he said, "We're going out. Wear a skirt. No panties."

As I stand in my guest bedroom and dig through racks of dresses, the question isn't *What will I wear?* What rattles in my head is *Do I trust him? Have I forgiven him? Will I tell him I love him?*

We share the same bed every night, hopping between my place and his. He wines and dines me, takes me to fancy parties with his fancy friends, slums with me at dive bars and restaurants, and accompanies me on visits with Bree and when I line dance at Gateway

Shelter.

I've spent the past three weeks analyzing his every word, every action, attempting to glean his intentions. We had the *I'm clean, he's clean, we don't need condoms* talk. And there hasn't been any suspicious interactions with other women. When I spy on him at the casino bars, he intercepts the bold feminine hands on his body. He doesn't so much as look at them.

Only one photo of Cole sits on my dresser—the one of him straddling his bike and smiling those adorable dimples at the camera. Gradually, mournfully, I boxed away the rest in the basement. The matter of the bike remains. Sell it? Keep it? Trace never mentions it, never pushes me to clear out the boxes downstairs.

I know he's not trying to trick me or impress me. He hasn't made any guilt-wrencher moves to imply a declaration of my love or forgiveness is necessary. I genuinely believe he simply enjoys being with me, talking to me, and watching me dance. No strings attached. Not even sex.

That's not to say he doesn't want sex. The man is hard more than he's not. He's in the shower right now, and I bet the stubborn shit is rubbing one out.

For me, abstinence was so much easier when I wasn't immersed in chiseled, scowly temptation day and night.

He works when I'm sleeping and dancing at the casino. Outside of that, we're never apart. This inseparable, celibate routine we've fallen into feels like a slow strangling death. He touches me chastely and kisses me sweetly, despite the sexual tension coiling around us and gasping for relief.

It's spectacularly effective.

He's worn me down with his patience and consistency. But in the end, it's his dedication that's my undoing. He's no longer an *if* but a *when*.

I still cling to doubts, but I trust Trace not to intentionally hurt me. I think he'll always be manipulative. It's in his nature. But will he manipulate me? Cheat on me? Fuck me and leave me?

He's moved past that.

I hope to God I'm right.

Selecting a turquoise dress with a flirty knee-length skirt, I slide it on with a pair of kitten heels. It's my night off work, and I've spent the last hour doing my hair and makeup.

I step into the dance studio and cue up a song that expresses everything I haven't had the courage to say to Trace. As I check my reflection in the mirror, *Say You Won't Let Go* by James Arthur streams through the speakers.

Mouthing the words, I gently sway my hips, lift my arms above my head, and close my eyes. By the time the chorus hits, I'm singing aloud and traveling through improvised steps. The music, the lyrics, the emotions I feel for Trace resonate inside me and accelerate my breaths.

When I open my eyes, I catch his reflection in the mirror and slow my movements to a graceful stop.

He leans against the doorframe behind me, chin down, one hand in the pocket of his khaki pants, the other holding a blue necktie. He's a heart-stopping sight, scowl and all.

"I'm ready. I'll just…" I move toward the stereo.

"Don't."

I freeze, pinned by the force of his gaze, and that's where I stay as the last half of the song plays.

The lyrics are a slow-burning confession of love, the push and pull of commitment, a plea to never let go. It's the ballad of us, and I know he agrees when his head lifts, eyes seeking mine.

As the song ends, I release the air from my lungs and wait for his reaction.

"I've never seen you dance to that." He doesn't move, his eye contact oh-so steady.

"It's one of those songs..." I drag a hand through my hair. "I wasn't ready to feel it before."

He straightens from the doorframe. "You feel it now?"

I feel so many things, but chief among them is acceptance. Acceptance of his mistakes and imperfections, his bad days and bad moods, and the scariest of all, his mortality. He might look like a god, but he's not invincible. He could die, abandon me in grief, but I accept that risk. Because I'm decidedly, irrevocably committed to fighting for a future with him.

"I feel it." My feet carry me forward, one shoe sliding before the other.

His lips part, and the necktie in his hand slips through his fingers, slowly pooling on the floor.

When I reach him, I flatten my palms on his chest, caressing the soft fabric of the button-up and savoring the rhythmic pound of his heart.

"Say you won't let go." I peer up into his crystal blue eyes.

"I won't let go, Danni." His arms envelope me, lifting me up his chest to touch his forehead to mine. "You're stuck with me."

Tension loosens inside me, replaced by waves of warmth, hope, *promise.*

I hug his shoulders and hook my legs around his hips. "I love you."

His breath catches, and he tightens his arms, burying his face in my neck. "I feel like I've been waiting my entire life to hear you say that."

"The hard-won victory." I smile and stroke the trimmed hair on his nape.

He leans back and stares at my mouth. "These are the moments worth fighting for."

"The moments of utter madness."

He captures my mouth in a kiss that transports us into passionate communication. The trembling slide of our lips confesses our fears. The rub of our tongues promises we won't take advantage of each other. The clash of our teeth vows we will fight for this, for us.

Fingers clutching, heads tilting, we plunge deeper, faster, into a boundless place where souls touch and dreams swell. Entwined together by an untamed force, we lick and moan and fuse with belonging and commitment.

It's a kiss that defines love, and when our lips separate, I feel it everywhere, stretching beneath my skin, growing, protecting, and persevering.

"Wow." He pants against my mouth. "That was..."

"As real as it gets." I lower my feet to the floor, rubbing my tingling lips.

His stunned expression makes me laugh. Then I laugh harder, because he just looks so perplexed.

"Are you ready to hit the road?" I ask.

"I'm rethinking that plan."

"Oh, no. You promised me a date without panties."

A growl vibrates in his chest. But rather than arguing, he snatches the necktie from the floor and holds it up. "With or without?"

"I don't like casual sex. You should wear the tie."

With a smirk, he moves to the mirrored wall and lifts his chin, efficiently tying the knot at his neck. "You assume we're having sex tonight."

"Don't fuck around with me, Trace Savoy, or I'll kick your ass."

"All I heard was *fuck* and *ass*."

"Dangerous words. Shall I pull out the thirteen-inch dildo for his pleasure?"

His chest hitches with an almost-laugh, and he stares at the floor, smiling to himself.

"What?" I step into his space, squinting up at him.

"You make me ridiculously happy." He trails his fingers across my cheek and tucks my hair behind my ear. "It's a novel feeling, like I discovered a magical cure. But with that comes the overwhelming need to lock you away and protect you."

Lock me away? I laugh. "I won't go quietly."

"I expect nothing less." He grabs my hips and throws me over his shoulder.

The air rushes out of me. I hang upside down, bracing my hands on his back as blood drains to my head.

He pivots toward a mirror and flips up the skirt of my dress, exposing my nude backside. "Goddamn, I wish you could see this."

I crane my neck, attempting to catch a glimpse of my reflection, but the angle's off. I see his hand, though, as it glides up my thigh and disappears between my legs.

"I fantasize about your pink little cunt and all the ways I'm going to tear it up." His voice is guttural and breathy, his fingers creeping, sinking, twisting into my pussy.

Liquid heat melts through my body and dampens my folds. I sag, boneless and panting, draped over his shoulder.

"Already wet." He thrusts his hand, stimulating my inner muscles and shortening my breaths. "So fucking responsive."

Pleasure rises, consuming me in pulses of electricity.

Until his touch disappears.

"Not yet." He presses a kiss to my hip, adjusts the skirt over my butt, and caveman-carries me out of the house, locking the door behind him.

"You're such a tease." I squirm in his hold as the driveway blurs beneath his swift long strides.

He laughs, dumps me into the backseat of the waiting sedan, and proceeds to tease me for the duration of the thirty-minute drive.

I don't know where we're going, and I can't find my voice to ask. His fingers are relentless, bringing me to the brink of orgasm and pulling back before I come. Over and over and over.

He keeps me in a heightened state of arousal, teasing and denying to the point of mindlessness. So mindless the driver's presence in the car fades into oblivion. It's not like I'll ever see him again. Trace's drivers are as consistent as his moods.

"We're here." Trace slides his fingers from between my legs and straightens my clothes.

That's not going to work. My insides clench so viciously I'm seconds from exploding.

"I need to come." I release the seatbelt and swing a leg over his lap, fumbling with the button on his fly. "Just fuck me. Right here."

The driver—an older gentleman in a black suit—steps out and shuts the door. Beyond the windows, the only building in sight is a gas station, surrounded by a packed parking lot and endless crop fields.

I mold my fingers around the hard shape of him beneath the zipper. "Pull it out, Trace. We can be quick."

He straightens his tie. "I'm thinking about Virginia in her granny panties."

My head jerks back, eyes wide. "What the actual fuck?"

"Guaranteed boner-buster." He lifts me off his lap and steps out of the car, pulling me with him. "This place has the best Bar-B-Q."

"It's a gas station," I grumble and trudge beside him, my hand locked in his and my thighs sticking together. "I'm dripping down my legs."

"Dripping is exactly how I want you."

The discomfort continues through dinner. He keeps his hands to himself, but those damn hooded eyes never stop touching me, caressing me, and making my pussy thrum.

And the gas station in the middle of nowhere? Turns out, it serves the best pulled-pork sandwiches I've ever tasted.

Bellies full, we're back in the car, riding along a dirt road in the middle of cornfields. I think it's corn. The sun closes in on the horizon, and all I see is tall stalks of rippling green against the fading blue sky.

I rest my head on Trace's shoulder. "Are we going to have sex in a field of corn?"

"No."

"On a horse?"

"No."

"In an abandoned shack with chainsaws and a musty mattress?"

He pinches the bridge of his nose. "That's a negative."

"But we're going to have sex. Just tell me where and how soon."

"Look out the windshield."

I lean forward and spot something huge and colorful flapping in the distance. "What is that?"

The car draws closer, bumping on the uneven road and jolting my excitement. As the ginormous object grows and lifts from the field, it takes on a round, recognizable shape.

"Get the fuck out!" I gasp as a hot air balloon blooms from a basket tied to the ground. "We're doing that?"

"We're doing that." He watches me with amusement.

I stare back at him, grinning. "Look at you, all sweet and melty, like a mushy-gushy cookie."

He grimaces. "Let's not blow this out of proportion."

I turn back to the balloon. "This is epic proportions, Trace. Huge gold stars for you, the kind that earn you blow jobs for days."

"I just want you." He grips my knee. "You for an eternity."

"Done."

When we exit the car, a middle-aged, tattooed woman with a pixie haircut strides across the field. "Mr. Savoy?"

"You must be Lori," he says.

They shake hands, and he introduces me.

"I'll be your pilot tonight." She tips her head back, smiling skyward. "What a beautiful night to fly. The thermals are ideal. We should drift along at an even speed without any turbulence. There's champagne in the basket. Feel free to board. We'll depart in a minute."

And that's how I find myself floating into a happily-ever-after sunset with the gorgeous, swoonable man of my dreams.

Except that man is Trace, and beneath the illusion of sweet romance lurks sinful intent and depravity.

Two-thousand feet in the air, I grip the handrail of the five-person basket, lost in the glowing curvature of the earth and the warm gentle wind lifting my hair.

That's the moment he attacks. My skirt goes up, and a forceful hand presses against my tailbone, immobilizing me against the interior wall of the basket. My gasp cuts off as he kicks my feet apart and drives a flesh-pounding palm against my exposed butt.

"Trace!" My lungs heave, and my backside catches fire. "Stop!"

He spanks me repeatedly, harder, faster, grunting with heavy breaths. I don't know which cheeks are redder—my ass beneath his strikes or my face, because holy shit, we're not alone in this basket. Lori is right behind us, piloting the burner.

I lift on my toes, fighting against the hand that pins me to the railing. But with every bone-jolting smack, my embarrassment begins to give way to heart-thudding anticipation.

The breathy noises coming from him isn't exertion. He's worked up. Three-weeks-without-sex worked up. All that control he exhibited on the way here is unraveling by the second, and when the tethers finally snap, his pent-up tension will be directed at me, on me, deep inside me two-thousand feet in the air.

Like a switch flipping inside me, the smarting pain crashes into a tendril of smoldering lava, seeping into my veins and liquefying my bones. I droop over the railing with my head hanging out of the basket.

The spanking stops. The hand on my back tightens, fisting the gathered material of my dress and yanking me back.

I look over my shoulder just as he lowers to his knees behind me and plunges his tongue between my legs. I get a half-second glimpse of Lori — with her back to us and bulky headphones on her ears — before blinding sparks of pleasure blot my vision.

The swirl of his tongue steals my breath and quivers my legs. I swallow without air, clawing at the wicker braiding of the basket and sinking against the pressure of his mouth.

God, he knows how to eat pussy. There's no gentle lapping or prudent licks. He gets in there, burying his face, working his jaw, and fucking me deeply with his tongue. Then his fingers join in, stirring the rim of my opening and gathering moisture. He slides his touch an inch back, and another inch, breaching the pucker of my rear hole.

"Did he fuck you here?"

The deep rasp of his voice swivels my head, and I come face to face with searing blue eyes. Sweet mercy, he's gorgeous, with his lips separated and swollen, the cords in his neck taut, and his bedroom eyes hooded with desire.

"Can she hear us?" I glance at the back of Lori's head and return to him.

"No." He bites the inside of my thigh. "We have ten minutes before she turns off the music."

Given the shortness of his breaths and the sharpening intensity in his expression, we'll only need a fraction of that time.

He presses his wet finger against my rectum. "Answer my question."

"Yes." My jaw flexes. "He fucked me there." *A lot.*

His nostrils flare, and his finger sinks past the tight clamp of muscle, slowly at first, then *fuck!* He penetrates me with ruthless thrusts. His mouth lowers to my pussy, and all I can do is hold on as he sucks and laves and rips moans from my throat.

My eyes roll back in my head, and my chest drops to the railing as my entire body dissolves into trembling bliss.

The finger in my ass curls at the perfect angle, applying exquisite pressure. The orgasm sneaks up and slams into me instantly, shockingly, violently.

I'm still coming as he surges to his feet, fumbles with his zipper, and pulls me back against his chest.

"Eyes on the horizon," he breathes at my ear.

I slump against him and stare forward. When his hand collars my throat and clenches, I shiver all over.

His dominance pushes all my buttons and sweeps the ground from beneath my feet. Every action he takes demonstrates exactly how much effort and energy he's willing to invest in me.

It's a trait I greatly appreciate after all the unassertive guys I've been with. *How do you want me to fuck you? I don't know. How about you just take control without asking? Okay, maybe I'll just lie here and do nothing while you suck my dick.*

With Trace, everything is on his terms, premeditated and carefully designed. The headphones on the pilot gives us privacy. The teasing on the way here ensured I'd be primed for multiple orgasms within the ten-minute time frame.

He's overbearingly controlling, but it makes me feel safe, protected. I love that he's such a prominent man — physically powerful and socially influential. No one would ever fuck with me. That's why I crave the power restraining my airway, controlling my movements, and pressing, hard and hot, against my pussy.

I'm sloppy wet, so when he drives his hips, his cock slides right in. But it's tight, and the stretch is incredible. With a deep groan, he buries himself to the hilt, strangling a gasp in my throat.

Then he moves — savage, vigorous thrusts that don't slow or relent. With my frantic pulse in his palm, he hisses past his teeth and grips my waist, his hips hammering and grinding with desperate urgency.

My body's his vessel, his flesh to pound, and he doesn't hold back, stroking me up and down on his cock and jacking himself off.

I fucking love it, need it. "More."

"I'll never get enough of you." His hand flexes

against my throat, his furious grunts panting at my ear. "Fucking love you."

"Yes, yes, yes..." I moan, reaching behind me to touch him, to hold him closer.

A growl erupts from his chest, and he pulls out, spinning and lifting me before slamming me down on his dick.

My legs straddle his hips. My arms encircle his neck, and I ride him, kiss him, and chase him into orgasm.

We come together, gazes locked, bodies writhing, thrusting, and joined as one.

"I love you, too." I rest my face against his, our noses sliding together, and breaths ragged.

After we regain our senses and straighten our clothes, he stands behind me, caging me against the railing in the safety of his arms. I spend the rest of the ride watching the sunset while he nuzzles and kisses my neck, whispering soft words and hungry promises.

I didn't understand the depth of his sexual appetite until he unleashed it. His wandering hands and fevered kisses don't leave my body, not in the balloon, not in the car on the way home, and not when he leads me into my house and locks the door.

He strips us both of our clothes in the dance studio, and only then does he release me to set a folding chair in the center of the room.

"Sit." He doesn't wait for me to obey and strides over to the sound system, mouth-wateringly nude. "Your taste in music is growing on me."

"You're a Beyoncé fan?" I lower into the chair, biting down on my smile.

I learned over the past few weeks that Stuffy Suit

Savoy listens to rap music, of all things.

"I went to that concert for you." He messes with the stereo, and the intro to *Close* by Nick Jonas & Tove Lo hums through the room.

Prowling back to me, he grips his hardening cock and begins to stroke. The song shivers with sex and seduction, but nothing compares to the predatory look in those blue eyes.

Shivers rain over my nude skin as he closes in, straddles my thighs with his legs straight, and fists the hair on the back of my head. The erection in his hand stands thick and hard and level with my mouth.

I wet my lips and stare up at him. "You want me to suck you?"

"Yes." An unbending response, issued from kissable lips.

I lift my hands to hold that beautiful cock.

"No." He yanks my head back by my hair, and his eyes smile blue flames. "Lock your fingers together behind the chair."

I follow his order, the position pulling back my shoulders and lifting my breasts. Nude and trembling, I ache to take him to the brink of pleasure and stare into his eyes as I send him over.

He trails a finger along my jawline and lifts my chin, holding himself within the reach of my lips. "If I never feel the touch of another woman, it'll be a tremendous blessing."

Warmth swells in my chest. "Don't worry. I'll beat them off you with a stick."

"Open your mouth, Danni."

I lower my jaw, and he touches the plump head of

his cock to my lips, gliding it around the curve of my mouth. Then he slides onto my tongue, inching in, groaning, fingers flexing in my hair.

Since we didn't clean up after the balloon ride, I taste myself on him and smell our passion in the trimmed patch of his hair. It's filthy and erotic and wildly irresistible.

His legs shake, and the rock of his hips starts slow and steady. He thrusts, and I lick around his girth. He grunts, and I suck harder, deeper. When he finally lets go and kicks into a pounding frenzy, I relax my tongue and glory in the claiming.

He gives me every ruthless, unrestrained inch of his desire, and I still want more.

It doesn't take long before he peaks, and when he comes, his mouth hangs open in ecstasy, his hands clenching in my hair and his eyes locked on mine.

Love means different things for different people. For me, love is when his happiness is vital to my own. The way he's staring at me now, eyes shining with soulful joy, I couldn't be happier or more in love.

That night, we lie entangled in bed, our bodies pressed together so tightly I feel the rhythm of his heart in my veins.

Before I met him, I lost the ability to dream. If I'm dreaming now, I want to stay awake for it. I want to feel every fucking minute of it.

I just want to feel him for as long as I have him, and maybe, just maybe, it'll be forever.

twenty-three

present

One month later, I grind my hips in the moving beam of light at Bissara. My bare feet slide effortlessly across the stage as dozens of gamblers and restaurant patrons look on in mesmerized silence. I might not ever be on Beyoncé's dance team, but this job is a wonderful consolation prize. I'm floating in a dream, caught in the rhythm, smiling, dancing, and hopelessly in love.

Since my shift only started thirty minutes ago, my energy is boundless, fluctuating through my limbs and loosening my waist.

Silver coin-sized sequins shimmy and shake on my hip-hugging panties. More adorn the black bra top and bands on my upper arms.

The belly dance costume would be as revealing as a bikini if it weren't for the floor-length chiffon panels that drape from my waist on the front and back. The shimmery fabric sways between my legs and exposes the length of my body on both sides. It's seductive and elegant, and I can't wait until Trace sees me in it.

I haven't spotted him in the restaurant yet, but he'll come. He always does, just to watch me dance.

Bending a leg in front of me, I balance it on a toe and rapidly tilt my pelvis, nailing the ending beats. The crowd erupts in applause as I bow and move into position for the next song in my set list.

Except the instrumentals that echo through the room aren't what I chose.

I falter, scanning the crowd as *Shape of You* by Ed Sheeran thrums through my chest.

Then I see him. Standing in the back corner. Tall and regal. Dressed in a black tuxedo.

I cherish this shivery feeling I get whenever I look at him and find he's already staring. And boy is he staring. It's the stare he gives right before he crashes in like a tidal wave, smothering, drowning, and sweeping everything away until there's only him and me and the breath we hold in our lungs.

"Dance," he mouths.

I don't have a choreographed belly dance routine to *Shape of You*. So I ad lib, rolling my pelvis and crossing my arms at the wrists over my head.

As he slowly prowls toward me, I try to focus on dancing, but I can't take my eyes off him. Why is he wearing a tux? And why did he change my set list to this song? I know he loves the shape of me. He's told me a thousand times. But there's a strange expression on his face. What does he have up his tailored sleeve?

He takes his time approaching the stage, that ice-blue gaze never straying from my body as I twirl and stretch and undulate my muscles. By the time the song fades to silence, he's standing beneath me, hands resting on the edge of the platform.

I take my bow, bending deeply, lower, closer, reaching out a hand to trail my fingers over his strong, clean-shaved jawline. Then I straighten to my full height and wait for the next song.

It doesn't come.

The restaurant is packed, and most of the diners return to their meals. Others watch with curiosity.

"Loving you is instinctual." His voice carries through the room, hushing the crowd.

My heart somersaults, landing somewhere near my throat. I'm shaking. Why am I nervous?

"Loving you is the best kind of self-ruination." He laughs to himself. "God knows, I needed some renovations. I still do, yet you love me anyway. Your acceptance is humbling." He stares up at me, his gaze naked, vulnerable. "I'm undeserving."

My chest hitches. "Trace—"

"Don't misunderstand me. I don't deserve you, but I won't let you go. You're mine, Danni Angelo."

Holding my eyes, he lowers to one knee.

The dining room falls quiet, but a drumming crescendo rises deep within me. It's the din of whispered words, laughter and tears, fears and kisses, and ten months of love. *With Cole.* All of it catches in my throat like a final breath.

But as I exhale slowly, it feels like a rebirth. The inception of something extraordinary. A new beginning. A second chance. *With Trace.*

My attention zooms in on his mouth, on the ever-present scowl that isn't moving, isn't asking the question that follows a bent knee.

Movement ripples through the restaurant, drawing my gaze. At least a half dozen servers stand at attention, spaced throughout the room, dressed in black suits, and holding empty trays.

One by one, they hold those trays over their heads, each with a letter painted in white on the bottom.

Seven letters.

Two words.

M-A-R-R-Y-M-E

My heart beats in overdrive, and tears swim in my eyes as I lower them to the man at my feet.

A ring is pinched tightly in his extended hand. His expression creases with uncertainty, but I'm already nodding my head.

"Yes." I drop to my knees and wrap my arms around his neck. "Yes, Trace. I'll marry you."

His relief is palpable, trembling through his shoulders.

The dining room explodes in cheers, but his gorgeous smile is all I see.

Until he kisses me, and suddenly we're not in the casino, not surrounded by a room full of people. It's just him and me, reaching toward each other, stretching and blooming as one through the cracks in a once-hostile landscape.

His mouth pulls back but not away, and his hand finds mine, raising it between us. He holds up the silver ring, and at first glance, it appears to be a simple band, bent to create a slight wave. But as he changes the angle, the twisted curves create the illusion of an infinity symbol.

I blink, smiling, and lift my damp eyes to his. "Infinity is a long time."

"It's not the length of time." He slides the ring on my finger. "But the depth."

My chest heaves with a nourishing breath, and I tug at the black bow tie around his neck. "You didn't have to wear a tux to propose to me."

A mischievous smirk slides across his lips. "Follow me."

He leads me toward the entrance of the dining room, passing happy shouts of congratulations on our way out. Through the gaming area and past the lobby, he doesn't slow until we reach the doors of the hotel ballroom.

"What is this?" I'm barefoot and half-dressed, completely unprepared for a formal function.

"Our engagement party." He ushers me inside and raises his voice to the waiting crowd of tuxedos and gowns. "She said *yes!*"

My breath quickens as I scan all the smiling familiar faces. Bree and David. Father Rick and Nikolai. Virginia and many of my other elderly neighbors. Friends I danced with in college. Students I used to teach. Even some of the staff from Bissara.

I squeeze Trace's hand, shocked and overjoyed. "What if I said *no?*"

"Ah, but you didn't." He kisses the top of my head. "Bree has your dress."

My dress?

She hurries toward me in a flurry of floor-length satin, simpering like a little girl.

"Lucky bitch." She grabs my arm and drags me into a connecting room off the corner of the ballroom.

Ten minutes later, I stand before her in a silver mermaid gown made from heavy silk. The fitted V-neckline gives me some sexy cleavage. The bodice bares my shoulder blades in a trendy racer-back style with a huge cutout just above my ass crack. The form-fitting mermaid skirt ruffles out in the back, cascading curls of silk into a gorgeous train.

I feel like I just inherited the keys to a magical kingdom. This life can't be real.

"You're breathtaking." Bree flattens a hand over her chest.

"He picked this out?" I slide my feet into sparkling silver stilettos.

"Yes, Danni. He arranged all of this."

"When?"

"A month ago."

The hot air balloon ride was a month ago. *The first time I told him I loved him.* The man doesn't waste any time.

"I didn't call Mom and Dad." She circles around me, tucking and straightening the drape of my skirt. "I thought you'd want to tell them yourself." She bounces up and down, squealing. "You're getting married!"

I stare down at the ring on my finger. *I'm getting married.*

Cole's face flashes through my mind, and my heart gives a heavy thump. That achy feeling will never go away, because I will always love him, always miss how happy I was with him, even if I found someone I love just as much.

Don't leave me, Trace.

"Ready?" Bree grips my shoulders.

At my nod, she laces her fingers through mine and leads me to the door.

I cross the ballroom, winding around tables and food and lively chatter. I squeeze Virginia's hand as I pass and wave at Nikolai across the room. But when I spot the gorgeous man in the black tux, everything around me fades to black.

He stands alone at the center of a dance floor, hands behind him, shoulders back. His lips might be curved down, but his eyes glow with happiness.

The skirt of my dress swishes over the floor and settles around my feet as I pause a foot away. "Are we going to dance?"

He nods to a man behind a portable DJ booth, and a heartbeat later, an electronic disco beat thumps through the room.

I burst out laughing, instantly recognizing the song. "I expected some slow romantic number, anything but *Get Lucky* by Daft Punk." I shake my head, smiling. "You're full of surprises, Trace Savoy."

"I intend to spend the next seventy years keeping you on your toes." He extends a hand. "Cha Cha?"

I toss my head playfully and sink into a hip roll. Then I strut past his waiting hand.

He grabs my wrist, spins me back in a handshake position, and just like that, we're dancing.

Cha Cha is a fast tempo dance, with sharp, staccato steps on the balls of the feet. Most of the hip action comes from the legs, flowing the entire body with the music.

I follow his lead, keeping my torso upright and my gaze on his.

His footwork is remarkably on point, fitting five steps into a measure and never missing a beat.

Watching him move ignites a low flame in my core. The sparkle in his eyes burns me hotter. My God, he's sexy as hell.

"You're good." I step forward, twisting side to side and back.

"I know." He swivels me around, pulls me back in, and holds my hands between us.

I laugh. "I can smell your arrogance from here."

He yanks me into a closed position, chest to chest, our hips rolling together.

"My favorite scent is your skin." Lifting my arm, he trails his nose across my wrist.

I love being pressed against his body. I want him soldered to me from lips to feet. "My favorite place is your arms."

His eyes flare as he rocks forward. I rock back on the diagonal.

"My favorite song is your laughter." He twirls me across the dance floor, his steps as steady as his eye contact.

I slide up against his chest and aggressively grip the back of his neck. "My favorite emotion is your scowl."

Chuckling, he struggles to hold onto that scowl.

For the rest of the song, we Cha Cha our hearts out. My cheeks ache from smiling, and my ribs feel too small to contain all the joy. Swinging, bouncing, bending backward, and blowing him a kiss, I follow him across

one *is a promise*

every square inch of the dance floor.
I'll follow him anywhere.

twenty-four
present

They say when someone appears in your dreams, it's because they miss you.

Well, they don't know shit.

The dream I just woke from starred a man who can't miss me. It isn't physically possible. Not anymore.

I don't remember much of the dream, but I recall his dark brown eyes and deep dimples so clearly it's as if he were in my bed, smiling down at me.

I lie on my back and press a hand against the ache in my chest, blinking away the fog of sleep.

Trace proposed two weeks ago, and since that night, Cole's been less and less in my thoughts. But he's never far from my heart. If there's an afterlife, I hope he's not missing me. I only ever wanted him to be happy.

As happy as I am now.

I roll toward the man responsible for my newfound peace and rest my smile against the curve of his bicep.

Face down in my bed and hugging a pillow beneath his cheek, Trace wears a gentle scowl, even in sleep. His blond hair falls rebelliously over his brow. Thick dark lashes fan toward sharp cheekbones and the scruff of day-old whiskers.

He's deliciously nude, the line of his spine cutting a groove between toned shoulders and a trim waist. I feather my fingers down that valley and follow the curved rise of his muscled ass.

Sweet lord in heaven, he has a great ass. Hard and round, it sits high and clenches tight, forming deep cleavage I love to play with. I consider slipping a finger into that shadowed dip, but he needs his rest. It's only six in the morning, and we didn't fall asleep until a couple of hours ago, thanks to my late shift at Bissara and his insatiable appetite afterward.

His breathing stumbles out of rhythm, and he cracks open an eye.

"You're awake?" His timbre rasps with groggy surprise.

I'm as shocked as he is. I never wake before him.

"Shh." I trail kisses over his shoulder. "Go back to sleep."

His lips bounce between a smile and a frown, and he creeps a hand toward my face, sliding his fingers across my cheek. A moment later, his eyes close and his touch falls slack.

I watch him sleep for a while, intent on drifting off

with him. But that doesn't happen. I'm wide awake and restless with the urge to drink coffee with the sunrise.

Slipping quietly out of bed, I pull on yoga pants, fuzzy slippers, and an oversized hoodie. After a pit stop at the bathroom, I make coffee and carry a steaming mug to the sitting area in the backyard.

St. Louis weather in October is unpredictable. The ground is warm from yesterday's heat wave. But this morning, the air is cold and cloudy, creating a ghost-gray fog low to the ground. So much for watching the sunrise.

I settle on the outdoor loveseat, relishing the ambiance of the mist crawling in around me. I feel like I'm enrobed in a cloud of mystery, in some faraway land, waiting for my Viking to lumber out and steal a kiss. And spank me.

A chuckle rises up, and I shake my head. Oh man, I have it bad.

I spin the engagement band on my finger. If he had it his way, we would've married immediately, but he respects my desire for a big wedding.

No, not a big wedding.

An over-the-top first dance.

Now that I've seen his hotter-than-Johnny-Castle dance moves, I can't *not* choreograph a routine that will put us in the history books of best-ever wedding receptions. But choreography takes time. So does all the practice I'll be putting him through. I'm thinking a Spring wedding.

Until then, we need to figure out living arrangements. He wants me to move into the penthouse, and I refuse to sell my house.

I still officially run a dance company, even if I'm

not teaching anymore. Who knows? I might go back to
that someday.

He says he'll buy me a new studio anywhere I
want, and therein lies my hesitation. I have a studio, built
with the bare hands of a man who loved me with his
dying breath. I can't let it go.

Trace isn't thrilled with the idea of moving into my
tiny bungalow with its green claustrophobic tub. But he's
here every night without a single complaint. Maybe I'll
just let my house sit empty and move into the penthouse.
That's what I should do.

With a decided breath, I finish off the coffee and
wade through the murky mist toward the back door. As I
reach the driveway, the hum of an idling car engine
slows my steps. It sounds close. Really close. *Weird.*

I turn my feet in the direction of the street — a street
I can't see because visibility is shit in this fog.

Walking toward the side of the house, I pass the
Midget. Trace's driver dropped us off after work early
this morning, so there shouldn't be any other cars in the
driveway. Except I'm certain I see a yellow one parked at
the end. A taxi cab?

My head tips, and the muscles in my neck strain as
I squint through the haze. Why is a taxi in my driveway?

The car door slams shut, and a dark figure emerges
from the mist with a duffel bag slung over one shoulder.
The silhouette walks like a man, the outline of shoulders
and biceps unquestionably masculine. And familiar.

My heart pounds in my ears, and my palms grow
damp.

He looks like Cole. Thinner. Slightly longer hair.
His gait a little more cautious.

It's a mirage. The density of the fog is playing

tricks on me.

But his eyes… Dark, warm, unforgettable Cole eyes.

The tremble begins in my chin and ripples inward, railroading me. I'm seeing things. It's the only explanation for the sudden need to empty my stomach.

Ten feet away, he drops his bag and stares at me out of a gaunt Cole face. "Danni."

The mug falls from my hand and shatters on the driveway. I'm shaking, swaying, panting sandpaper breaths from a chest too tight to heave. I can't rationalize this. It isn't real. It can't be real.

I reach for him, and my legs don't work right, lurching me forward and throwing me off balance as a low keening sound claws from my throat.

His arms come around me. Strong arms. Intimate arms. I know the shape, the golden skin tone, the dusting of dark hair.

Except there are no tattoos.

I drag my gaze to his neck, to the pristine skin above the collar of the t-shirt. No snake. No ink anywhere.

"You're not him." I push against his chest, my heart rate careening out of control.

"I know I look different." He grips my head with both hands and puts his eyes inches from mine. "Take a deep breath and really *look*. It's me, baby."

My face crumples as I stare into the liquid brown eyes that never stopped haunting me. Tears gather at the corners, clinging to his dark lashes, and the sight of his agonized expression sucks all the oxygen from the atmosphere.

"How?" A sob escapes, but I fight back the next one. Everything inside me goes cold and still, my voice a scratchy whisper. "How is this possible?"

"I have a lot of explaining to do, but there are things I can't… I just need to hold you for a minute." He cups the back of my head and pulls my cheek to his chest. "Christ, I missed you so much." The heavy tempo of his heart pounds in my ears. "You have no idea how much I love you."

My body melts against him for a fraction of a second before my brain fires.

"No!" I twist out of his embrace and stumble back, my hands shaking violently. "Where have you been? It's been four and a half years! How could you do this to me?"

"Shhh. Baby…" He reaches for me, his eyes burning with desperation. "I'm here now."

"I buried you!" I swat him away as painful memories flash behind my eyes. "The ashes…the funeral… I *mourned* you. Goddammit, I cried myself to sleep every night for years. Why didn't you call me? Message me?" My voice tumbles into an anguished cry. "Why didn't you come home?"

"I'm so sorry," he chokes. "It kills me to see you hurting. Please don't cry."

"Tell me!" My muscles cramp against the relentless pain.

I can't stop staring at him, devouring the sharp angles of his too-thin face, reacquainting myself with his fierce mannerisms, the confidence in his movements, and the compulsive way he looks at me. I never thought I'd see him again, and my brain struggles to make sense of what's standing right in front of me. How is he here?

Whose ashes did I bury? Why isn't he explaining his absence?

"It's complicated." The despair in his eyes hardens. "Trust me, I would've been here if I could."

"No, that's not good enough. You ruined us, and I need to understand why!"

His jaw flexes, and his brows dig in. I know that determined look. He wants to touch me, comfort me with his body, and he'll hold me down if he has to. I brace for a struggle.

He steps toward me, shoulders squared, and halts at the sound of the back door opening behind me.

Trace.

Sharp pain stabs through my chest, stopping my heart. The world around me stands still, holding its breath. This is happening, and I can't stop it.

My past and my future.

My first love and my second chance.

Two hearts from two separate lives colliding helplessly, cruelly together.

Cole's furious gaze snaps over my shoulder. "What the fuck?"

His face turns red-hot, eyes wide and agonized, expressing all the nuances of shock as he watches a man step out of my house at six in the morning.

I turn my neck as Trace disperses the fog with his slow approach. Shirtless, clad in pajama pants, he stares at Cole with an unreadable expression.

My stomach feels rock-hard, my throat strangling in a fist of dread. I inch backward, reaching a hand toward Trace.

"You're with him?" Cole thrusts a shaking finger at

Trace, teeth gnashing. "Are you fucking him?"

"You died." My whisper is tormented, torn from the darkest hours of my life. "You weren't here."

Trace stiffens beside me, and I rethink my answer. I'm with Trace. I'm sleeping with him because I love him.

I open my mouth to explain, but Trace speaks first. "You're late."

Three and a half years late. I can't breathe beneath the debilitating shock.

Cole's alive.

He's been alive all this time.

And he didn't come home.

Trace laces his fingers through mine, squeezing painfully hard. "You told me to take care of her."

A chill slithers up my spine, and my blood turns to ice. "What did you say?"

Cole stands a few feet away, biceps bunching as he scrapes his hands over his head repeatedly. "You weren't supposed to make contact." His expression contorts between devastation and rage. "I told you to watch over her, not fuck her."

They know each other. Trace fucking knows Cole and never thought to mention it?

I yank my hand from his and wrap my arms around my shaking body. "How do you know each other?"

"We used to work together," Trace says in a hollow voice.

"Auditing for the government?" I gape at him, silently begging him to tell me this is all some kind of joke. "You own a casino. I don't understand. Why didn't you tell me you knew him?"

He and Cole share a look, communicating

something that's beyond my realm of understanding. Or rather, beyond my security clearance.

The deployment in Iraq. The silence at the government building. The fake funeral. The removal of tattoos.

"You're not an auditor, are you?" I ask Cole on a thin breath, shaking from head to toe.

"I can't say, Danni." Cole doesn't remove his glare from Trace.

"You lied to me." My skin tingles, and disorientation sweeps through me as I turn to Trace. "You lied, too. You knew Cole and never told me."

More tears fall, and I bury my face in my hands. *I need to step back. I need to think.*

"What is that?" Cole rushes forward and grabs my wrist, his eyes zeroed in on the engagement ring. "No." His whisper crashes into a pained guttural noise. "No, no, no!"

He yanks his arm back and stumbles. Every visible muscle in his body goes taut as he spins away and paces like a caged animal, shoulders heaving, hands stabbing through his hair. The tortured sounds coming from him threaten to bring me to my knees.

When he whirls back, he looks absolutely destroyed. "You missed me so much you fucked my best friend? And now you're what? Getting married?"

Best friend.

How deep does the deceit go?

My shoulders curl forward, wracked by an onslaught of grief and betrayal.

"I didn't mean that." Cole rushes toward me and frames my face with shaky hands. "I'm not upset with you. I put you in a terrible position and kept things from you. I had no right to expect you to wait around for a dead man."

The ache in his voice crushes me, and I feel his terrified pain as if it were my own. Because I never stopped loving him.

None of this is my fault, and he knows that. He's raging and losing his shit for one reason. The woman he loves is engaged to someone else.

"How long, Trace?" He lowers his hands and claps his gaze on the silent, brooding man at my side. "How long did you wait before you preyed on her?"

"He didn't prey on me!" I stand taller. "I worked at his casino for four months before we got together."

"Three years." Trace shifts beside me, his tone calm and steady. "I was in love with her for three years before I made contact."

Three years? The ground spins beneath my feet.

"She started dating," Trace says. "I did exactly what you wanted me to do. I kept the men out of her bed." His voice hardens. "Which I would've done anyway because I love her."

Anger boils through my veins. I could easily direct it at both of them, but I bare my teeth at Cole. "You disappeared for over four years. You died! And you didn't want me to find happiness again?"

Cole turns away, a hand splayed over his mouth. His posture coils tightly, and he releases a low growl, full of warning.

Before I can blink, he spins around and slams a fist into Trace's face.

Trace falls back but remains on his feet. As blood trickles from his lip, he doesn't move to wipe it away.

With his arms at his sides and his expression blank, he shows no signs of fighting back.

Cole, on the other hand, rears back his arm again.

"Stop!" I ram a shoulder into his rigid body, causing his strike to hit air. "You were dead! You had no claim on me!"

"*You* thought I was dead," Cole seethes, flexing his fists at his sides. "But Trace knew."

My mind spins as the last six months tumble into a new light.

What would your fiancé think about the dipshit you were with tonight?

I'm not going to fuck you.

It's just not in the cards for us, sweetheart.

If Cole was in this room right now, where would I fall? Would you shove me aside to get to him?

Trace chased away every man who came near me. He purchased the restaurant I danced at. Set my schedule so I never had a weekend off to date. Refused to date me himself. Pushed, pushed, pushed me away, all while being overly-fixated on my attachment to Cole.

Because he was watching me for Cole. And at some point — long before I met him — he fell in love with me.

Under the malicious waves of comprehension, it dawns on me. The set up with Marlo wasn't to hurt me. It was a last-ditch attempt to stop himself from stealing his best friend's girl.

Only it didn't drive me away. None of it did. Because I love him, too.

My heart sinks beneath an impossible realization.

I love two men, and they're both here, staring at me with the kind of desperation that destroys a person.

"You knew Cole was alive?" I whisper and lift my gaze to Trace.

Heartache drains the light from his beautiful blue eyes. "I knew there was a chance."

up next

ONE IS A PROMISE is only the beginning.
The Danni-Trace-Cole love triangle continues with:

TWO IS A LIE
THREE IS A WAR

two

is a lie

Two lies.
Two men who don't share.

I never stopped loving Cole. Not when he left me. Not
when he disappeared for three years. Not when he
crashed back into my life in a violent explosion of
testosterone and fury.
His sudden reappearance questions everything I thought
I knew, including how I came to love another man.

Trace is an intoxicating breeze of seduction over ice. My
rock. My second chance at forever.
And he's committed to annihilating the competition.

The battle that ensues wrenches me back and forth

between them.
Fighting and fucking.
Resisting and submitting.

Together, they entangle me in a web of lies, rivalry, and desire that weaves as deeply as their devotion to me.

I love two men, and if I can only have one, I choose none.

three

is a war

Three means war.
Three sides vying for forever.

Cole.
My first love.
The bad boy with the dangerous smile and passionate temper draws attention like a lit fuse on dynamite. But his dark molten eyes spark only for me.

Trace.
My second chance.
Over six feet of Norse god in a tailored suit, he calculates every move and seizes my hungry breaths with an iron fist.

Me.
The free-spirited dancer, torn between two men with no resolution in sight.
I tried leaving, staying, refusing, and surrendering.
What options do I have left?

I love two men, and I do the only thing I can. I fight.

books by
pam godwin

DARK COWBOY ROMANCE
TRAILS OF SIN SERIES
Knotted #1
Buckled #2
Booted #3

DARK PARANORMAL ROMANCE
TRILOGY OF EVE
Heart of Eve
Dead of Eve #1
Blood of Eve #2
Dawn of Eve #3

DARK ROMANCE
DELIVER SERIES
Deliver #1
Vanquish #2
Disclaim #3
Devastate #4
Take #5
Manipulate #6
Unshackle #7
Dominate #8
Complicate #9

STUDENT-TEACHER / PRIEST
Lessons In Sin

STUDENT-TEACHER ROMANCE
Dark Notes

ROCK-STAR DARK ROMANCE
Beneath the Burn

ROMANTIC SUSPENSE
Dirty Ties

EROTIC ROMANCE
Incentive

DARK HISTORICAL PIRATE ROMANCE
King of Libertines
Sea of Ruin

playlist

Dangerous Woman by Ariana Grande
Cupid Shuffle by Cupid
Try by Pink
Hips Don't Lie by Shakira
Stay by Rihanna
We Found Love by Rihanna
One More Night by Maroon 5
Down by Marian Hill
Talk Dirty by Jason Derulo
XO by Beyoncé
Criminal by Britney Spears
Dancing On My Own by Calum Scott
Say You Won't Let Go by James Arthur
Close by Nick Jonas & Tove Lo
Shape of You by Ed Sheeran
Get Lucky by Daft Punk

pam godwin

New York Times and USA Today Bestselling author, Pam Godwin, lives in the Midwest with her husband, their two children, and a foulmouthed parrot. When she ran away, she traveled fourteen countries across five continents, attended three universities, and married the vocalist of her favorite rock band.

Java, tobacco, and dark romance novels are her favorite indulgences, and might be considered more unhealthy than her aversion to sleeping, eating meat, and dolls with blinking eyes.

pamgodwinauthor@gmail.com

Printed in Poland
by Amazon Fulfillment
Poland Sp. z o.o., Wrocław